Additional Praise for
Beautiful Country

"This unsettling book about the moral encounter between America and China is a study of privilege, innocence, and risk. It is a tragedy of manners and a portrait of Beijing—amplified and torqued and unmistakable." —Evan Osnos, winner of the National Book Award

"A coming-of-age story that vividly encapsulates the complexities of the modern encounter between China and America. Indeed, this is in many ways the quintessential 'Chimerican' novel for the millennial generation. Disarming in its candor, addictively readable." —Niall Ferguson, author of *Kissinger: 1923–1968: The Idealist* and *Civilization*

"Compelling and authentic . . . a story of China as told by an outsider. Through the perspective of a young American, we can see a different side to our country and ourselves—one that is unfamiliar, but real." —Yu Hua, winner of the James Joyce Award and the Grinzane Cavour Prize

BEAUTIFUL COUNTRY

BEAUTIFUL COUNTRY

J. R. THORNTON

HARPER ● PERENNIAL

NEW YORK ● LONDON ● TORONTO ● SYDNEY ● NEW DELHI ● AUCKLAND

HARPER ● PERENNIAL

HarperCollins books may be purchased for educational, business, or sales promotional use. For information please e-mail the Special Markets Department at SPsales@harpercollins.com.

FIRST EDITION

Designed by Diahann Sturge

Library of Congress Cataloging-in-Publication Data has been applied for.

ISBN 978-0-06-241191-4 (pbk.)

16 17 18 19 20   OV/RRD   10 9 8 7 6 5 4 3 2 1

For Tom Mallory
1988–2005

Author's Note

This is a work of fiction. All characters, including the narrator, are entirely imagined and bear no relation to any living persons.

姦. *Jian*, the Chinese character for *woman* repeated three times, implying conspiracy or treachery. I was reminded of it as I watched the three female immigration officials huddle over my passport. They spoke to each other in rapid whispers that came out in machine-gun bursts. They glanced at me, looked back at my passport, and then flipped through the pages—again and again. It was unnerving. I was alone in this new country and barely spoke the language.

I didn't understand enough Chinese to know exactly what the problem was, but I suspected it had something to do with my visa. I reached over the counter and tried to point out the visa page in my passport, but the first immigration official jerked my passport away and snapped at me. The three women huddled together. I heard one of them repeat *shi si sui*, the words for fourteen years old, several times, but I didn't understand much else. I guessed they couldn't figure out how or why a fourteen-year-old boy had a diplomat-level visa. Someone at the Embassy had arranged it as a favor to my father. Since retiring from investment banking, my father had served as a senior business advisor to the Chinese government on privatizing state-owned enterprises.

Trying to explain the situation to these women would only complicate matters.

I had been at the desk for close to an hour, and for the last thirty minutes, I had been the only passenger left in the immigration hall. Finally, the two women who had been called over to help shook their heads with an indifferent sense of disapproval and walked away. What made these women finally give up, I don't know. Whatever the reason, the first immigration official reluctantly stamped my passport and waved me on. Along the back wall, four armed guards stood motionless with arms pressed behind their backs and feet shoulder width apart. I walked past the guards and down a long, still corridor to the baggage claim. I expected to see other travelers. But there was no one else. Only me.

By the time I arrived at the baggage claim, my bags were circling alone. Too tired from the sixteen-hour flight to chase them down, I sat down and waited for my bags to circulate around the oval track. The baggage claim area was stark and unlike those in other airports I had passed through at the beginnings of holidays in Italy and France. The billboards featuring tanned models who beckoned with their blue eyes and white smiles that decorated the Florence and Nice airports were nowhere to be found. In their place were official notice boards and signs with unintelligible Chinese characters. The carousel's metal plates scraped together as they rounded the corner and beat a steady rhythm like an oversized metronome marking the room's silence.

I hauled my bags off the belt and headed toward the exit. As I walked past the customs counter, I realized that this was the first time I was leaving an airport on my own. It felt strange not to be following an adult with a trolley loaded with bags. I looked back and saw the long columns of trolleys perfectly aligned, and I remembered how my older brother Tom and I used to take them and race them around like pushcarts as we waited for our father or our nanny to collect the bags. We stopped a few years ago. It was what kids did, Tom said. I dropped my bags to pull out the photograph my father had given me of the young Chinese woman he had hired to act as my guardian for the year. Victoria—with her straight black hair and glasses—would be waiting for me on the other side of customs.

The walk was long and the emptiness of the airport made me wonder if my flight was the last to land. The strap of my heavy duffel bag cut into my shoulder. As alone as I felt walking down that long hallway, I suppose I felt a sense of relief to be going to a place where nothing was familiar—no shared language, no remembered faces, no recognizable landscape, nothing to remind me of what had happened. I had no idea what I would be heading into—it would be harder than I, at the time, had the ability to imagine. But looking back—knowing what I know now—I would never send my son off like that.

The truth is that it was never my decision to go to Beijing. My father decided I would go, and that was all there was to say. I've come to understand that he must have believed time and distance were correlated, that somehow the farther away he sent me the faster things would heal. Perhaps he didn't understand that memories have a way of finding you wherever you are.

I knew I needed to leave home, I knew I needed to be somewhere else for a while, but I didn't understand why I had to go to Beijing. I wanted to go to Florida where I could play tennis for six hours a day against the top players in the United States. I once told my father that, but he dismissed me and said it would be much better for me to go to Beijing. I didn't agree with him, but I didn't object because I didn't want to disappoint him. If our father had decided to ship Tom off to Beijing, he would have stood up for himself. But I have never been very good about confronting my father. I suppose my hesitation came from a fear that he would think less of me.

Maybe it was Tom's imagination that had allowed him to resist in ways I could not. I remember once when Tom was twelve, he convinced all the kids in his class to act in a play he had written.

He allowed me to believe that I was his assistant director, writer, and general sidekick. The work was titled *Macbeth in the Internet Age*—the plot was true to Shakespeare, except that Macbeth's addiction to surfing the Web with Dunsinane's recently acquired high-speed internet derailed his ambition, and Lady Macbeth had to carry out the gruesome murders by herself. Tom ended his play with me walking out onstage with a shark mask and asking the audience, "What do you want out of life?"

He died on a Saturday in January when he was sixteen and I was thirteen. The official cause of death was listed as "MDMA intoxication." The drugs he and his friends took were cut with something toxic, and Tom's body had reacted badly to it. That was what it said in the newspaper anyway. It didn't make sense to me at the time. I didn't even know what any of that was back then. All I knew was that there must have been some mistake because drugs were something drug addicts did, not my older brother.

The day after he died, I locked myself in my room and refused to open the door. My father had to call a locksmith to remove the lock completely. He didn't want there to be any chance that I did it again. I don't remember a lot from those first few weeks, but I do remember being afraid to fall asleep because I was scared of the dreams and nightmares I might have. And I remember always feeling as if I were on the verge of throwing up. It wasn't just sadness. It was some horrible combination of anger and guilt. I remember feeling that in some way it was my fault. It wasn't, of course, but that guilt nevertheless was there. I couldn't escape the thought that if I had done something differently that night, Tom would still be alive. If only I hadn't gotten mad at him over the PlayStation. Or if I had asked him to take me to see a movie, or if I had told my father that I had a math test I needed Tom to help me study for. If I had done that, he never would have left to meet up with his friends. And he wouldn't have died. I couldn't get that out of my head.

The day after he died I took a tennis racket and started smashing it into my PlayStation as hard as I could. I only stopped when our housekeeper came in and wrenched the racket from my hands. By the time she came in, the game console was already scattered across the floor, broken fragments of plastic and metal. The last time I saw Tom we had an argument over that PlayStation. I had told him he wasn't allowed to use it anymore because he always cheated when we played. I smashed it into pieces because I couldn't bear looking at it anymore. Every time I looked at it, I was reminded of that conversation and it filled me with this terrible guilt over what I had said to my brother the last time I had seen him alive.

After that incident, my father canceled a business trip and drove me out to East Hampton to spend a week at his sister's summerhouse. The Hamptons were deserted at that time of year and we had the house to ourselves. Getting away for that week helped. It was too much being at home. Everywhere I looked I was reminded of Tom.

I didn't want to go back to school, but the therapist they made me see told my father that I should start school again. She said being reintegrated with my peer group would help with my recovery. I don't think it was the right decision. Everyone at school treated me differently. They were too nice; their averted eyes and muted voices made me more aware of Tom's absence. My friends had become afraid to laugh or make jokes in front of the boy whose brother had just died. I could tell that my presence had become a burden on them.

I couldn't get myself to care about school. I didn't do my homework, I didn't study for tests, and I began to get Ds and Fs when I had previously received mostly As and some Bs. But my father only pulled me out of school after I got in a fight with Jake Green during a game of basketball at recess. Jake started cracking jokes about my brother and when he didn't stop I ran over and pushed him so he fell down on the ground, and I started kicking him as hard as I could in the stomach. He started crying but still I didn't stop, and then I kicked him in the face, and I broke his nose. I don't remember stopping, even when there was blood all over my sneakers. My father pulled me out of the school after that. He pulled me out because the school told him that they were going to expel me if he didn't. I finished the eighth-grade syllabus with tutors at home.

I started playing tennis again around the time I was sent back to school. While I struggled in school, I did well in tennis. Each day I would exhaust myself up to the point where I had nothing left in me. All my energy and emotions were concentrated on the simple action of hitting a ball back over a net. My father must have picked up on the fact that tennis was helping me, because about a month after he pulled me out of school, we started talking about the idea of my taking a year off to play tennis.

It was about that time that one of his business associates, Mr. Richard Zhang, came and stayed at our house for a weekend to discuss a real estate venture my father had proposed setting up with him in China. He and my father spent most of the weekend in my father's study talking, but on Saturday afternoon they came out to the tennis courts to watch me practice. At dinner that night, my father quizzed Mr. Zhang about the tennis standards in China. It turned out that one of Mr. Zhang's close friends was a senior official in the Chinese government and currently served as Minister of Sport. Over dinner, I saw the idea of sending me to China begin to take shape. Theoretically, my father asked Mr. Zhang, would a foreigner be allowed to practice within the Chinese State's sport system? Could Mr. Zhang's friend arrange for that to happen? Did he know any good language schools in Beijing? I watched as each potential obstacle was dismissed by Mr. Zhang, who either had a ready solution to each problem or simply said that he was sure that something could be arranged. As my future was being decided in front of me, I waited for the one question I longed for my father to ask. *What did I think about the idea?* But the opportunity never came.

It took me some time to understand that sending me to China was my father's way of protecting me. That was the way he was. I never had the kind of relationship with my father many of my peers had with theirs who were present at every soccer match, every science fair, every school play. Though I knew he cared deeply for me, he was aloof and reserved, rarely showing signs of approval, which of course made me strive for it all the more. Besides, I had my older brother, Tom. Tom was not only my hero, the person I looked up to more than anyone else in the world, he was also my best friend. After his death, my father became even more remote.

I think that his aloofness allowed him the illusion of control. I have no memory of my mother. She died when I was only two and Tom was five. It happened just after she had dropped Tom off at kindergarten. The weather was bad and a truck in front of her hit a patch of black ice and lost control, jack-knifing and sending my mother's Range Rover into an airborne spiral down an embankment. Sometimes late at night Tom would wonder out loud to me that if he had taken five more seconds to get dressed or to eat his breakfast or to give her one last kiss before he got out of the car, she would still be alive. I have no memory of my mother. I used to envy Tom for his, but now that he's gone, I am glad I don't remember her. No one should have to feel that kind of loss twice.

Before I left for China, my father handed me a copy of a letter his father had received from his father—a short note written by my great-grandfather, a Presbyterian minister, who counseled his son that in confronting choices, the three most important things to remember were duty, honesty, and courage. Duty was about shunning temptation and fulfilling your responsibilities to others. Honesty was about always being truthful. And courage was about having the strength to do the right thing. I never knew whether this point of view came from the New England fierceness of my great-grandfather's maternal line or the Scottish stoicism of his paternal side, but I suspected the latter. If you had asked me, before that year, about courage, I would have given you a crisp, clear answer. On the tennis court, it was straightforward. Courage was about honesty, about always being brave enough to tell the truth—the ball was either in or out, nothing unclear or ambiguous.

I guess the message in this handed-down letter was my father's version of a St. Christopher's medal, but over the course of the next year, I realized that what my father had passed on to me was, at best, incomplete. I came to understand that duty and honesty and courage were lines that crossed and overlapped—they weren't always straight or compatible. The difficulty was in knowing which of the lines was most important.

三

As I walked through customs out into the airport lobby, I searched for a woman who matched the photograph I had been given. Victoria Liu had worked as a journalist for a news network in Guizhou Province. She had recently come to Beijing with her husband, who was an artist, but she hadn't been able to find any work in the city as a journalist. My father had interviewed Victoria on one of his trips to Beijing and thought she would be a good person to look after me.

My father had told me that most Chinese people who deal with Westerners have two names, their real name and an English name. In China, the meaning of their adopted English name is very important. Men preferred strong, masculine names like Michael or Jack while women often chose the names of flowers such as Lily or Ivy or Violet. Victoria's real name was Zhong. She later told me that she had chosen the name Victoria as her English name because of Victoria Beckham.

I heard someone call my name. A slender young woman with short, spiked black hair, tight jeans, a neon purple sweater, and orange and brown rubber-topped tennis shoes waved at me with one hand as she held a pink cell phone to her ear with the other.

Could this be Victoria? I looked back at the photo and then back at her. The two women looked nothing alike, but the board she held had my name misspelled, *Chas Robretsn*.

The woman tucked the sign under her arm, spoke a few words into the pink cell phone, and then approached me with a wide smile. She held her hand out and introduced herself as Victoria and then pulled the pink phone out again. She said she was calling the driver to pull the car up. As she spoke on the phone I examined my new guardian more carefully, unsure what to make of her. She seemed cooler than I had imagined. I felt relieved she didn't appear to be too strict or overbearing.

I followed her out to the curb where we waited for the car. The air was thick, and even though it was early August, the sky had the kind of white-gray look that presages the coming of snow. The thick, smog-filled air obscured the horizon, and buildings appeared as little more than hazy outlines, like faded charcoal lines drawn on a cloud. Victoria waved her hand as a black Audi sedan pulled up. Once we were in the car, Victoria called Richard Zhang, who had offered to let me stay with his family in Beijing, and informed him that we were on our way.

"Maybe one hour to get to Beijing. Not long way, but traffic very bad." Victoria tumbled through her words. I was tired and after a few minutes I closed my eyes and dozed off.

I awoke to the sound of fireworks. It was dark and we were in the midst of the city. Cheaply built apartment buildings, four or five stories tall, lined the streets lit by dim orange streetlamps. All around us fireworks exploded in the night air. The rockets traced blurred red and green and yellow lines through the dark smog. There seemed to be no pattern as to how and when they were set off. Unlike the precise, choreographed performances I had seen on the Fourth of July, these fireworks were fired in a series of mistimed, unordered volleys.

We drover farther and passed by a roadside stand selling fireworks. Discarded firework casings, fragments of charred cardboard, littered the street like confetti. To my amazement, I saw men with their wives and children setting off fireworks right next to the stand, in the middle of a busy city street. A car even had to swerve to avoid driving over a bundle of freshly lit firecrackers. It was chaos.

"What's going on?" I asked Victoria.

"Fireworks have been banned for more than ten years," Victoria said. "They just changed the rule. Today is the first day they are allowed again."

"They can just set them off right here? In the middle of the city?"

"Sure," Victoria said. "Why not?"

The slow stop-and-start traffic made me queasy. I opened the window and looked at the acres of buildings that surrounded us, specters in the dark smog. The air was so heavy and stale that I had difficulty taking a deep breath. Everywhere I looked, people were moving. Men and women on bicycles, men and women walking, all pushing toward home at the end of the day. I wondered what Tom would have made of this scene. When we would drive to New York City or to the Hamptons, Tom would make up games for me to help pass the long sit-still hours in the car. A box in a passing car became a box filled with stolen jewels, a sleeping passenger would turn into a kidnapped victim who needed rescuing, and an old man in a vintage Cadillac became a Mob kingpin whom we had to tail. It seems silly now, but back then Tom made it all feel real to me. As we got closer to the center of the city, I saw fifty or sixty bicycles standing in a row. Victoria noticed what had caught my eye, and she commented, "Everyone rides bikes to the bus and subway station."

"Don't they have to worry about them getting stolen?"

"Stolen?"

"The bikes."

"Oh yes," she said. "You have to lock them. But even if you use lock, your bike still getting stolen. At least two times, every year."

I checked my watch. We had been in the car over an hour and a half. I leaned my head back and tried to fall asleep again but I had no luck. I was nervous about meeting the rest of my host family. My father had told me the Zhangs had kids who spoke English. He hadn't known how old they were though. We made a series of turns and, in one case, I could have sworn our driver went into the lane of oncoming traffic to bypass the clogged lane we were stuck in. I tapped Victoria and mouthed my concern, but she just smiled and said, "Don't worry, Driver Wu very good." She smiled again and gave me a thumbs-up.

"Is that what you call him?" I asked. "Driver Wu?"

"Yes, that's what he likes to be called. It's a sign of respect. Like how you say professor or doctor. This a very good job."

We drove through a series of construction areas beside a murky, dark green lake and a small park before stopping in front of a six-foot white gate. Behind the gate stood four identical high-rise apartment buildings, twenty stories tall. Two armed security guards appeared from the gatehouse and approached our car. Victoria explained that we were coming to see the Zhangs. One of the guards nodded and returned to the gatehouse where he picked up a phone and dialed a number. The second guard remained by our car holding his rifle.

"Why do they need guards?" I asked Victoria.

"You have to be very careful, there many robberies. The Zhangs worried about kidnappings. So many people come to Beijing from the country and many people very desperate." The first guard hung up the phone and shouted something to the second. The white gate retracted into the wall and allowed us to pass. Victoria took out her pink phone and called someone, speaking too fast for me to understand. "Just tell to them that we're here," Victoria said.

Mrs. Zhang, who was waiting outside the apartment building, was dressed in navy slacks and a white blouse. She spoke rough English and addressed me by my last name. After introducing herself, she turned to Victoria and the two spoke for some time. I was tired and wanted to sleep. Finally there was a pause in the conversation. Mrs. Zhang turned to me. "*Hao de*," she said and paused. I had learned in the few lessons I had taken with a tutor before I left that *hao* meant good or okay. "Okay," she said in English. "We go now."

She led us to the elevator and told us that their apartment was on the sixteenth floor. On the elevator wall I saw a list of elevator rules written in Chinese and English. They were fairly standard, except for rule number two: "2. PLEASE DO NOT PLAYING AND GAMBOLING IN THE ELEVATORS." I smiled at the thought of four elderly Chinese men hunched over a smoky card table in the center of a crowded elevator. I wondered what the real story was behind that rule.

The elevator opened onto an empty gray corridor. At the end was a bright red door with a huge, golden door-knocker. A savage-looking animal, a dragon or a lion perhaps, glared back at me, its teeth gripped tight around the golden ring that hung from its mouth. Mrs. Zhang ignored the knocker and pressed an intercom to the side of the door.

I heard the sound of several locks being undone before the door swung inward. A small woman who looked to be in her forties or fifties peeked her head around the door. Mrs. Zhang shooed her out of the way and walked into the apartment. Victoria and I followed, but the driver hung back in the hallway with my bags. Mrs. Zhang took her shoes off and handed them to the woman who had just opened the door. The woman, whom I took to be a maid, was holding three pairs of slippers, the cheap, thin kind you find in hotel rooms. I saw that Victoria was now also wearing the slippers, and I noticed that Mrs. Zhang was staring at my shoes. I took them off and took the last pair of slippers from the maid. They were too small, and my heels stuck out far beyond the end of the soles.

Mrs. Zhang gave Victoria and me a quick tour of their home. She explained that they had bought three apartments and connected them. First she led us through two sparsely furnished living rooms, which she said they used to receive guests. The walls were painted white and were bare except for several large and elaborate paintings of flowers and mountainous landscapes. The chairs in the dining room had a shiny gloss to them, and the large sofas that sat in front of the television had a plastic quality that made them look unnaturally clean. She showed me her family's living quarters. I was surprised to find a European-style four-poster bed in the master bedroom and a large bathtub in the middle of the room. The tub was white and had gold taps in the shape of swans. Mrs. Zhang smiled and nodded her head when

Victoria told her how beautiful the room was. I could tell by Victoria's reaction that she was overwhelmed by the opulence and size of this apartment.

Several months later, Victoria told me that she and her husband had been saving up for several years to have enough cash to buy their own apartment. She told me that in Beijing, it had become common for government officials and businessmen to launder their "gray money," money that came from bribes and corrupt deals, by buying second and third apartments in cash. The practice had artificially inflated the housing market to the point where just finding a place for herself and her husband had become extremely difficult. The luxurious bathtub placed in the middle of the gigantic bathroom was an extravagance she would never have even contemplated.

Mrs. Zhang brought us back to the dining area where a maid served tea. She passed around a bowl of small packages of nuts. I took a sip of the tea. It was green and tasted like bitter licorice.

"You don't like?" Mrs. Zhang laughed at my expression.

"No, no, it's good," I said. I raised the cup to my mouth and pretended to drink.

"This is called Long-Jing tea, from Hangzhou. Very expensive," she said.

I noticed a bowl of sugar packets on the table, and I picked up several, emptying three into my tea. Mrs. Zhang, who had been talking to Victoria, looked back to me and saw what I was doing. "Ah!" she exclaimed. "No, no. For coffee. Okay, no matter." I raised the tea to my lips again and took a small sip. It was better.

Mrs. Zhang explained that for security reasons, I must always wait in the building for Victoria. Under no circumstances was I ever to leave unescorted. "Not safe," she said. She also said they had only one key to their apartment. It stayed with their live-in security guard. The key never left the house unless they were all going on vacation, in which case Mr. Zhang kept it. "They can make a copy," she explained. "So we only have one key." She never did explain who "they" were. Mrs. Zhang told Victoria that we were to use one of their four drivers. Driver Wu would be free to take me to school in the morning and tennis in the afternoon. She said that she had made these arrangements with my father and that these instructions were not to be modified in any way.

In all the months I lived in Beijing, I never heard or read about any kidnappings and robberies, but I didn't know if that was because they did not happen or because they were not reported. I wondered if my father had arranged all of these precautions to protect me or to supervise me.

I finished the remainder of my tea and declined a second serving. Mrs. Zhang then clapped her hands, and a servant appeared. She rattled off something in Chinese, and the servant disappeared only to return a few minutes later with two small children. Due to the One Child Policy, it was unusual for a Chinese family to have more than one child. The Zhangs had lived in Hong Kong, I suspected, so they could have more children, and had just moved back to Beijing because, as Mr. Zhang had told my father, the children's written Chinese was very poor. They had attended the American International School in Hong Kong, where half the classes were in English, half in Mandarin. Ten-year-old David arrived holding a Nintendo DS in front of him as if it were a steering wheel. Mrs. Zhang laughed that David was never without his Nintendo. He stood motionless staring at the tiny screen in front of him until his mother said something to him that sounded like a reprimand. He looked up and waved a hand. "Hi," he said.

"Okay, you two talk now, yes?" Mrs. Zhang said. It was a command, not a question. David clearly resented the interruption from his video game, and he gazed at me sullenly. There was an awkward silence. Exhausted from my flight and wanting only to lie down, I was not thrilled by the prospect of having to struggle in conversation with a grumpy ten-year-old.

"David," Mrs. Zhang said sharply. Her tone got his attention. "Chase plays tennis, very good," she turned to me. "Yes. David likes to play tennis, too."

"Do you play a lot of tennis?" I asked.

He shrugged his shoulders. "Sometimes," he said.

"How about soccer?"

David shrugged again and did not answer. Mrs. Zhang hid her irritation with a laugh. "David plays too many computer games. I hope you will inspire him to play sports," Mrs. Zhang said.

David's six-year-old sister, Lily, was dressed in a pink Disney princess outfit and was hiding behind her nanny. Victoria knelt down to say hello, but Lily hid her face in the back of her nanny's leg. Mrs. Zhang told Lily to speak, but she just burrowed her face deeper into the folds of her nanny's skirt. Finally a small hand stretched out from behind the nanny and waved a timid hello.

Victoria squeezed me on the shoulder and said that she was going to go home. She said good-bye to Mrs. Zhang and the two spoke in Chinese for a few minutes. When they had finished, Victoria turned to me and told me that she would pick me up the next day at 10 a.m. and take me to the tennis center where I would have my trial with the team. Mrs. Zhang nodded her approval.

"Tomorrow?" I asked. "In the morning?" Victoria's words caught me by surprise. I knew I was scheduled to have a trial, but I assumed it would be several days from now, after I had a chance to adjust to the time difference.

"Yes, tomorrow," Mrs. Zhang said. "Don't worry, everything already organized."

Her words gave me the sense that there would be no use in trying to postpone the trial a few days, and in any case, I was too tired to protest. Victoria waved good-bye and disappeared with the maid who had let us in.

Mrs. Zhang brought me back to the kitchen where two maids were washing dishes. She explained that if I wanted any food when they were not home to feel free to help myself. She also showed me the room next to the kitchen where the maids lived. In this dark room, with low ceilings and not larger than twelve by nine feet, were a pair of bunk beds that had been set up side by side. Four women were living in a space smaller than the size of the single dorm rooms my friends were currently occupying at New England boarding schools. "If you need something just ask them," she said. "You want water?"

"I'm fine. Thank you," I replied.

She clapped her hands, and one of the maids from the kitchen appeared. Mrs. Zhang spoke so quickly that I could only understand *shui*, the word for water. The maid disappeared and reappeared with her arms full of plastic water bottles. "Okay," Mrs. Zhang said, "we go now."

Mrs. Zhang brushed past the maid and walked through the kitchen to the door at the back. I turned to the maid and extended a hand to take the water bottles from her. She shook her head and lifted her chin for me to follow Mrs. Zhang down what appeared to be a narrow, dark hallway. The maid followed behind us carrying the water. It looked as though the hallway was used for storage. Tall, thin picture frames were stacked in layers against the wall. I paused to take a closer look. The maid didn't see me stop and knocked into me, spilling the water bottles. Mrs. Zhang spun around. Her smile disappeared and she chastised the maid in a fast staccato outburst.

The maid hid her face and began picking up the water. I bent over to help, but Mrs. Zhang snapped, "No, no. She do it. We go now."

We ascended a narrow staircase at the end of the hall to a small, dark annex that consisted of one bedroom with a small bathroom. The walls were painted white and were entirely bare. Across from the doorway was a narrow window with opaque glass. The room was not as small as the one occupied by the four maids, but still, the full-size bed took up most of the room, with a cupboard, one bedside table, and a desk taking up the rest. There wasn't enough room between the bed and desk for a chair. The bed occupied far too much space, and the position of the desk made it impossible to open the cupboard door all the way. I was about to ask where my bags were when I saw them tucked in the space between the far side of the bed and the wall.

Mrs. Zhang raised her arm. "Okay, yes? You will stay here. It's okay?"

I wondered if two of the four bunks I had seen before had been in this room. "I hope I'm not taking anyone's room," I said.

"No, no," she assured me, "this room was empty. Empty room."

I wasn't certain I believed her, but there was nothing I could do about it. Mrs. Zhang told me there would be breakfast on the table in the morning. Satisfied that I was settled in, she departed.

Finally alone, I collapsed on the bed and closed my eyes and listened to the lawless percussion of fireworks exploding in the night air. Everyone back home would be waking up soon. I thought about the friends that I had left behind who would be getting ready for another day at school. I thought about the school dances and the parties that I would never attend, and the jokes and stories that I would never be a part of. Here I was, seven thousand miles away from home—$\frac{1}{32}$nd the distance to the moon—in a small white box of a room on the sixteenth floor in a country in which I was a stranger. I could disappear and no one would know.

It was dark when I awoke. My mouth was dry and my legs ached, and I had no idea where I was. I reached down to rub my legs and noticed I was wearing jeans. I sat up and looked around. I had fallen asleep on top of the bed, but someone had placed a blanket over me. On the bedside table were a dozen bottles of water and a digital clock that had not been there the night before. The clock read 5:27 a.m. I stood up and reached my arms out to find the light switch. The light stuttered and then filled the room with the fluorescence of a hospital. I turned it off.

After I showered, I pulled my duffel onto the bed and dug through piles of neatly pressed tennis clothes and looked for my lucky yellow Nike shirt. The clock now read 5:55. I was awake but not alert. Everything was slightly off, as if it were raining in my head. I remembered what Mrs. Zhang had said about breakfast. I was starving but I didn't go down to the kitchen. It was too early, and I didn't want to wake anyone. But I also dreaded having to cobble together bits of my meager Chinese to communicate with one of the maids.

I cleared a space among the clothes strewn about my bed and pulled out my laptop and watched a film I had started on the plane. I tried not to think about the tryout, but the more I attempted to keep my mind off it, the larger it loomed. I wished Mr. Zhang hadn't scheduled my tryout with the team for the day after I arrived in China.

The film finished, and I still had two hours before Victoria would arrive. I called my father, but it went straight to voicemail both times. I checked and rechecked my tennis equipment, regripped my rackets, and stenciled a red "Wilson" logo on the strings. Satisfied that I had done all I could do to prepare, I called my father a third time. He picked up but told me that he couldn't talk. He was at a business dinner and would call me tomorrow to find out how the trial with the tennis team went. He hung up. I sat there for fifteen minutes and then I called him once more, hoping that there was a chance he had finished dinner. But he hadn't, and so I told him that I'd been trying to call Victoria and must have accidentally hit redial. It was still nice just to hear his voice again.

When I came down for breakfast, Mrs. Zhang had just left with David and Lily. The housekeepers were clearing away the children's breakfast bowls of clear broths and noodles and plates of thinly sliced meats. I startled them, and they disappeared into the kitchen before I had a chance to greet them. On the dining room table, someone had left an unopened box of cornflakes. I walked into the kitchen and opened the refrigerator. One of the younger maids appeared. I asked her for milk. She shook her head. "You know, milk. Um . . . cow?" I said and followed with my best imitation of a cow's moo. She gave me a bewildered look and started laughing. I looked in the refrigerator and saw nothing that resembled a carton of milk. Hoping to avoid dry cornflakes, I drew a picture of a cow that looked more like a goat. The maid smiled and opened a cupboard and pulled out a cardboard box from which she took a plastic bag. I shook my head and pointed to my poorly drawn picture again and raised an imaginary glass to my mouth. Undeterred, she pulled a pair of scissors from a drawer, cut off the corner of the bag, and poured the contents into a bowl. It was milk.

She followed me to the dining room and watched me pour the milk on the cereal. The milk was warm and had a metallic after-taste, and I tried not to think about what chemicals negated the need for refrigeration. I smiled at her and gave her a thumbs-up. She nodded her head and disappeared. I walked back to the kitchen to look for some sugar. As I was opening cupboards, she appeared again. I tried to mimic sprinkling sugar onto my bowl of cereal. She nodded and disappeared and reappeared with another box of unopened cornflakes. I was about to head to my room and get my Chinese-English dictionary to find the word for *sugar* when Victoria called to say the traffic was very bad, and she would be late. As I put the phone down I kicked myself for not having asked her how to say *sugar* in Chinese.

I abandoned hope of improving breakfast and instead had a closer look around the Zhangs' living room. Next to the huge television was a small room that contained the Zhangs' massive DVD collection. On all four walls the room had shelves from floor to ceiling. Every shelf was filled. The titles ranged from Disney classics such as *Aladdin* and *The Lion King* to Chinese films I had never heard of to the films that were still in theaters in the United States.

The tables were covered with framed photographs. Some appeared to be from holiday trips—the Zhang family together on a tropical beach, in front of the White House, with Western friends on the Great Wall, David and Lily holding a tiger cub. Then there were endless photos of Mr. Zhang with all sorts of famous and important-looking people. There was a picture of Mr. Zhang with President George H. W. Bush, one of the whole family with the former Chinese president, Jiang Zemin, one of Mr. Zhang and his wife with Bill and Hillary Clinton, and one of them with a very young boy dressed in Buddhist robes who I learned later was the eleventh Panchen Lama, the highest-ranking Buddhist Lama after the Dalai Lama. The young Panchen Lama was a divisive figure because the Chinese government had controversially intervened in the selection process and chosen him against the wishes of the Dalai Lama. There were many more pictures like those, with people I didn't recognize but I could tell must be important. My father had told me that Mr. Zhang was a wealthy businessman, but that was all he had really said. The pictures made me question if there was not more to the story. I began to wonder who Mr. Zhang really was.

五

I began playing tennis when I was six years old. My father had been a very good junior player and had captained the varsity team at Yale his senior year. Some of my earliest memories of Tom are watching him play tennis with our father. Once Tom learned how to serve, our father started taking him to eight-and-under tournaments all around Connecticut and New York on the weekends. When Tom turned nine, our father hired Lukas Bartek, an ex-professional player from Slovakia, to be his private coach and paid an athletic supply company to construct a backboard behind our tennis court. I think he envisioned Tom using it to practice during his free time, but Tom never did. I am not sure that Tom ever loved tennis, not the way I did, at least.

Tom might not have used that backboard much, but I certainly did. After years of being dragged along to Tom's lessons and tournaments, I couldn't wait to start playing myself. Every day after I finished my homework, I used to take my miniature racket and go out to the backboard where I played imaginary matches against Sampras, Rafter, and Agassi. I never lost. By the time I had my first real tennis lesson, I could already claim seven

French Opens, four U.S. Opens, and, most importantly, eleven Wimbledon titles.

Despite my illustrious success in my own backyard, it was at about age nine when I got serious about tennis. Once I started the fourth grade, I began practicing with Lukas. He was the best coach I ever worked with. Lukas had grown up in the brutally competitive Soviet-run Czechoslovakian sports system and had been ranked as high as three-hundredth in the world on the professional tour before a shoulder injury prematurely ended his career. While he had exchanged his homeland for that of the United States, he had brought with him the methods and intensity of the sports system he had grown up with—as well as the attitude that if you were an American kid, you were, by definition, spoiled.

Prior to working with Tom and me, Lukas had trained some of the world's top junior and professional players and demanded the same work ethic from us as he did from them. He used to say that if you finished practice without throwing up, then you hadn't worked hard enough. Lukas proved to be too tough for Tom, who lost interest in tennis by the time he was fourteen and gave up the sport altogether the following year despite our father's strong disapproval. But for me Lukas was a phenomenal coach. He demanded a lot, but under his guidance, I became one of the top players in the country for my age group. When the decision was made that I would take a year off from school, Lukas had urged my father to send me to train at the elite Laver Tennis Academy in Florida and was adamantly against me going to China to train. Both he and I thought there was a very real chance that I could become a top professional tennis player. After it had been confirmed that I was leaving for China, Lukas took a job coaching a player on the West Coast.

The National Training Center was south of Beijing's central district. Despite being relatively close to the Zhangs' apartment, it could take over an hour to get there because of the traffic. When the traffic was particularly bad, Driver Wu would often pull out of our lane into the opposite lane of oncoming cars.

The outskirts of Beijing had a sameness to them—two- and three-story buildings, shops, apartment buildings—many built at the exact same time so that the result was a succession of identical structures, all in varying states of dilapidation. We turned down a road dense on both sides with gray concrete-block buildings, and rundown shops. At the end of the road in front of a formidable gate stood a green-uniformed soldier with a red star on his cap. He held a machine gun across his chest. Driver Wu rolled down his window and gave my name. I showed my passport and Victoria handed over her national ID card. The guard checked a list and then opened the gates. Driver Wu parked the car in a small lot behind the gatehouse and told Victoria that we would have to walk the rest of the way.

Fifty feet from the gates, a giant five-faced statue towered in front of a collection of dreary cinder-block buildings and cast a long, wide shadow onto the tarmac below. I gazed up at the huge statue as we walked by. It began with a gray-colored stone column that rose thirty feet into the air. Atop the thick column were five athletes representing different sports: javelin, sprinting, tennis, discus, and shot put. They pointed outward in five different directions, their bodies meshing together in the center. They had been sculpted so that their bodies were flawless with lean rippled muscles, but their faces lacked any clearly defined features, and there was no joy in those cold, stone-gray faces. There was something unsettling about that statue. The way that the figures with their sad, not-quite-human faces seemed to represent athletic ideals rather than individuals—as if their identities had been lost.

The center seemed deserted. It was supposed to be one of China's main athletic facilities, and I had expected to see athletes running, stretching, or just walking around the complex, but there was no one around, not even any maintenance workers. I was worried that we had gotten the address wrong, but Victoria assured me we were in the correct place.

We wandered into a gym. The room was poorly lit, and water dripped from a brown stain on the ceiling into a plastic bucket by the door. In the corner was a stack of free weights. The weights were of different brands and materials, a hodgepodge collection that looked as though it had been assembled through random donations. There were two bench presses, one multipurpose weight machine, and a spin bike that was missing the seat. Everything looked at least fifteen years old.

The ratty old gym equipment convinced me that we had come to the wrong place. There was no way that this could be the national training center. Most of the Best Westerns and Holiday Inns I had stayed in for national tournaments had better equipment in their small gym rooms. We turned around to leave when a guard appeared in the doorway. He held a machine gun and questioned Victoria. He sounded angry. Victoria replied and I recognized the word for tennis court. He barked a message into his radio. We stood in silence as he waited for a response. His fingers never left the machine gun, and he looked at me with what I can only describe as hostility. Finally a reply crackled over the radio, and the guard nodded to Victoria. He escorted us out of the gym and toward a second building. When the guard was three strides ahead, I asked Victoria why he had been so upset. She whispered that every Thursday high-ranking government officials came here to play tennis with members of the men's team. That guard could have lost his job if anyone had discovered that we had been allowed to wander into the building. He was responsible for securing it, and we had nearly walked into the officials' reception area. We should have never been allowed to wander around unsupervised.

Inside the second building, I heard the unmistakable sound of tennis balls being hit clean and hard, and I knew we had come to the right place. I thought back to the decrepit gym and wondered if my father had realized the training facilities would be so poor. Maybe once I explained all this to him he would let me transfer to the Laver Tennis Academy.

It had been nearly a week since I had last played, and I was anxious to get on the courts. I knew that once I felt the ball on my racket and the bounce-hit rhythm of a rally, I would be back in a world I knew well, and I would feel more at home.

After a few minutes, a tall, unsmiling woman appeared and walked toward us with long strides. An old wooden racket was tucked under her arm. She was dressed in a white warm-up suit and dark sunglasses and wore white gloves, but she didn't offer either Victoria or me her hand to shake. *"Jiang Jiaolian,"* she said. She looked at me and pointed to herself and said, "Madame Jiang." She turned and motioned for us to follow her. She led us down a corridor and pushed aside a blood-red-colored curtain to reveal six indoor tennis courts. Two teenage boys were hitting on the first court and three more stood to the side, unpacking their rackets.

Madame Jiang yelled out, *"Bo Wen!"* The boys on the first court stopped playing and one of them came over. He was tall and thin, with long black hair tied back with a yellow bandanna. He bounced on the balls of his feet as he walked. He smiled at me and held out his hand.

"My name is Bowen," he said in English. The rhythm of his speech was slightly off. It was like he had seen the words written on a page but had never heard them spoken aloud. I shook his hand and introduced myself. Madame Jiang cleared her throat and said something to Victoria and motioned for her to translate.

"She wants the two of you to play a set," Victoria said.

Tennis courts need to be resurfaced every few years to be kept in playable condition, and I could tell just from looking at them that these courts had not been touched for at least a decade. If courts aren't resurfaced regularly, the surface wears away and they become increasingly difficult to play on. With wear outdoor courts become scarred with cracks and bumps, while indoor courts can become so polished and slippery that the ball flies off the surface as if it were ice. I followed Bowen to the first court, dropped my bag at the net post, and walked to the baseline to begin warming up.

As I had expected, the courts were slick and fast. Bowen, the only left-handed player in the group, spent little time warming up. He played like a typical indoor court player—sending the ball extremely fast and low over the net with barely any topspin. The technique of applying heavy topspin to the ball had been drilled into me by my coach, day after day, and was ideal for the slow Florida clay courts but totally useless on these slick indoor courts.

When Madame Jiang noticed that the boys on the other courts had stopped playing to watch our warm-up, she yelled something sharp that I didn't understand. They immediately resumed play on their courts.

I could tell from my first few shots that I wasn't going to play well. After thousands of hours on the court, every time you hit the ball, you know at that one-millisecond point of contact how good the shot is going to be. That day my arm felt detached from my body, as if it belonged to someone else, and every time I felt I was starting to settle into a rhythm, I sent a ball flying wildly long.

I hadn't realized that the trial was going to consist of a brief warm-up and a set. I had expected I would practice with the team for several days, play a few sets at the end of the week and then hear the verdict. In America, if you joined a team practice to be evaluated, you would be asked first to drill. You might be asked to play points or tiebreakers at the end of practice, but you would never be evaluated by having to play a set right at the beginning.

Bowen came to the net and stood his racket on its head. He played with a red thin-beam Wilson racket, the same racket that Roger Federer used. It was a difficult racket to play with because it gave you little power and required perfect timing and coordination due to its small sweet spot. Very few players on the pro tour other than Federer were able to play with it, but those who could were rewarded with excellent feel. Bowen lifted the racket and held it so the butt pointed toward me. He pointed to the red "W" Wilson logo on the butt. "M or W?" he asked, stumbling over the letters. I wondered how much English he knew. "W," I answered.

He nodded his head and said, *"Hao de* (Good)," and spun his racket with his left hand. It may seem like a small thing, but this one gesture, spinning the racket to see who would serve first, made me feel at home. So many things here at first seemed to be the same as in America, but on closer inspection they were different, imitations or alterations of the original; this gesture of spinning the racket was the first familiar gesture I had seen, and as the racket twirled, for a short second I was no longer in Beijing, but at the indoor center near my house in Connecticut. But then the racket tripped on a crack in the court's surface and came tumbling down, and I was back on the other side of the world once again.

Bowen won the toss and chose to receive. I expected that Madame Jiang would give us new balls for the set, but Bowen just picked up the dead balls that we'd warmed up with and sent them flying toward me. I played a terrible first game, double-faulting twice and sending two sloppy forehands long past the baseline. Bowen, on the other hand, played his first service game close to perfection. He approached the baseline and cracked his serve fast and hard, and it skidded low on the court. Bowen flowed around the court, so perfectly in sync with the game it was as if he saw everything two seconds before it happened. He seemed to know where I was going to hit the ball even before I did. When Bowen hit his ground strokes, his thin arms moved laconically in a loop, bringing the racket up and then dropping it down below the ball. Then, just before the point of impact, his racket became an extension of his arm and his muscles uncoiled to whip the ball back across the net at seventy or eighty miles per hour. A tennis ball stays on the strings of a racket for only a few hundredths of a second, and yet that minuscule fragment of a second was all Bowen needed to get the ball to do whatever he wanted.

I knew from the start of the warm-up that I was outclassed. Bowen simply played on a different level than I did. He was profoundly talented, there was no other way to say it. His movement, his anticipation, his reading of the game, his timing, everything was exquisite. I knew I would never be able to play the way that he did. It was as if the game of tennis had somehow been woven into the threads of his DNA.

At 4-0, I feared I was going to get blown off the court without even winning a game. I looked over at Victoria on the sidelines for support, but she was texting on her pink phone. I walked to the back of the court and stood there for twenty seconds, looking down at my strings. I needed to figure a way to get back into the match. I approached the baseline and took several deep breaths to try to focus my mind. I cracked a first serve, hard, down the tee—ace. I was starting to get a feel for the slick courts and began hitting slice serves so that the ball skidded low and fast. Bowen missed returns on the next three points. I was still a long way off from being back in the match, but at least I had gotten myself on the scoreboard. Madame Jiang yelled across the courts to ask what the score was. Bowen shouted back 4-all. I was confused—I had only won one game. I thought I must have misunderstood him, but he smiled at me and raised his eyebrows.

That moment always comes back to me—Bowen acknowledging to me that he was up to something and that I was somehow part of his plan. I would come to see that it was his supreme confidence in himself and his ability that permitted him to tease fate. I passed the balls to Bowen and he got ready to serve the

4-all game. Madame Jiang came over to our court and watched with her hands folded behind her back. Bowen won the game easily to go up 5-4, and I won the next game by hitting winners that I suspected he had set up for me. Bowen controlled everything that was happening. At 5-all he went into another gear and raised his game and effortlessly pulled ahead and won the set 7-5. When Bowen won the last point, Madame Jiang nodded her head, as if to say, *This is how it should be.*

By fabricating such a close score with the gift of three fictitious games, Bowen had ensured that I would be considered good enough to practice with the boys. At the time, I had no idea why he had done it. Maybe he knew that if he played his best he would keep me off the team and he did not want that responsibility; maybe he wanted someone new to practice with. I wasn't sure, but I was glad he had let me back into the match. It wasn't until months later that I understood what he had been up to.

六

The next day Madame Jiang began the practice by rolling out a shopping cart of over three hundred tennis balls. The boys left their rackets on the bench and stood in a wide circle. She threw everyone, including me, three balls, then she sliced the air with a sharp command, and all five boys started juggling. At first I thought it was some sort of joke. But they continued juggling, and I saw that they were taking it very seriously. Madame Jiang walked to the cart and started throwing each boy an extra ball. It was something straight out of the circus. I had absolutely no idea how to juggle, but I did my best to copy the other boys. I kept dropping balls and having to run after them. I would take as long as I could to chase the ball to minimize the time I spent humiliating myself. Madame Jiang threw an additional ball to all the boys except me and then threw two more to Bowen and a tall boy who wore thick eyeglasses. At the end of the drill, Bowen was juggling eight balls, and Lu Xi, the boy with the thick glasses, was juggling seven.

After juggling, Madame Jiang paired us up to begin drilling from the baseline. She motioned for me to go on the court with Chang Yang and Mao Xiao. Both boys were only about five foot six. Chang Yang was wiry and muscular, his physique more like a gymnast than a tennis player. Mao Xiao was broad, with thick wild hair that hung like a mop and bushy eyebrows that almost met in the middle. I would find out later that the other boys on the team had several rather amusing, but somewhat cruel, nicknames for Mao Xiao that were derived from his last name, 毛 (*Mao*)—the same character as the *Mao* in Chairman Mao's last name (毛泽东—*Mao Zedong*). That character, when not used as a last name, means *hair*. His first name, *Xiao*, was written 恔, which means *cheerful*, but it was pronounced the same as 小 (also *xiao*), which means *small* or *little*. Given his size and appearance, it was an unfortunate name to have and unsurprisingly my teammates gave him several nicknames including *Xiao Maozi* (which translates roughly to *little hairy guy*), *Xiao Zhuxi* (the Little Chairman), and *Xiao Mao* (Little Mao).

We played "two on one" with two on one side of the court hitting only down-the-line shots, and one on the other side returning their shots crosscourt. They hit the ball hard and fast but they lacked consistency, and it was difficult to get a long rally going to establish a rhythm. Several times Madame Jiang came on the court and chided us for our bad footwork. I couldn't understand a word she said. I think she was trying to show us to take fewer but bigger steps and then sidestep back to the center of the court. She demonstrated herself, but her demonstration made no sense. Her footwork was all wrong. She pushed off from the court with the wrong foot and instead of doing a split step she crossed one foot over the other.

Madame Jiang then stood at the net with her large shopping cart and fed the balls side to side. One forehand, one backhand. We each hit six shots and then the next player rotated in. This drill was elementary, and, for us, it had no purpose except to practice repetition of technique—something I had stopped doing by the age of twelve.

In the year that I spent in China, Madame Jiang never once adjusted or corrected anyone's technique, but would have us do this drill over and over again to no purpose. She offered no comments as to where we hit the ball; it didn't matter if we hit them all crosscourt, down the line, or in the bottom of the net. It was a stark contrast to the methods I was familiar with in America. Since I was nine years old, I had spent every summer and winter vacation at tennis academies in Florida. At those academies, every drill we did during practice was chosen for a reason and was designed to achieve a specific goal or purpose. We would work on specific shots: running forehands, topspin lobs, angled passing shots. We would practice predesigned patterns like a quarterback and his offensive line rehearse their plays. The coaches did video analysis of our technique, designed specific fitness and workout plans that were tailored to each individual player, charted statistics in our matches, and carefully monitored our progress and improvement over time. In China there was none of that. There was just a woman who clearly knew very little, if anything, about tennis and her shopping cart of three hundred tennis balls that were so old some of them barely bounced. When I saw what these players were working with, I was amazed that they were as good as they were.

Without warning, Madame Jiang stopped the drilling and told us to play sets. She paired me with Mao Xiao. I had him figured as the type of player who would get frustrated if I mixed up my play and didn't let him hit the same shot twice. I played better than I had the day before, and won 6-3. Then I played Chang

Yang, who was wilier than Little Mao, and lost 6-4. Bowen had been keeping his eye on my matches. When practice was over, he sat next to me on the bench and began rearranging his bag. He asked me in English, "How old you?" I told him I was four-teen, but he didn't understand my rough Chinese response. I pulled out a piece of paper from my tennis bag and wrote, "*Shi si sui. Ni duo da* (Fourteen, how old are you)?" He examined my Chinese characters. He smiled and looked at me and nodded his head in approval. I asked him how old he was. He pointed to his chest and answered my Chinese in English, "Me too. You make the team. You good for fourteen." Bowen faltered over the word *fourteen.*

Madame Jiang noticed us talking and slapped her racket hard twice on the net, which was her way of telling us to stop talking and hurry up with the ball collection. Bowen moved on with his ball hopper picking up balls. Looking down at the ground, he mumbled in broken English, "Madame Jiang, no speak." I as-sumed he meant that she didn't speak English. He looked up to see if she was watching. She stood on the far side with her arms crossed. He looked back down and said without looking at me, "Madame Jiang—no play tennis."

After practice, the entire team went to the gym to work out with weights. In America most academies do not allow boys under fifteen to train with weights. The view is that before age fifteen, bones have not developed enough and weights could cause injury. I explained this to Victoria, and she translated for Madame Jiang. Madame Jiang shrugged her shoulders to sug-gest she didn't care. She told Victoria that I should come back the following day. She gave no indication whether or not I had made the team. She obviously was aware that my introduction to the team had come down through the Minister of Sport. I sensed Madame Jiang didn't like having someone imposed on her. As tough as Lukas had been, I knew he cared about me and wanted me to do well. It was difficult to work hard for a coach when you knew they didn't care, and there were many days when I wished Lukas was with me in Beijing.

七

The traffic back to the Zhangs' was even worse than the day before. For over forty minutes we were at a dead stop. Victoria pulled a book from her purse and opened it. I asked her what she was reading. She looked up and turned the cover to me.

"*One Hundred Years of Solitude*," I read aloud. The title was written in English but the text was in Chinese.

"Did you read this one before?" Victoria asked.

"No, I've never heard of it. Who is it by?"

"By?"

"Who wrote it?"

"Oh," Victoria said. "*Ma-er-ke-si*. You know him? In China, now he is very popular." Victoria pulled out her phone and toyed with it for a few seconds and then held it out to me. "You see? Number one in China now."

I looked at the screen and saw that Victoria had pulled up the best-seller list on a website that looked as if it were the Chinese equivalent of Amazon. *One Hundred Years of Solitude* by Gabriel García Márquez occupied the top spot. It was followed by *The Catcher in the Rye*, a book by a Chinese writer, *The Great Gatsby*, and *Love in the Time of Cholera*. It surprised me to see old books like *The Great Gatsby* on a recent best-seller list. I asked Victoria about it, and she told me that many Western classics had only started getting translated into Chinese in the last few years. She pointed to the third-placed book.

"Do you know Gao Fei?" Victoria asked.

I shook my head.

"He is a very popular writer here. He is Chinese though. But many people said that he copied Ma-er-ke-si. So I bought this book because I want to see if that's true."

"Is it?"

"I don't think so. Maybe the way they write is a bit similar. But—" Victoria held up the book. "The feelings in this one are different from Gao Fei's books. In Gao Fei's books, you can feel the spirit of China. In this one, there is a different spirit."

"Is he the best writer in China?" I asked.

"Gao Fei? He is good. Many people like Da Ning more. I do. But his books are very criticizing the government. So nobody will say he is best. He doesn't win the prizes. Gao Fei wins many prizes." Victoria paused. "Do you like to read?" she asked.

"I read some," I said. "Mostly for school though. My brother liked to read a lot."

"Why not? What is your most favorite book?"

I thought for a moment. "Last year I had to read a book called *To Kill a Mockingbird*. I liked that one."

Victoria smiled. "You will find that one for me, and I will buy you one book Da Ning wrote that is my most favorite one."

Several soldiers stood at attention along the street, guns across their bodies in a ready position. I was about to ask Victoria why there were so many armed guards everywhere with such serious-looking machine guns, but before I could, Driver Wu told Victoria a motorcade would be coming through. Almost as soon as Victoria translated this for me, a motorcade of black Audi A4s came up beside us in the emergency lane. Driver Wu looked back at us and smiled.

"What's going on?" I asked Victoria.

"They're government officials," Victoria said. She pointed to the back of a passing car. "See, they have white license plates."

Every car in the convoy had a white license plate with red and black lettering instead of the usual blue plates with white letters. "What does that mean?"

"That's how you know they're officials. They always have the Audis with white license plates. They can use the emergency lane. They don't have to follow the rules."

I would come to understand that there were a lot of things in China that I could not explain, for example how Driver Wu always knew when a motorcade was coming, or when he could cross into the wrong lane, or when he should obey the traffic cop standing in the middle of a busy intersection, and when he could ignore him.

I yawned and let my eyes close for a second. I was still fighting off jet lag, and the exhaustion and disassociation came in waves. I leaned my head against the window and tried not to think too much about what I had traded for this year. I forced myself to stay awake by trying to translate the road signs we passed.

The traffic had slowly started moving again. When I asked Victoria why there was traffic going into Beijing at this time, she just laughed and said there is always traffic, it doesn't matter which way or what time. Driver Wu decided to try a shortcut, and soon we were going through narrow single lanes and alleyways. It was slow, but at least we were moving. At a crossroad with a light

I saw two boys playing a makeshift game of badminton in the street with the heads of two broken badminton rackets attached with twine to some sticks. I tapped Victoria on the shoulder and said, "Isn't that dangerous?"

Victoria shrugged her shoulders. "They will be okay." I thought about David and Lily Zhang and tried to imagine them being allowed to play badminton on the streets, but I wasn't able to picture it. These children were part of a different China.

Victoria pulled out her cell phone and scrolled through some of the features. I asked her if it was new. She nodded. "Pink is very hard to get. I had to wait for six hours!" On our long car rides, Victoria often placed her pink cell phone on the seat next to her. Sometimes she would pick it up and play with the features or send text messages to friends. Sometimes she would just hold it and admire it.

My father had told me that the Chinese had the biggest cell phone system in the world. They had leapfrogged technology; many Chinese went from no phones to cell phones. In many places they didn't even bother installing landlines. During my time in China, Victoria upgraded her cell phone twice. She would spend hours learning all the features of each new phone. Cell phones were one of the few Western consumer goods that were affordable but expensive enough to be prestigious. To her, a phone was a fashion accessory in the same way the newest pair of shoes or an expensive bracelet would have been.

After a gruesome two hours we made it back to the Chao-yang District where the Zhangs lived. I had asked Victoria about Beijing's famous fake DVD shops, and on the way back to the Zhangs she told Driver Wu to stop at a dismal-looking store with

DVD VIDEO in large soot-covered red letters emblazoned on its windows. I had seen at least a dozen of these stores on the way home. When we went in I was surprised to see titles that had not come out yet in America. I looked at the price, 10 RMB, slightly more than one dollar. The store had all of the new movies and most of the popular TV shows. The television show 24 had just finished season two in America and it wouldn't be out on DVD for another six months, but here it was, right in front of me. It cost the equivalent of five U.S. dollars as opposed to the fifty dollars it would cost when it would come out in the States. I couldn't wait to message my friends back home once I had internet hooked up in my room. I ended up getting the season of 24 and three other DVDS for nine U.S. dollars total.

Victoria and I crossed the street to the Zhangs' apartment building compound. With the building in sight, I convinced Victoria—and it did take some convincing—that I'd be able to survive an elevator ride by myself. I rang the doorbell and waited a few minutes. One of the maids opened the door. She said something to me that I didn't understand. I waved and headed to my room. She called after me in a tone that sounded urgent, and I turned to find her pulling on my shirt and pointing at my shoes. I dropped my bag and bent down to unlace my sweat-stained shoes. She didn't wait for me to take them off but pulled them off my feet before I had a chance to. Shoes in hand, she scurried back to the doorway.

I heard the sound of her bolting the three locks as I trudged through the living room toward the kitchen. I was pleased to see the living room was empty. My legs ached, and my back was sore from hitting serves. I walked down the dark hallway and up the stairs to my annex. My legs burned as I walked up the stairs. Lukas would have made me stretch after practice, but here there was no one checking that I did the things I was supposed to do.

After showering I felt the familiar haze of jet lag return. It became harder and harder to keep my eyes open. I was in the middle of putting on socks when I fell asleep.

I awoke not knowing where I was. I checked my watch—seven fifty. Morning or evening? The haze in my mind cleared as my stomach awoke: "Dinner." I picked a fallen sock off the ground and slipped it on my right foot. My thighs burned even more than they had before, and pushing myself off the bed was an excruciating task. I descended the stairs step by step, trying to bend my legs as little as possible.

I pushed through the door into the kitchen, expecting it to be swarming with maids cooking and cleaning, but it was empty. There was no one at the dinner table either. It was then that I heard an exclamation from across the room. David was sitting in front of the television, eating his dinner on a table in front of the sofa. I walked over and sat next to him. He was watching some sort of wrestling event. He glanced at me before turning his attention back to the television.

"What is this?" I asked.

"*WrestleMania*," he said, without breaking eye contact with the television.

I focused on the program. At that moment, a scary-looking bearded guy with a long blond ponytail and a swollen torso accented by a sleeveless biker jacket climbed into the ring. Two men who appeared to be identical twins waited on the other side of the ring wearing matching all-black outfits. They also both had long ponytails and appeared to be wearing eyeliner. I wondered how this, of all things, had made it to Chinese television. "Who's playing?" I asked.

"You mean fighting? This guy is the best. His name is Triple H. He's fighting the Hardy Boyz."

There was silence and I tried to think of something else to say. "You think he's gonna win?"

"Of course, he's the best."

"You speak English really well," I said.

"Yeah, I know. We speak English in schoo—Woah! Did you see that?" David jumped up from the sofa and gestured at the television. Triple H had just landed a massive hit on one of his opponents. David punched his fists in the air and brought them down on an imaginary Canadian foe. "That was awesome!" he shouted.

"So, where is everyone?"

"Dunno. Lily is doing homework."

Perhaps alerted by David's shouts, a maid appeared in the living room. Upon seeing me, she disappeared to the kitchen and returned a moment later and placed a tray of food in front of me. There was a cup of soup and a bowl filled with some sort of brown gelatinous material next to it. A bowl of white rice and a small plate of meat that looked vaguely like pork made up the rest of the tray's offerings. In the coming months, whenever I could convince Victoria, I tried to eat at the few Western restaurants I discovered around the city. It wasn't that I was opposed to eating the local food, some of which I found delicious; it was more that it was just so foreign that it became exhausting after a while. The Hard Rock Cafe proved to be an unlikely savior during my year in China. Its mozzarella sticks and chicken fingers neither looked nor tasted like they did in America, but they were close enough. And they proved to me that the world I left behind still existed.

I asked David how they could get *WrestleMania* on television, and he said they could get a lot of other channels too, and he showed me where CNN, BBC, and HBO were. We watched Triple H a little longer. David jumped up and down on the sofa throwing punches and kicks as if they would somehow help his hero, Triple H, but David's efforts were in vain as the Hardy Boyz proved too much, and Triple H limped out of the ring with a promise to return. I remembered the new DVDs I had just bought. I patted David on the back and told him I was going to my room.

The quality of the first DVD was shockingly bad, very grainy, and there seemed to be a black furry patch in the bottom left corner. About four minutes into the film, the furry patch moved, and I realized it was the head of a person. Someone had brought a camera to the movie theater and recorded the film. I ejected that film and tried another. That was how I learned it was a mistake to buy movies that had just come to the theaters. The slightly older ones already on DVD were much better quality. This rule generally applied unless it was award season. During this time the movie companies sent out DVDs of all the new and still-in-theater films to film critics. Somehow these discs made their way to pirates. Once in a while I'd get a DVD that had "This movie is strictly for Academy Awards judging purposes only" scrolling across the bottom.

This became my routine. Most days I would get home from tennis and go straight to my room until it was time for dinner. Sometimes David was waiting for me. I could tell he wanted me to hang out with him, but I didn't want to be anyone's older brother. But sometimes the emptiness of my room would get to me. Sometimes those four walls reminded me of a story Tom used to tell me about a World War II tail gunner who was a grandfather of one of the kids in his class. The tail of his plane was shot off by a German fighter pilot, and while the others in the plane went crashing down to the ground, the tail of the plane spiraled slowly down to earth, and so he stayed in the tail until he got close enough to jump out with his parachute. I don't remember all of the details of the story except that Tom liked to retell it—he liked to imagine what it must have felt like to be eighteen years old and have time to think about how to save your life. Sometimes I couldn't get that story out of my head, and the more I tried to think of something else, the more difficult it became until finally I would have to leave my room and join David, who was usually playing video games or watching TV. I watched a lot of films with David that year. We became experts in all the James Bond films. Sometimes when David and I shared a TV dinner together, he would pick a Bond film and challenge me to recite entire scenes from it. I attempted an English accent—one that I imagine was quite terrible, but to David it sounded like the real thing. Back home my friends and I used to watch a lot of funny shows like *The Simpsons* and *Saturday Night Live*. But I didn't watch many of those in China because David didn't get the humor, and I don't know why, but I never enjoyed watching those shows by myself. I think it's because I had no one to laugh with.

On the fourth morning I was awakened by the ringing of my cell phone. It was my father, who said he was calling with good news. I thought for a second that he was going to tell me that he had changed his mind and that he was sending me to Laver. But the good news was that I had passed the trial for the Beijing team. I wouldn't be able to play tournaments, but I could train with them every day. I thought back to the match I had played with Bowen and suddenly I resented him for giving me those games.

"Dad, the facilities and stuff here are really bad. I don't think the coach really knows what she's doing."

"What are you talking about?"

"All the gym stuff is super old. All the balls we play with are dead. I feel like I'm going to get worse over here. I thought the whole point of this was to get better. And if I can't play tournaments—"

"Look, this is going to be what you make of it. The best way to improve is by playing with better players. The players there are good, yes?"

"Yeah, I mean they're good. But the coaching is terrible."

"Chase, you've had years with some of the best coaches in the world."

"There are good players at Laver, too. Lukas told me the U.S. national team just moved there. All the best guys in my age group are training there now."

"Is that what this is about?"

"What do you mean?"

"For the last time, you're not going to Laver. We're not having this discussion again."

I felt like punching the wall. I wanted to protest, but I said nothing, and there was a long silence on the line. I didn't understand why he was so against the idea of me going to Laver. I knew it would be so much better for my tennis to spend the year there, and Lukas had said the same thing.

"Has Victoria gotten you set up with Chinese classes yet?"

I didn't answer right away.

"Hello? Can you hear me?"

"We're going there this morning."

"Okay, that's good." He paused. "How do you like it so far?"

"Like what?"

"Beijing. Fascinating, right?"

I gazed out my narrow window at the city that grew in a cloud of fog. The specters of buildings and cranes grew fainter and fainter the farther away they were, slowly blending into the white-gray fog until the fog overwhelmed the city entirely and even the faintest traces of the city's skyline disappeared into a cheerless wall of white-gray nothingness. It was a disorienting feeling, not being able to see the horizon. You lost all sense of perspective and location. It made you feel like you were in the basket of a balloon lost in the clouds.

"Yeah, it's good," I replied, not meaning a word. I wished that I did like it here. It was an interesting place. But it was a difficult place to be alone.

Victoria called me at half past eight to tell me she was downstairs. I told the Zhangs' security guard I was leaving, and he unlocked the door and let me out. As I walked around the car, I noticed that it had a white license plate. I wondered how Mr. Zhang was able to have government license plates on his cars. I didn't understand exactly what he did, but I knew he wasn't a government official.

Soon Victoria and I were off to the language school. I had a bad headache that I chalked up to still being jet-lagged, but Victoria said it was probably the pollution.

"In Beijing we have an expression that we are buried up to our necks in pollution," she said. "Many foreigners get headaches. After some time the headaches won't be so bad, but you will always notice the color of the sky. Most days the sky is gray, it's not blue, sometimes you don't see the sun for a long time. Even for me the air is bad. I don't think I ever get used to it."

The car ride was long, and we went slowly until Driver Wu decided to go into the lane of oncoming traffic. Victoria looked at me and smiled triumphantly. It would be impossible otherwise. "Take us two or three hours," she said. "Don't worry, Driver Wu knows what he's doing." We wove in and out of the oncoming lane of traffic.

During the car ride Victoria chatted with Driver Wu. I caught snatches of what they were saying but had to rely on Victoria's translations for the most part. Driver Wu explained that he had been in the Special Forces branch of the military but had left about ten years ago to become a bodyguard and driver. He had worked for the Zhangs for most of those years. He said something about his eight-year-old son and video games. I think he was worried that his son played them too much.

There was so much congestion both ways that even our ability to cross over into the opposing lane of traffic did not help that much. We turned into a maze of *hutongs* to reach the school. Several times we were reduced to going foot-speed down these small alleyways because someone was on a three-wheeled bike in front of us and there was no room to pass. The car stopped outside a dilapidated five-story building with a rusty fire escape running up the side. On the outside of the building was a sign that read: BEIJING WOMEN'S PUBLISHING HOUSE.

"Is this the school?" I asked Victoria.

"Mmm hmm," she said.

"I don't think it is."

She pulled a piece of paper from her purse and studied it for a second. "This is it," she said. "Floor five."

The Taiwanese Language Institute occupied the top floor of this cheaply constructed office building. It had been founded in New Jersey in 1956 and in that same year had set up a school in Taipei. The school had been unusually successful teaching Chinese to Westerners and had expanded to mainland China during the past decade. A former banker whom my father knew had moved to Beijing to take part in what he thought would be the equivalent of the dot-com revolution. He had spent a year doing a crash course in Mandarin at this school believing he would be perfectly positioned to make a fortune on the economic rise of China if he could speak the language. He claimed to have become nearly fluent and had highly recommended the school.

We arrived at the school an hour late. I had missed my first class. I sprinted up the four flights of stairs and down the hall to the office and burst through the door. Two women looked up at me, surprised. One was the *Xiao Zhang*, the School Head, and the other one was the school secretary.

"Sorry, there was a ton of traffic. We were stuck for over an hour." I was out of breath and panting for air.

"Oh, it's okay. Today really bad traffic. Your teacher is still not here yet. Anyway, just don't be late again," the principal said.

"Where should I go now?"

"Room twelve, you have five minutes before the next class starts. So you can just wait in that room." She handed me a piece of paper and pointed across the hall.

I was glad I had gotten off so easily. Lukas had instilled in me a deep fear of ever being late to anything. He had a strict rule where I had to do ten sprints for every minute that I was late to tennis practice.

The waiting room was eight by ten feet. A bombed-out sofa and four metal chairs lined the wall. A young man who looked like a college student was slouched on the sofa reading the *China Daily*. He had a low buzz cut and was wearing sweatpants. He looked as though he was at least partially of Asian descent. A second man, whom I put in his mid- to late thirties, sat in one of the metal chairs. He was well dressed in expensive-looking jeans and brown leather driving shoes, and he had his hair slicked back with hair gel that was shiny under the room's bright light. He was reading a newspaper that I recognized as the salmon-colored *Financial Times* that my father read.

I nodded hello and sat down. The man with the slicked-back

hair looked up from his paper and asked me what brought me to this place. I explained that I was taking a year off from school and was planning to take Chinese classes.

"How about you?"

"I'm doing an intensive course here," he said.

"For how long?"

"Six weeks." He held out his hand and introduced himself as Josh Waring. The younger guy in the sweatpants raised himself off the sofa and shook my hand as well. His name was Tao Campbell and he was from Lubbock, Texas, and he had been in Beijing for one month. He said that he had been a student at Texas A&M but had realized halfway through his junior year that he had no idea what he wanted to do with his life, so he had dropped out and worked at his dad's car dealership for six months to pay for himself to come to Beijing and learn Chinese. Tao said he was planning on staying until his money ran out. Josh whistled and said that what Tao was doing was gutsy. I asked Josh what he was doing in Beijing, and he told me that he had just left a boutique investment bank to come to China to start his own business with a Chinese guy he went to business school with. Josh said he had done some work for his old investment bank in China, and it struck them that there were great inefficiencies in the market. Such an environment allowed for smart investors to mine the inefficiencies. Josh spoke with the confidence that he was one of them.

"Isn't it hard as an American?"

"Of course," Josh said. He twisted a gold watch around his wrist and added that he would have never considered starting anything in China if he didn't have Chinese partners. He smiled and said, "China is all about connections. And my business partner is hooked up over here. His family is close with the Premier. We're gonna make a killing."

"Who's your teacher?" Tao asked.

I looked at the piece of paper. "Ai Lu. Room twelve." Tao leaned over and looked too.

"Oh, *Lu Laoshi*. She's great, I—" Tao said. He was cut off by the built-in PA system, which began playing a high-pitched Chinese folk song at a loud volume. "That's the bell," he said over the music. I walked down the hall in search of room twelve.

Ai Lu was a small, wiry woman, probably in her fifties. She wore a dress with a pattern of green and red owls and held a clear glass thermos of tea with all sorts of flowers and herbs floating in it. She told me to call her Lu Laoshi (Teacher Lu) and then she asked me to introduce myself. I began in English but she immediately stopped me, and, with a kind smile, told me to speak Chinese. I told her that I wasn't very good yet, but she said it didn't matter and that making mistakes was the only way to learn. I told her my name and age, and I tried to talk about my hometown and my hobbies. It was frustrating. There were so many simple words that I had no idea how to say. She asked me about my family. I told her that I was an only child and that my father was a banker and my mother was a teacher because I hated the way people looked at me when I told them my mother had died. But it was a mistake to say teacher. She got excited by that and asked me a bunch of questions about what kind of teacher my mother was and I had to lie on the spot.

Like many people I met in China that year, Teacher Lu had a background of incredible hardship. I would later learn that she was from Beijing and had lived in the city until she was fifteen when, during the Cultural Revolution, she was sent to a labor camp twenty kilometers outside of Beijing. She said that she had to spend six years there, but that it wasn't so bad, because she had been able to bicycle home to her parents' house in Beijing on the weekends. Her brother had had it much worse. He had been sent to a labor camp in Inner Mongolia and only came home once during those six years. She told me that when he came home he was thin as a starving dog, and his hair and clothes were covered in lice.

The thing she disliked the most about the labor camp was that it meant she couldn't attend school. For six years the only book she was allowed to read was Chairman Mao's "Little Red Book" of quotations. After the Cultural Revolution finished, she went back home and applied to take the *Gao Kao*, the national university entrance exam. She told me that the Gao Kao was incredibly competitive that year because it was the first time since the beginning of the Cultural Revolution that anyone was allowed to take it. Less than 1 percent of people who took the exam were accepted to a university that year. Because her schooling was interrupted when she was sent to the labor camp, she had to teach herself three or four years' worth of material for this exam in a matter of months. She taught herself calculus and physics and learned English by listening to illegal foreign radio broadcasts at night. Even still, it wasn't enough and when she took the exam she didn't earn a high enough score to get into a university. But her cousin did, and when Teacher Lu heard that her cousin had been accepted into the foreign language instructor program at Beijing Teaching University, she decided that she would retake the exam the next year and then apply to the same program that her cousin got into. She did just that and, the next year, ended up getting into the program. After she graduated she did a PhD in

English and then applied to study abroad in America where she did two years at Middlebury College. She had thought about staying in the States, but ultimately decided that it was better to come back to China where her family was. She also said that she wasn't sure if she would have gotten a green card because during those two years at Middlebury, the FBI visited her four times because they had gotten reports that she was a Chinese spy.

While she might have fallen into education by accident, Teacher Lu was one of the best teachers I have ever had. She never stayed seated for more than a minute or two. She hopped around in our small classroom and sometimes leaned so close to me and pinched the air with staccato hand gestures that I felt as if she were trying to pick sounds from my mouth. When I would not know the answer or make a mistake, her eyelids would flutter and the rest of her body would freeze, but when I responded correctly she would jump up and clap her hands and say some phrase of praise so rapidly that I never could decipher the words.

My first text was an introductory book on pinyin. Pinyin is the system of writing that uses the English alphabet to spell phonetically the sounds of the Chinese characters. Some of the sounds that are used in Chinese, however, are not even sounds in the English language. The *u* is pronounced like the German *ü*, *zh* is pronounced sort of like *j*, and the *c* is pronounced *ts*. It is difficult because all of a sudden you have to make sounds that you have never made before. For example, to pronounce the word *cai* meaning dish (as in dish of food), you need to press your tongue against your teeth and make an almost hissing sound. It is like combining a *t* with an *s* into a *c*. I spent most of that lesson reading column after column of three-letter words to improve my pronunciation. By the end of two hours, my jaw was sore from forming so many new words.

One of the tricky things about Chinese is that multiple characters will often share the same phonetic spelling; for example, 妈 (mother) and 马 (horse) are both spelled *ma*. The way one differentiates them when speaking is in the tone in which one pronounces them. There are four different pronunciation tones. The first tone is flat. The second tone goes up with the word as if at the end of a question in English. The third tone goes down and then up. The fourth, the easiest, is down. It sounds similar to a command or an angry remark in English. I found this fourth tone to be somewhat amusing as its harshness can often make it seem to an observer that two people are having a very angry conversation, only for them to burst out laughing seconds later. Each of these four tones gives the character a different meaning. *Ma* pronounced with the first tone, *mā*, means mother, while *ma* pronounced with the third tone, *mǎ*, means horse.

However, it gets even trickier when different characters share both phonetic spelling and tonal pronunciation. 消 (to vanish), 削 (to peel with a knife), and 箫 (a bamboo flute similar to a pan flute), are all spelled *xiao* and all are pronounced with the first tone, *xiāo*. In cases like this, one has to rely on context in which the word is being used to realize its meaning. Tones, however, are very important to the Chinese as a mark of education, and a Westerner who can speak using the proper tones is held in far higher esteem than one who cannot.

I made certain that in the first lesson I learned how to say, "Where is the sugar?" I repeated "*Tang zai nar?*" several times to get the tones right. I finished my Chinese lesson at twelve, went down the stairs, and saw Driver Wu and Victoria waiting for me in the car. Josh was perched on top of a brand-new Vespa motor scooter that he revved into gear. He sped off and disappeared around the corner. I envied him for his ability to come and go as he chose.

九

Victoria was in the front seat reading. She marked her place in *One Hundred Years of Solitude* and listed the choices for lunch— there were several local places that served good dumplings or we could go to *Kenduji*. I asked her if Kenduji was Kentucky Fried Chicken, and she said she thought so. She said Kenduji was the most popular fast-food chain in China, more so than even McDonald's, and it was, she said, very good. I could tell she wanted to go so I thought I'd give it a try.

The menu board was all in Chinese, but thankfully it was complete with pictures so I was able to make a selection rather easily. Victoria told me what to say after I told her which item I wanted. After listening to her pronunciation several times I gave it a try. "*Wo yao dian di wu ge* (I would like to order number five)." I mumbled the words, and the woman behind the counter looked at me with a funny expression on her face. Victoria nodded encouragingly. I tried a second time, but this time the woman behind the counter started laughing. She waved over a second employee. I felt the other customers turn to look at me and I froze and stood there feeling horribly self-aware and not knowing what to do. Victoria came to my rescue and rattled off a few sentences in Chinese. She looked at me, smiled, and said, "You need to work on your pronunciation and tones. But otherwise it was good."

There were no tables at KFC so we went around the corner to a small park and sat on a bench and ate our lunch. It didn't taste the same as American KFC. The chicken was spicier and had more flavor and I actually liked it better. I asked Victoria where she had learned such good English.

"In school. Everyone in school has to take English. If you want to go to university you have to take an English exam."

"Really?"

Victoria nodded her head. "English is one of five exams you have to take."

"Even in small towns?"

"Yes, everyone who was accepted at Guizhou University had to do well on the English exam."

"Is that where you went?"

"Yes, I studied English and literature. Then I worked for the Xinhua News Agency. I was a journalist. I left to come with my husband to Beijing, but to find a journalist in Beijing is much more hard. So when my friend who works for CCTV asked me if I knew anyone who spoke good English and could act as your guide, I said I would like to apply."

The language school was only about fifteen minutes from the tennis center. When we arrived at tennis, Madame Jiang and Victoria spoke while I unpacked my bag. Victoria made an effort almost every practice to chat with Madame Jiang. I assumed it was just her outgoing newscaster personality. I would later understand her friendliness to be something much more subtle and complex. Victoria turned to me and translated. Madame

Jiang had given her the schedule—tennis practice from one to five every afternoon Monday through Friday. Saturday morning nine to eleven. They would begin to start practicing for the National Championships at the end of the year. I would not be able to play any of the official or arranged matches, but I could practice with the team. Madame Jiang did not bother to say welcome or introduce me to the other two boys I had not played with. I could tell she felt I had been forced onto her program. Victoria later told me that my presence made Madame Jiang nervous, that she was probably apprehensive that I would be a spy of sorts, that I might report things that were not correct or different from the Western way of doing things. Just as practice was about to begin, Madame Jiang was called into the pavilion for a phone call.

As I waited for Madame Jiang to return, I looked over at my new teammates. I was disappointed to see that Bowen, the boy I played with on the first day, wasn't there. The other four Chinese boys had dropped their bags about ten yards away from me and were standing in a close circle, talking and laughing. I stood there twirling my racket in my hand over and over. They continued talking, ignoring me.

These boys were the best junior players in the region surrounding Beijing. In China, four cities—Beijing, Shanghai, Tianjin, and Chongqing—held the same status as provinces. By population, each of these cities was the size of a midlevel country. Tianjin was the smallest at around ten million people, roughly the size of New York City or Israel, while Chongqing was the largest at over thirty million, a population larger than that of countries such as Australia, Saudi Arabia, Venezuela, and Canada, and was a city that most Westerners had never heard of. These numbers were understated as they only reflected the official number of residents in each city and did not include the millions of nonregistered workers who illegally immigrated every year and lived in China's major cities.

The cities competed against one another every four years in national games that encompassed all major sports—a sort of internal Olympic Games. Within each city existed an infrastructure that was charged with finding and developing the city's best talent in each of these sports. Just as the USSR had handpicked talented, athletic children and earmarked them as future Olympic athletes, such as gymnasts or divers, the cities did the same to recruit for their sports teams. The Beijing Tennis Commissioner had selected my teammates along with over fifty other boys when they were seven or eight years old and put them in a training camp. Each year some of them would get cut either because they lacked the raw talent, or the commitment, or the competitive instinct to win. The state had decided these boys were going to be tennis players, and that is what they became. The boys took classes in the morning and practiced from one to five in the afternoons. Although they were technically enrolled in school, the classes were little more than a formality, and the boys I knew had very little education. Those who were cut from the team were left with nothing except the skills they had developed on the tennis court. The lucky ones were the players who were cut when they were still young enough to learn to do something else. That was the paradox of the system. It doomed those who succeeded within it. The training methods and level of instruction were so poor that it would be almost impossible for any of these boys to reach the level they needed to become professional, and the system took away any opportunity for success in another field. It was tragic, but for many of these boys I knew that the highlight of their life might be winning a medal at the National Games.

There was a cynical side to these National Games. The mayors and the government officials who oversaw sports took these National Games very seriously, as success reflected their leadership ability and competence. The more events and medals a city won, the better it was for the careers of all the government officials involved. In most cases, these government officials had no background or interest in sports, but were occupying a position, such as Beijing Tennis Commissioner, that they would hold for two years before being promoted to an entirely different government department. My guess is that most of these officials did not care about the welfare of the athletes they were charged with developing. They cared about medals, not about the athletes. It was as if these boys had been reduced to pawns within the game of Chinese politics.

Victoria came up behind me. "Go talk to them."

"I can't. What would I say?"

"Just go, it will be fine." She stressed the word *fine* as if I were making a big deal out of nothing. I noticed that the sounds of conversation and laughter had quieted. Without needing to turn and look, I knew that there were four pairs of eyes staring at the two of us. I didn't know these boys at all, but I understood how Victoria, my minder, would be viewed in the eyes of someone who had been left to fend for himself since he was nine or ten years old. Her presence instantly set me apart from them and marked me as someone who came from a world of privilege that they had never known.

"Okay, okay," I said to Victoria. "It's time for practice. You should go now." I walked reluctantly toward the group of boys, feeling their gaze with every step. "*Ni hao* (Hi)," I said. They were silent. One of the boys I hadn't met yet spoke. "Heyy-lll-ooo," he said in an exaggerated imitation. The other boys burst out in laughter and turned back to their conversation.

I bent down and untied and retied my shoes, taking as long as I could. The boys resumed talking. This was just the beginning. Why did I have to come here? I felt this surge of frustration and anger toward my father for leaving me here.

Madame Jiang's cold voice snapped through the dry air, bouncing off the corrugated steel walls and echoing around the cavernous structure. Before the echo was finished, I heard the squeals of rubber on acrylic and looked up to see my teammates racing around the corner of the court. I put my thoughts aside and chased after them.

The rhythm of China was different from the West. There was no formal religion and therefore no day set aside for worship. The sameness of my everyday routine meant that the weeks had a way of running into each other. During the Cultural Revolution, Mao had abolished religion after deciding he no longer wanted to compete for his people's affection with deities and other such inconveniences. Some Chinese had recently begun experimenting with different religions, curiously trying one, and then another, knowing that they were searching for something but not exactly sure what they were searching for.

At home I had been known as a chronic oversleeper, but in Beijing I began waking every day at 6 a.m. Not because I had to wake up that early—Victoria didn't pick me up until 8 a.m., but because I realized that between 6 and 8 a.m. I could catch many of my friends back home during their boarding schools' mandatory study hall periods. At the end of the first week, Mrs. Zhang arranged for someone to set up an internet connection in my room, and I was able to break my isolation by chatting with friends who were happy for a reason to procrastinate. During their nervous early days of boarding school, my friends were just as lonely and eager for an old friend to talk to as I was. Some of them would ask me about Beijing, but none of them really seemed to understand or care about what I told them. They didn't even know the questions to ask. As the year went on and they developed new friendships, their time and enthusiasm for our conversations lessened, and I could tell that my absence had relegated me to a nuisance from the past. I sent messages to a few of them offering to bring back pirated DVDs and asking what they wanted but only one of them replied. That was one of the toughest parts about my time in China, feeling my friendships slip away and not being able to do anything about it.

Every morning I would descend the stairs, retrieve a bottle of water and bowl of cereal from the kitchen, and retreat back to my annex. I never saw any point in sitting alone at the oversized dining room table. Mr. and Mrs. Zhang traveled a lot and were not around very often, and David and Lily would spend a maximum of five minutes eating before an anxious nanny ushered them out the door to school. Besides, it made me uncomfortable the way the maids hovered, watching me, attempting to anticipate anything I might need. At 8 a.m. one of the maids would open the front door and escort me down in the elevator to the building's lobby where Victoria was waiting to take me to Chinese class. After three hours of class I had an hour-and-a-half break before tennis during which I would eat lunch with Victoria and go over what I had learned in class.

It was a strange feeling living in a place and not understanding the language; it was as if I had become both mute and deaf overnight. I was so unconnected to anything around me that at times it almost felt as if I didn't exist. But with each lesson the sounds and characters began to seem less alien, and I could feel that I was beginning to make progress in turning the silence of my deafness into sound. While my Chinese was improving, I still lacked the vocabulary to have real substantive conversations. One of the difficulties with Chinese is that if you haven't learned a word, really the only way to guess the meaning is from the context in which it is used. It's not like Spanish or French where you can infer what something means from Latin roots or similarity to an English word, which makes immersion learning much more challenging. Rapid-fire interactions between native speakers were still as unintelligible to me as they would have been to any of my friends back home. Because of that, I had yet to make much of a connection with my new tennis teammates. It wasn't for a lack of trying, but there is only so much interaction you can have with another person when you don't speak a common language. Besides Bowen, only Chang Yang spoke any English. One day after practice Chang Yang told me he had an English name, "Random."

"You have a random name?" I asked.

"No, my name is Random."

"Random?"

"Yes, my name is Random," he repeated. "My teacher give to me. You have Chinese name?"

"No," I said. "Only an English name. Chase."

"Cha-se," he repeated. The way he pronounced it made it sound more like *Chay-Suh*. I hadn't seen Bowen since the second day. His absence at practice was yet to be mentioned or explained to me by anyone. I asked Random about Bowen but he didn't answer.

The second Monday I arrived at practice fifteen minutes early and found that Bowen was still missing. The same four boys I had practiced with the week before were on the first court, positioned around the net, playing a game of mini-tennis in the service boxes. At the academy where I trained in Florida, my friends and I often played the same game before and after practice. The smaller area of mini-tennis favored skillful hands, trick shots, and misdirection. The game was a favorite of mine. Excited to have found a common ground, I snatched a racket from my bag and ran to the net so I could sub in for the player who made the next mistake. None of the four boys registered my presence. I was beginning to get the sense that they were suspicious and perhaps resentful of my being able to walk into their training program. They had worked hard to be where they were. They had been playing in the same program for as long as they could remember and most likely were fearful of losing their place.

I asked Random if I could play. "Next game," he said. I waited. The four boys kept playing, and despite one of the boys losing two games in a row, the "next game" never arrived.

I stopped about halfway through practice that day because of pain in my elbow and wrist. I had been experimenting with changing my technique to suit the courts better, but slapping the ball low and flat had put strain on my arm. I explained it to Madame Jiang through Victoria. Madame Jiang nodded, uninterested, and said I could rest if I wanted to. I asked Victoria to ask her where the medical trainer was. Madame Jiang simply said, "*Mei you* (don't have)," and turned her focus back to practice.

I sat on the ground to the side of the first court, my back against the corrugated steel wall and watched the other boys practice. The whole group, Madame Jiang included, was on the second court. Madame Jiang stood at the service line on one side with a shopping cart of balls, racket in hand, the four boys in a single-file line behind the opposite baseline. I watched as the boys rotated in one at a time and slapped forehands and backhands as hard as they could, not seeming to care where the ball ended up. Rather than improving, the boys were reinforcing terrible habits. Had Lukas been on the court, the sight would have made him apoplectic. Madame Jiang was making these boys worse.

Bowen appeared dressed in jeans and a loose-fitting gray T-shirt. He saw me and walked over and sat down beside me.

"Why you don't play?" he asked.

"I injured my arm." His eyes moved upward to the ceiling and he mouthed the words slowly. "My arm, it hurts," I said to clarify. I tried to think of the word I had learned that morning for hurt. "*Tou teng*," I said, pointing to my arm.

Bowen laughed and pointed to his head. "This is *tou*." I realized I had used the compound word for headache (literally *head-hurt*). I hid my embarrassment behind a smile, pointed at my elbow, and said, "*Dui, Dui. Zhe teng* (Right, right. This hurts)."

Madame Jiang spotted Bowen sitting next to me and shouted something at him. He sighed and stood up and started to walk toward the exit.

"Where are you going?" I asked.

"I have to go," Bowen said.

I scanned the courts. Victoria was nowhere in sight, and Madame Jiang's attention was back on the boys on court two. Having no desire to sit by myself and watch more mindless drilling, and sensing Bowen was my best chance to make a friend, I jumped up and followed him. "Wait, wait," I said. "I'll walk with you."

Bowen stopped in the doorway. He glanced at Madame Jiang. "Okay." He seemed hesitant. It had been dark every day by the time I had finished practice, and it felt odd to step out of the complex into the brightness of the day. Bowen was several yards ahead of me, so I jogged to catch up. "Where are we going?" I asked.

"I go to . . . uh . . . *zenme shuo* (how do you say) . . . *sushe* (dormitory)?" He looked at me questioningly, but I was unfamiliar with the word. "Where I live," Bowen said.

"Oh, okay. Your dorm."

"Yes, dorm."

"How come you haven't been at practice? Are you injured? *Teng ma* (hurt)?" I asked, making sure I got it correct this time.

"No." He paused as if he was searching for the words to explain. "*Mei guanxi* (never mind)."

We walked along the cracked, gray pavement and followed the curve of the athletic stadium. We passed the five-sided statue that guarded the entrance. One guard and then a second emerged from the stadium's periphery. They marched side by side, chins held high, red-starred caps pulled down low, black automatic rifles pressed tight across their chests into their starched and pressed green uniforms. Neither acknowledged us. I wondered if their guns were loaded.

Bowen interrupted my thoughts. "Why do you come to China?"

"I want to turn pro when I'm older. So I'm not going to school this year. Just playing tennis," I said. Knowing it was something I was going to be asked a lot that year, I had practiced my answer a thousand times in my head. But when I heard it, it sounded false. It was the truth, it just wasn't the whole truth.

"Me, too." Bowen's sudden intensity surprised me. "I want to be professional player, too. Wimbledon." He struggled with the word and tried again. "Wimbledon. I am going to win Wimbledon."

"My club at home has grass courts," I said. "But I'm terrible on grass."

He frowned. "But why do you come to China? I think maybe it is better in America, no?"

"Well, my dad is here a lot for work," I said. Both of us knew that this was an incomplete answer. I wasn't sure I knew the true answer myself. Bowen didn't press me on it. We had now left the stadium and were following a brick path that bordered an artificial soccer field. Trees covered with a thin layer of dust lined the brick path. But they were barren and seemed pathetic compared to the maples and oaks that colored Greenwich every fall with impossible shades of red and yellow.

"So in America you are number one?"

"Me?" I asked, surprised. "No, no. In the twelve-and-under I was number fifteen. Now in the fourteen-and-under I am lower."

"Oh," Bowen said, clearly disappointed. "I am number two in China for under fourteen. Dali? You know him?" I shook my head. Bowen stopped and pointed back in the direction from which we had come. "He plays here. He is tall, hits ball like this." Bowen screwed up his face, grasped an imaginary racket in his two hands, ducked low into an exaggerated athletic stance, and sidestepped to the left, pulling the pretend racket back as he did. He stopped and shadowed a double-handed backhand, slow and awkward, grunting loudly as he did it. I laughed out loud, recognizing it as the backhand of the tallest of our teammates.

"Okay, yeah, I know him," I said.

"He is number six," Bowen said. "The others are not so good, maybe numbers twenty, twenty-five. So you practice here now? How long?"

"For one year, I think," I said.

"Good. I can practice my English." He patted his chest and opened his hand to me as if he was offering something. "Maybe we can play doubles." I knew we couldn't because foreigners were not allowed to compete in the national tournament, but I sensed this was his way of making up for the other boys.

I felt a hand on my shoulder and saw that Bowen had stopped walking. To our left were several rows of identical one-story bungalows that extended far down the brick path. Most wore their years poorly, their green doors pockmarked with brown patches where the paint had flaked off, and their whitewashed walls chipped and divoted. Bowen pointed down one of the tiled avenues that ran perpendicular to the bungalows, cutting the rows into columns. "Okay," he said. "I go here. You should go back. Maybe Madame Jiang will look for you now. She can be angry." The thought made him frown, but only for a second. He began to walk away but stopped and turned back to me. "Hey, what kind of music do you think is beautiful?"

"Coldplay, Outkast." I could see the names meant nothing to him. He listed some names that he said were famous, but I didn't know them and have still never heard of them again.

"Okay, I will give you, uh—" He searched for the word.

"CD?"

"Yes." He beamed. "I will give you CD."

I walked back to the courts quickly with my head low. Bowen's warning had made me anxious about Madame Jiang's reaction to my leaving practice. I passed several uniformed guards. In all my time at the center, I never got used to their presence. I broke into a jog and rushed past the five-sided statue and up to the indoor complex. As I approached the main doors of the indoor center, I imagined an irate Madame Jiang waiting for me, and I imagined the conversation I would have to have with my father about my skipping practice. I felt an anxiety I had last felt while waiting outside my principal's office after I had gotten into that fight with Jake Green.

But when I walked in, Madame Jiang didn't even register my presence. She must not have realized I had been gone. Or maybe she just didn't care.

Bowen was back with the team the following week. After Monday's practice he pulled out a CD from his tennis bag and held it out to me with a wide smile on his face. He asked me if I had brought one of American music for him and I told him that I had forgotten but that I would bring one the next day. I tried listening to his CD that night but I couldn't get it to play on my computer. The following day I gave him a *NOW* pop music compilation that I had brought from America. He studied the glossy album artwork and flipped it over and stumbled over the names of artists as he tried to read them aloud. He ran over to the other boys and showed them what I had given him. None of them seemed that interested, but for the next week Bowen would pull me aside before and after practice and ask me questions about the different artists and how to pronounce their names.

After two weeks of practice, I began to get to know my teammates quite well. I wasn't sure if it was because he spent so much time talking to me, but I began to get the sense that Bowen wasn't quite part of the gang. The other boys would walk to practice together in a group. But Bowen would already be at the courts alone, running sprints or hitting serves. When we would have water breaks, the other boys would stand in a circle and chat and joke, while Bowen came over and sat by me. I noticed other things about my teammates too. You can learn a lot about a person's nature by the way they play a sport—whether they are conservative, impulsive, imaginative, bold, optimistic, pessimistic, a risk taker, a cheater—it's all coded in the choices a player makes. Lukas always said that a hard-fought game of tennis laid bare one's soul.

The boys on the team had differing levels of commitment to practice. With the exception of Bowen, they played with a sense of obligation and duty as if they were going to work every day. Random treaded water, waiting for the time to come for him to leave. Only Bowen had his heart in it, or at least that is how it seemed to me.

I would later learn that Random was the only boy who didn't come from a desperately poor background. I don't know how she found out, but Victoria informed me that Random's father had recently made money in a shirt business—selling cheap white shirts to the growing Chinese workforce over the internet. So Random had a safety net underneath him. I guess because he knew he had a better future than the other boys, he had developed a protective attitude toward some of them. I once asked one of the boys if I could borrow some tape for blisters on my hand, but Random shook his head and said I shouldn't ask for anything from them because they couldn't afford to give anything.

In the first two weeks I was paired with Little Mao quite a bit. He said he was sixteen, but he looked older. His teeth were so crooked and at such odd angles to one another that I guessed it must have been hard for him to bite food properly. He hit the ball flat and hard and never varied the way he played. He stayed on the baseline and was uncomfortable at net. I had figured out on the first day that the way to beat him was to frustrate him by mixing up the speed and placement of the ball. A chip, followed by a lob, followed by a heavy forehand would rattle him, and he would miss by overhitting. If you gave him the same ball every time in a rally, he would lock onto the rhythm and send a winner streaking past you. When we did drills such as figure eights or side-to-side movement, Little Mao almost never missed. He was like playing the backboard.

Dali was the opposite of Little Mao. Whereas Little Mao was small and worked hard, Dali was tall, thin, and extremely talented but the laziest player in the group. Little Mao could not hide his irritation at Dali's squandering his talent. He would look over in amazement at Dali doing a tough drill with ease and then later react with disgust as Dali tanked another match because he didn't feel up to it. He always looked for the shortcut in a rally, and he was happier to let a ball go than to lunge after it. But even though Dali was the laziest out of all of us, his raw ability meant that when he actually tried, he was the second-best player in the group. I also liked his name because it reminded me of the artist.

Then there was Lu Xi, whose last name, 路 (Lu), meant *path* or *road*, and whose first name, 希 (Xi), meant *hope*. We called him Hope for short. Hope was agile and graceful and played a way that was reminiscent of the bygone era of serve and volleyers like Stan Smith and John McEnroe. He wore glasses and old tennis whites. He showed up and went to work like a dutiful accountant and never showed any emotion at practices. The only thing he would do if he missed a volley at net was to push his glasses closer to the bridge of his nose with his index finger.

Despite practicing every day for months with Hope and Dali,

I never really got to know them well. Hope was only seventeen, but there was something broken about him, almost as if all emotion had been drained out of him. The only time he ever really seemed content was when he was on the tennis court. He had a good serve that depended more on placement than power, and he often came to net. All his tennis clothes, I later learned, were hand-me-downs from his uncle who had been the men's number one player for Taiwan. I once tried to speak to him about Taiwan, but he did not want to tell me anything. He kept to himself, even among the other Chinese boys. Hope and Dali were both seventeen and would soon be moving on. Either they would be good enough to make the men's team, or they would be deemed not good enough and dismissed from the program. No second chances, no safety nets, no soft landings. Only Dali didn't seem to care about the outcome.

Over the time that I spent playing with these boys, I came to understand the risk with which they had to live life. They were given one opportunity, just one. It was theirs to manage, and there was no one to help them. I guess things had been decided for me too, but it was different. I was expected to apply myself as my father had done and as his father had done before him, but if I was not doing well at something, there was an alternative plan, and there was always someone watching out for me.

Of all the boys, Bowen was by far the most naturally gifted and the best player. He was never without his yellow bandanna tied around his shaggy head of hair that he held up high in a sort of defiance against the world. As a lefty, he nailed his serve consistently at high speeds, and he could place it almost anywhere. Each shot took him at least three feet closer to the net, so he just attacked and attacked until his opponent returned a weak shot.

Bowen would then send the ball to the open court with so much precision and power that most times his opponent wouldn't even bother to chase it. By the time two weeks had passed, I could tell that Bowen had consciously played me in such a way as to bring out the best in my game. It was as if he had flipped his understanding of how to win into an understanding of how to lose, but in a way that still made it look as though he was trying.

Bowen was always asking questions about America and what it was like. He noticed my clothes—if I wore a T-shirt that I had gotten at a national tournament that had the location of the tournament printed on it, he would ask me about the city—San Antonio, Fort Lauderdale, Palm Springs, Dothan. He was especially curious about the Orange Bowl. At the start of one practice I fished out a bottle of Advil from my tennis bag. My elbow hurt from hitting the hard flat balls. Bowen asked me what Advil was.

"It's medicine for my elbow. To make it stop hurting so I can play."

"Does it work?"

"It helps."

Practices in Beijing started differently from how they did at home. In America, we would warm up by first stretching and then jogging twice around the court and then turning sideways and sidestepping around the court. Next came alternating crossover steps that twisted your body from side to side. Sometimes our coaches would ask us to get our rackets out with the covers on and swing them in shadow strokes to warm up our shoulders. The routine had been thoughtfully crafted to minimize injuries and gradually increase the level of exertion.

Without fail the Chinese practices almost always started with juggling. Perhaps Madame Jiang thought it would train us to keep our eyes on the ball. Occasionally she would interrupt practice and tell us to run laps around the outdoor track that was part of the sports complex. The randomness of her inclusion of this conditioning exercise was disruptive to practice. Only once can I remember her ever instructing us to run laps at the end of practice.

Though I hoped my time in Beijing would greatly improve my tennis, what little instruction was given during the tennis drills was incorrect, and I found myself regressing. None of Madame Jiang's footwork drills made sense. When we were doing an overhead drill, she chided me about my footwork. As I had been taught by Lukas, when jumping back for an overhead I would push off my right foot, scissor kick, and land on my left. But Madame Jiang tried to get me to do the opposite, to jump off with my left foot. It made no sense to me. I knew what she wanted me to do, but the movement was so awkward and made it much harder to generate any height or power. Bowen looked as if he were playing badminton. I resisted what she was instructing, and she got frustrated with me. Bowen said to me quietly, "Do what she asks." I did as Madame Jiang instructed even though I knew it was wrong. She was pleased and smiled and nodded her head. When the drill was over and we were picking up balls, Bowen moved close to me and repeated what he had said when I had first practiced with the team. "She doesn't know how to play tennis. Only volleyball." He lifted his chin toward her. "She doesn't know anything about tennis."

"What do I do at the next practice?"

"Do it both ways. When she looks at you—left foot, when she is not—right foot. She forget soon. Just wait."

A few summers before Tom died, my father took us on a trip to visit good friends who spent every summer in a beautiful but crumbling villa in Tuscany just outside the small town of Marlia. My father's friends didn't have children and didn't know what to do with Tom and me so we were free to do whatever we wanted in the day. Tom had gotten a video recorder for his birthday and for those two weeks he filmed our exploration of the run-down villas in the surrounding countryside. We would spend the evenings watching and editing the day's footage. It soon took shape as *And So We Venture Forth*, a film, Tom declared, that would rival any documentary of exploration he had watched on the National Geographic Channel. For the next two weeks Tom and I snuck into falling-down villas, private chapels, stables, and, in one case, a frog-filled tunnel that connected the main house to a kitchen house. We lit our way with flashlights, and every so often in the film, Tom's voice would softly say, "And so we venture forth." At the bottom of one of the hills we explored, Tom found the plot for his movie in a large fountain that graced the entrance to a sixteenth-century villa. Tom took the opportunity to introduce himself to the camera and said, "In the spirit of other great explorers, he, Thomas Ott Robertson, being of low birth but high ambition, hoped"—*hoped*: he repeated as if to emphasize the odds against us—"to find the source of the fountain." He filmed us going through the bamboo gardens and paths that led to a large stone tank that collected rain and spring water that ran off the hill. At the end of the film, Tom balanced the camera on the ledge of the holding tank and walked around to face the camera. He described our affinity to the world's greatest explorers: Captain James Cook, Sir Ernest Shackleton, Hernando de Soto, Sir Walter Raleigh. Tom put his arm around me and concluded, "And so we ventured forth." He made me promise that every year, with or without him, I would do something worthy of the *And So We Venture Forth* Club.

On the weekends, Victoria and I would take trips around the city, to markets, to museums, to old Buddhist temples, and to monuments from both the Communist and Imperial eras. I looked forward to those trips and I think Victoria did too because she told me once that she planned to do the same thing when she had a daughter. It was a nice break from the everyday routine of Chinese lessons and tennis practice, and we got to visit a lot of really interesting places. It gave us the chance to talk about a lot of things too, and it was nice just to have someone to talk to.

I also felt as though those trips helped me learn about China in a way that books never could. Victoria showed me how the buildings of Beijing held the history of China in their bricks and mortar. She showed me the old city wall that had once been the outermost layer of the city and had protected the citizens against centuries of invaders. But the wall now stood useless, miles from the city's expanded limits. Like most things from the past that no longer had a use in modern-day China, the wall was seen not as a part of history that should be preserved, but rather as an inconvenience. Large sections of the wall had been torn down to make way for new real estate developments and thousands of bricks had been stripped from the remaining sections of the wall to be auctioned off at exorbitant prices to China's new wealthy elite as symbols of their wealth and prosperity. The Zhangs had several of those gray stone bricks displayed on a bookshelf in their living room, next to the picture of them with the Clintons.

My favorite afternoons were the ones where we just wandered through the hutongs, the fast-disappearing network of winding, narrow alleys that spidered through Beijing. We visited old courtyard houses and tea shops that had been in the same families for hundreds of years. People walked or rode bicycles everywhere. Elsewhere in the city it felt as if the pace of time had been set to fast-forward. Every day more hotels opened, more malls were planned, more factories sprouted up, more jobs were created, more people bought cars and laptops and iPods and designer clothes, and more and more parts of the old city disappeared. But in the hutongs, time crawled reluctantly forward and it was easy to get lost in those narrow alleyways.

On our wanderings around Beijing, Victoria and I would play a game to see who could find the sign with the most amusing English translation of the Chinese characters. Our game soon developed into a serious competition. We named it the *Translation Olympics*, and there were multiple different events. There was the VENDOR & RESTAURANT category, the winner of which was a laundry shop with CLEENING SERVICE FOR CLOVES written in English below the Chinese sign. The silver medal in that category went to the restaurant whose motto was SMART NOSHERY MAKES YOU SLOBBER, and promised that their food was "guaranteed not to cause pregnancy." The small *jiaozi* (dumpling) store around the corner from the language school that advertised FRA-GRANT AND HOT MARXISM lost out because of its lack of subtlety. Then there was the PROHIBITED ACTION category in which NO STRIDING narrowly lost out to DO DRUNKEN DRIVING. Honorable mentions in that category went to NO LOUDING, THE GRASS IS SMILING AT YOU—PLEASE DETOUR, and KEEP OFF THE LAKE.

My favorite was the HEALTH & SAFETY category. BE CAREFUL OF CAUTION took the gold over PLEASE SLIP CAREFULLY, and a sign that clearly meant to say CLEANING IN PROCESS but instead read EXECU-TION IN PROCESS. In the INDIVIDUAL FREESTYLE—a category for translations that didn't fit into the other categories—a fire extinguisher labeled HAND GRENADE stormed away with the gold medal. It strikes me now that many of the Chinese I encountered that year were just like these translations. They forged ahead and didn't let their lack of understanding or grammar worry them. They didn't wait for conditions to be perfect. They just kept push-ing forward.

One of the first places in Beijing that Victoria took me was to her husband's art studio. One Saturday morning, a couple weeks after I first arrived in Beijing, Victoria picked me up at the Zhangs' and told me that she was taking me to a place called 798. As Driver Wu sped away from the Zhangs', Victoria told me a little bit about where we were headed. She explained that about ten years ago a group of artists had taken over a number of aban-doned military factories on the outskirts of the city and turned the spaces into studios. The area was now called Art Zone 798 or just *Qi Jiu Ba* (798) for short. The name came from Factory No. 798, one of the largest factory buildings in the complex.

Art Zone 798 turned out to be a collection of cinder-block

buildings organized along a grid. We pulled in and parked, and Victoria called to a man smoking a cigarette in front of one of the buildings. I assumed he must be her husband. He was quite small and looked to be in his early forties. He wore paint-spattered gray work pants and a hooded sweatshirt. He waved to Victoria and threw his cigarette on the ground and walked toward us.

The man exchanged a few words with Victoria and then the two of them stopped talking and looked at me. Victoria laughed and slapped the man on the shoulder. She switched to English. "Well . . . say hello to Chase!" He spoke to me in Chinese, but I didn't catch a word of what he said. "Ah!" Victoria said with mock severity. "*Yong Yingwen!* Use English! His Chinese is not that good yet." She smiled at me. "But he is practicing—right, Chase?"

"Hello. My name is Z," he said. "Very pleased to meet you."

I extended my hand and shook his. "Z? Is that your real name?" I asked.

He laughed. "It is not the name my mother gave me, no. But it is the name I used for art." He shrugged. "So yes, you can call me Z."

"Your English is very good," I said. "I'm impressed."

"I spent ten years studying and living in New York." He lit another cigarette. "Want to see my studio?"

As we followed Z, Victoria pointed to the cinder-block buildings. "This all used to be factories. To make guns."

"When?"

"Oh, I don't know," Victoria said. "Long time ago. Maybe more than forty years. Now it's all artist studios here. And restaurants. All of them but they used to be factories for guns. That's why it's called Factory 798. All factories that make weapons for the army are given number seven."

"Why number seven?"

Victoria looked at me quizzically and laughed. "I don't know! That's just the number they choose."

We followed Victoria's husband to the studio that he shared with three other artists. He walked over to where some futon mattresses surrounded a low table. He unplugged a kettle from the wall, refilled it, and plugged it back into the wall. While the water was getting hot, he walked around his studio with me. It was much larger than I had expected and had high ceilings with large skylights that filled the studio with sunlight. Z stopped in front of a large canvas with eight *Wizard of Oz*–sized munchkins dressed in military outfits standing in a row. Behind them was a large airplane parked on a runway. He stood waiting for my reaction. "Cool," I said. "I've never seen anything like it."

After our tour, we walked to the corner of the studio and sat on the mattresses and drank green tea. Victoria asked me what I thought of her husband's paintings. Did I think Americans would like them? I could tell that Victoria was hoping I would buy one. I told her that I liked them, and the next time my father was in Beijing we should show them to him because he knew a lot more about art than I did. Victoria seemed satisfied with my response. She asked Z to show me other artists' studios.

We walked to a second studio in a nearby building. The walls were covered with large canvases bearing images and slogans taken from old Communist propaganda but painted in a style that was more reminiscent of Andy Warhol's. I assumed the artist was mocking the embrace of the Communist Party in China, but when I asked Z and Victoria if the artist really believed the slogans, they nodded and both said yes. Victoria said they would take me to the studio of the most successful artist in China, Zhang Xiao. She explained that one of his paintings had just sold for over $500,000 in an auction in Hong Kong. Zhang Xiao's studio was at the end of a long row. As we were coming to the door, I suddenly heard the surreal sound of American accents echoing inside the gallery. I was hit by that sense of surprise you feel when you run into a close friend in a place you're not expecting them to be and you have to double-check it's them. It had been four or five days since I had seen another American and a week since I last spoke to my father and had heard American-accented English. Just as we walked in, I saw an American couple, accompanied by a scruffy-looking woman with peroxided blond hair, heading for the exit. The blond woman was an art guide of some sort. She spoke in loud nasal tones and punctuated her speech with wild arm movements. When she saw me, she stopped talking abruptly and all three of them gave me puzzled looks. I realized they were obviously very confused by what an American boy was doing wandering around the outskirts of Beijing with a Chinese couple. It struck me as a funny situation and I decided to mess with them. I nodded at them and with a straight face said, "Nimen hao," in my best Beijing accent. They looked about as bewildered as I've ever seen anybody in my life and it took every ounce of effort to contain my laughter until they had made it through the door.

Zhang Xiao's studio was twice as large as Z's. On every wall were these massive portraits of ordinary Chinese people all painted in shades of pale grays and greens. The way they had been painted made them look almost like cartoon characters. Their heads bulged at the top and then narrowed to a point at the chin. They had huge, balloon eyes with enormous dark pupils and tiny mouths with thin, pursed lips. The faces were stoic, their lips closed and silent. But underneath that stoicism I could sense a terrible sadness that came through in their eyes. It made me feel as if all these people held stories that had never been told to anyone. Stories that were begging to be told, but would always remain suppressed. Many of the paintings were of incomplete families. A mother and a daughter, a solitary man, a father and a baby. I felt as if their sad, haunted gazes followed us around the darkened studio.

Z suggested that we all have lunch at the restaurant he had just opened. Victoria explained that Z and two other artists from his home province, Guizhou, had started it together. She explained that opening restaurants had become a popular thing for artists to do in China. The restaurant provided them with food to eat, money to pay some bills, and a gallery space to exhibit their work.

The restaurant, which had the less-than-creative name The Three Guizhou Men, was about a two-minute walk from Z's studio. The entrance was marked by a bright red sculpture that Z had made especially for the opening. It resembled a sort of totem pole composed of three comically squat men stacked vertically, their arms raised overhead, supporting the figure of a man above. A hostess wearing an elaborate headdress and costume that I suspected was traditional Guizhou formal dress greeted us outside and brought us to a table in the back. Almost immediately after we had been seated, dishes of steaming vegetables, rice, and meats started appearing. Z did what I had noticed a number of Chinese do: he took his napkin and tucked a corner of it under his plate and then used the end of it to wipe his mouth or his hands.

Z explained with great care that these dishes were the dishes his mother used to make. When our waitress brought us a plate of sliced peppers and beef, Z got very excited. He stabbed his chopsticks at the bowl. "This is my favorite. Try, try."

Victoria laughed. "It's not easy to find authentic Guizhou food here in Beijing."

Z pointed to the ceiling where there were sets of characters painted in red on the arches. Victoria explained that the writings were old Maoist slogans and asked me if I could read them. Of the three, I could only translate one, 女人擎半天, as "Women hold up half the sky." The other two Victoria translated as "We shall heal our wounds and we shall continue fighting until the end," and "Once all struggle is grasped, miracles are possible."

"I like those," I said. "They're nice. What are they from?"

"Mao Zedong," Victoria said.

"Chairman Mao?"

"From his Red Book," Victoria said.

"Oh," I said, somewhat surprised. "Isn't that weird to have his quotes on the wall? I would think that they're not really that relevant anymore."

"They're Mao's statements."

"I know, but does everyone believe in them still?" I asked.

"Of course."

"Even now?"

"Yes," Z cut in. "He make mistakes, but he is great man. Before him China had many problems. The Nationalist government was very corrupt. Many people were poor. Mao changed that and he rescued China from the Japanese dogs."

He swore in Chinese and spat on the ground after he said "Japanese dogs." It confused me to see such vehemence toward the Japanese paired with such positive feelings toward a man that had always been put in the same category as Hitler and Stalin in my history books. "But what about the Cultural Revolution?" I asked. "The Great Leap Forward? Didn't a lot of people die?"

"It's complicated." Victoria nodded at her husband. "He was there, you know? For the Cultural Revolution. I am too young, but he is older. He was sent to the work camps."

I wouldn't have brought it up if I had known. Perhaps sensing my awkwardness, Victoria added, "It's okay. You can ask him about it, he doesn't mind." I hesitated, but Victoria said, "If you want to know, you should ask him. He doesn't mind talking about it. Most people do though."

"What was it like?" I asked.

Z took a long breath. "My father was a teacher. That meant that things were very bad for us. He was the first one to commit suicide in our village. After that they sent me to the Dadu River State Farm. I was eleven. Seventeen when I can go home. It was hard, hard work." Z's face darkened and I saw that under his easygoing exterior a harder side existed. "The comrade in charge, Controller Qiu, he was a bastard." Z reached over his shoulder and rubbed his back. "I still have scars." He paused. "But I can't remember his face. I only remember always being hungry. We ate anything we can find. Insects—*zenme shuo*—ah yes, worms, and when we can't find those we ate the dirt, we ate the bark off trees, anything." He paused. "This why I am so small. My head is too big for my body. I should have been much taller. Never enough food."

Z paused and encouraged us to sample more dishes that had been placed on the table. It was all really good but there was so much of it that I was already full. Not wanting to be rude I took another spoonful of the peppers and spicy beef dish. Z picked up a small bowl of rice and ate hastily. He explained that he rose to become the farm's youth deputy party secretary. "When I applied to be the youth party secretary, at the end of the application, I was required to write, 'I will stay on the Dadu River State Farm for the rest of my life.'"

He bowed his head for a moment before looking up. "I could never bring myself to write that sentence. It seems crazy now—but back then, not knowing what the future would be, to write that would break all the hope I hid in my heart. I was not given the head position. I knew I should have said it. I was hungry, and I would have gotten more food as the head. But I just couldn't."

He reached across the table, picked up a dish, and offered it to me. "Please," he said. "Delicious. Very spicy," he added. "You like spicy?"

All the tables in the small restaurant were now filled. The conversations from other tables seemed to bounce hard against the cement walls and floor. I had to raise my voice to be heard.

"What happened?" I asked. I leaned forward to hear his answer.

"You mean how did I get back home?"

"Yes."

"We were out in the fields and this boy, he was two years younger than me but was senior in the camp because his family were peasants, he said that we were going home. Just like that. No warning, no explanation. He said they didn't tell him why or how, but this old flatbed truck arrived, and we climbed on it, and it stopped on the outskirts of Guiyang, and I walked home. After we left those fields, we never came back. I had been away from home for over four years. I remember I went to my house, and only my mother was there. She had been beaten in prison and could never work again. My sister had been sent out to the country a few months after I had left. She was two years younger than me." He laid his chopsticks down on the table. "Ruo never came back. My mother never got over that. Even to this day she still likes to think that Ruo will come back. That she is alive and will return. I have to believe that she got sick and died. There was so little food and no medicine."

Our waitress came with a platter bearing barbecued meat piled high in a mound with diced chilies and peppers. Victoria pointed a chopstick at it. "This one is too spicy for him," she said to Z.

Z waved his hand in front of him. "Let him try, it's fine."

"Thank you. I'm okay though," I said. "I'm quite full."

"*Chi bao le*," Victoria said. "That's how you say I'm full. *Chi bao le*."

I mouthed the words silently, thinking about all that Z had told me. A question struck me. "So when did you learn to paint?"

"After I got home. First I just started to draw. I drew the things I couldn't forget. Controller Qiu beating that old woman. Peng'er falling down in the fields that day, and never getting up. The Red Guard leading my father through the streets with a rope around his neck. Mocking him. Throwing things at him." He paused for a moment to pull his emotions back around him, and I saw his eyes were misted. "The drawing helped me find happiness again. It was a way to tell the story of things I never thought I could talk about. I think it helped other people, too. So I kept drawing and got better and better, and then I taught myself how to paint. Art felt safe."

"So what do people think of Mao now?"

Victoria answered for her husband. "We see good and bad. Some bad things happened, but they see that Chairman Mao loved China, he wanted to free China from foreigners. He wanted to help the people."

"But it seems like nobody wants to talk about the bad things he did. Only the good things," I said.

"It is not so simple," Victoria said. "He was a great leader, and he did what was best for China."

"I just don't get why you defend him like that. Surely your parents must have suffered, too."

Victoria pursed her lips and said nothing.

"Why won't you talk about it?"

"Chase, you are not so smart."

"What do you mean?"

"No talking tells you how hard it was. Maybe for some people it is too hard, too difficult to talk about."

"How so?"

"It's like a scar that is left dry and solid," Victoria said. "Don't touch. If you touch it, it bleeds. Better to leave it alone so slowly, slowly, slowly the scar heals around the edges and gets smaller and smaller. Takes a lifetime to heal, maybe even three lifetimes."

I looked at her to see if she believed what she was saying. There was no joy in her eyes. I saw the same sadness I had seen in my father's eyes after Tom had died, and I realized that what she had said was true. My father and I had never talked about what happened to Tom. The three of us sat there in silence for a few moments.

After that afternoon, I learned not to ask direct questions. I learned to let the answers reveal themselves. In the United

States, most people are only too pleased to talk about themselves. But not in China. I did not know whether it was an innate or learned reaction, a national characteristic, or a form of survival. The Chinese that I came across were happy to listen, but most of them did not want to talk.

The year I was in China was the year that the world seemed to wake up to its importance. There were plenty of Westerners running around looking for opportunities that were, almost without exception, vague and ill-defined. They even showed up at the training grounds of the national Beijing teams. Every two or three weeks, a coach from a tennis academy in Spain or Germany or Australia or the United States would appear. The head of the academy would train with us for an afternoon and show us new drills and hand out T-shirts emblazoned with the logo of his academy. And then he would disappear. Once at the beginning of practice when we were sitting together waiting for Madame Jiang to finish speaking with the visiting professional, Random said to me, "Watch, everyone is going to practice very hard. They hope for a scholarship to his academy. But we are too old. They are looking for younger kids."

I could never figure why these recruiters came. It was not as if the Chinese boys represented any potential business opportunities for these academies. They expected students to pay tuition, and these boys were poor. The boys would try to shine so they might have a shot of getting noticed by one of the coaches and given a scholarship to their camp. Over time the boys developed the sense that everyone who came through was interested in cashing in on China and that there was no chance they would be rescued by one of the foreign coaches.

All, that is, except Bowen. Without fail, whenever anyone came, Bowen lifted his game to an even higher level and played flawlessly. I remember on one occasion watching Bowen decimate Juan Esparcia, the founder of the top tennis academy in Spain that bore his name. Esparcia had once been a top world-ranked player himself. He moved beautifully despite being at least fifty pounds overweight. He tried to impress on us the need to constantly be moving during the point. "It's a dance," he said. "Never stop dancing."

He had asked us to play a game of king of the court with him, and he had planned to whip us all to demonstrate his point about movement. He had no idea that Bowen could hold his own with him. As we watched this Davis Cup veteran under pressure from Bowen, Little Mao repeated what Random had said: "He thinks he is going to get a scholarship, but he won't." He spat on the ground after he spoke.

Within two games Bowen had control and was beating Esparcia at his own baseline game. I had never seen another player mimic the style of someone else so completely. At 4-2, Bowen switched to his game of attack, and Esparcia was finished off completely. I looked at Random and raised my eyebrows in approval. "Pretty good," I said in Chinese.

"Won't matter."

"Why?"

"He is too old."

"But he is only fourteen."

He shook his head. "Sixteen, he is sixteen."

"What? He's fourteen." I looked at him in confusion. Bowen had told me himself.

"Bowen is sixteen." Random waved me over and leaned his head in close to mine. "Everyone here," he said, "is one, maybe two years more than they say. I say sixteen, but I am seventeen." He pointed to each of our teammates one by one and listed their true ages. I was amazed to discover I was the youngest on the team by nearly two years.

"Does she know?" I asked Random, lifting my chin toward Madame Jiang.

He laughed. "Everyone knows but no one says anything. All the players in China do it. Even if we don't want to, we have to. If we don't lie then we have to play guys two years older than us."

I was stunned. Of course I had heard stories about this sort of thing. Stories of North Korean gymnasts who somehow had remained fifteen for three consecutive years, or the occasional rumors about Eastern European tennis players who showed up in Florida at age "twelve," already over six feet with facial hair. But I had never been confronted by it in person. I had never seen it in such a blatant and unapologetic form as this. Random's cool attitude about it threw me off and made me question the truth of what he was saying. Bowen wouldn't have lied to me. I assumed that Random had made this up, perhaps out of envy of Bowen's talent.

"Well he's still very good for sixteen," I said.

"He's still too old for an academy."

"How do you know?"

"I just know."

"Come on, how do you know?"

"I was one of them."

"Where?"

"Bollettieri."

"Is that where you learned English?" Random's English was much better than the other boys.

He nodded.

"Why did you leave?"

"I was too young. I got homesick. It was four years ago, and I couldn't speak English very good. My parents, they could not afford to come over. I wish I had stayed though. Much better than this." He waved his hand around the complex. "I hate this. I don't want to play anymore. Now my parents can afford to send me to America again, but it is too late."

Random's words stuck with me. I thought about how I had sometimes tanked practices in the States when I was feeling tired or didn't want to play. For Random, each minute on court at a place like Bollettieri represented hours of work and sacrifice made by his parents to give him the same opportunity that I took for granted. I thought about the times I had cracked rackets in anger during matches. Throwing a tantrum like that wasn't an option when you couldn't afford a new racket.

Another time an Australian coach came to practice with us. Madame Jiang, as she almost always did, brought out the basket of balls and had us all begin practice with juggling. I had gotten better at it, but I still didn't see the point. Usually Bowen took six or seven balls, but this time Madame Jiang handed him three and snapped at him when he tried to take more. Not to be deterred, Bowen adjusted his bandanna so it was loose, and while he was juggling he shook his head so his bandanna fell over his eyes. He continued to juggle flawlessly. Madame Jiang became furious at him for shifting the attention to himself, and she ordered him to do fifty push-ups clapping between each one. Bowen smiled at her as if to say, "Finally you are going to let this coach see how athletic I am." He sprung into a handstand, walked on his hands to the baseline, flipped backward to his feet, and then did fifty push-ups. Madame Jiang stood over Bowen. I turned to Random and asked, "What's her problem with him?"

Random pulled the corners of his mouth down. "She thinks she is too good to be coaching us. She still hasn't given up the past. My father told me she was a famous national volleyball player. She was meant to win the gold medal in 1980, but China didn't participate in Olympics because of politics. So she missed the chance to be the first Chinese to win the gold medal." Madame Jiang saw Random talking to me and shot him a harsh look. He resumed juggling and whispered, "She is still angry about it."

Bowen completed his fifty push-ups, and on his last one, he clapped his hands twice. The Australian coach stood up and applauded. He was obviously charmed and amused and impressed. Bowen would have to deal with Madame Jiang's anger later.

After the professionals left, Madame Jiang would follow a sort of watered-down version of their drills. Because there was no methodology or theory underpinning her training routine—as she did not completely understand the purpose of the drill—she would have us do some version of it, but it was always a little off. After about two or three weeks, she would stop asking us to do the drills and would return to the practice she had devised.

Among the senior leadership, tennis is a popular sport in China. As Victoria and I had inadvertently learned, every Thursday the indoor courts were reserved for senior government officials. Often several members of the men's team would be required to play with these officials. On a few occasions the top women players were brought in to play. China had no men ranked in the top 500 of men's world tennis, but they did have several women who were breaking into the top 100 in the world. The highest-ranked player was a girl named Peng Ai. She was originally from Tianjin and had trained at the same facility as Bowen. Bowen had heard that she was coming, and he was determined to watch her play. She had gotten to the quarterfinals of the U.S. Open and was Beijing's only hope for the 2008 Olympics.

How Bowen learned that she was coming I do not know, but somehow he found out. "Watch for Thursday," he had said to me, and sure enough on Thursday, Peng showed up and practiced with us for two hours. Madame Jiang assigned Hope and Bowen to hit with her. We watched as the two of them drilled Peng. She was big and strong and hit flat and hard with two hands on each side—two hands for her forehand, two hands for her backhand. Several times in the rallies when Peng hit a ball out, Bowen caught it on his racket strings before it hit the court without ever letting it leave the strings. It was almost as if he made the ball disappear, and then, with the deft grace of a gifted magician, he made it reappear. This display of hand-eye coordination and racket control delighted Peng, and she asked Madame Jiang if she could play a set with Bowen. Madame Jiang didn't like the idea, and Bowen tried to act neutral about her request, but he was, I could tell, thrilled. Madame Jiang said Bowen had to go to the gym. He contradicted her and said he could go after he played a set. Madame Jiang had been boxed in, and there was nothing she could do. She made the rest of us run sprints on the court, but we did our best to watch Bowen handle Peng's power. Peng liked to take control of the points, and once she had control, it was almost impossible to win the point. Bowen started taking the ball early and hitting it on the rise. Bowen knew that he was throwing her off her rhythm. Peng started to lose confidence and make unforced errors. She was a baseliner and was uncomfortable at net, so Bowen created situations that forced her to come to net and hit volleys.

Bowen finished the set 7-5. Peng stayed on court with him and chatted for a while after the match while Madame Jiang clenched her jaw. We had been given instructions by Madame Jiang not to chat with Peng. She told us that Peng didn't want to be bothered with conversation. Peng spoke to Madame Jiang before she left. We finished practice, and I asked Bowen what Peng had said. We spoke quietly and quickly while we were getting a drink at the water fountain to avoid Madame Jiang's irritation. He told me that Peng was playing an exhibition match against a teammate from Beijing that evening for the officials. She had invited him to come watch and told Madame Jiang the same thing. As he wiped his arm against his mouth at the fountain he said, "Madame Jiang didn't say yes."

"Did she say no?" I asked.

"No, but she didn't say yes, which is the same thing."

十四

The next day I arrived at practice early and found the courts empty. A few minutes before practice was scheduled to begin, all the boys except Bowen came in. They walked in a tight group and spoke in hushed voices. They looked upset. I went over and tried to listen in to their conversation, but I didn't catch enough to understand what they were talking about and none of them offered to clue me in. I pulled Random aside and asked him what was going on. He said Bowen had gotten in trouble, and now we were going to have a hard practice. "*Bowen yinggai huidao Tianjin* (Bowen should go back to Tianjin)," Little Mao blurted. I asked Little Mao what he meant. I thought he said something about how Bowen had been on the Tianjin team, but I didn't hear him clearly and when I asked again, none of the boys would clue me in on what he had said. A few minutes later Bowen came in with his head held high. He seemed to be looking over all of us.

Madame Jiang arrived and ordered us to stand in a row. She walked back and forth with her hands behind her back. We felt like convicts awaiting our sentencing. She said Bowen had, against permission, slipped out to watch Peng play her exhibition match and was caught in the high bleachers of the indoor facility. So, as punishment, he and all of us would have to run the bleachers. The boys all looked back at her and showed no emotion. No one made a sound. She lifted her chin toward Bowen and said he was going to lead. Bowen looked at her and smiled condescendingly.

"*Keyi, mei guanxi* (Sure, no problem)," he said with the same nonchalance as if she had asked him to hand her a tennis ball.

Bowen had not even had time to put down his tennis bag. He started walking toward the indoor courts. The other boys hoisted their tennis bags onto their backs.

"Aren't we coming back?" I asked.

Random answered, "Bags might get stolen." It was as Victoria had warned, everything in China was vulnerable—even at a state-run athletic facility that had a guard posted at the entrance and several who patrolled the grounds.

As we walked toward the stadium, Little Mao repeated, loud enough for Bowen to hear, "Bowen should go back to Tianjin. He only thinks about himself." Dali didn't say anything but he looked at Little Mao and nodded in agreement.

"He doesn't have a choice," Random said.

"Madame Jiang didn't have a choice either," Little Mao snapped back. "And now we have to pay for that."

I sped up my pace so that I walked just behind Little Mao. I hoped that his temper would cause him to drop his guard and reveal more about why Madame Jiang had such an intense dislike for Bowen. But he said nothing further, and we marched toward the stadium in silence. I wanted to ask Little Mao what he meant when he said Madame Jiang didn't have a choice, but I knew there was no point. All direct questions I asked my teammates were met with cryptic answers and subtle remarks that seemed to reveal little, if anything. As my time in Beijing progressed, I came to realize that it was hopeless to wait for a clear, direct answer. To find answers to my questions, I would have to learn to pick up the subtleties in what my teammates said, how they said it, and perhaps most importantly, what they did not say.

I could never get any of them to explicitly tell me why Madame Jiang had it out for Bowen, but I came to understand that she had never been consulted about Bowen joining the team. He had been imposed on her. The cities are autonomous in China, and the officials wield a lot of power. My guess was that a superior had informed her one day that Bowen would be joining her team. She had to accept it, but she didn't have to like it, and she didn't have to treat him well. And when he was defiant and refused to submit and be broken by her training practices, it infuriated her all the more, and eventually the dislike grew into something stronger.

The facility was locked, and we had to wait for Madame Jiang to open it. Bowen stood facing the door, not wanting to look back at us. Hope stood directly behind Bowen and patted him on the shoulder as if to say, "I'm with you." He left just enough room for Madame Jiang to get by to open the door without him having to step aside.

The building was cold and dark, and Madame Jiang disappeared to turn on the lights. Three loud thwacks echoed across the courts and the lights came on. She returned and pointed where we should run. Up the steps of the first aisle, over thirty feet, down the steps, over thirty feet, up the next aisle, over thirty feet, down the next aisle. She waved her hand in a circle indicating that we should continue all around the stadium until she said stop. She said something abrupt that I did not understand, and then she clapped her hands, her white gloves muting the sound. Bowen took off and went up the bleachers three steps at a time. We followed—Hope, Little Mao, Dali, then me, and finally Random. Hope set a conservative pace. He didn't skip any steps. Little Mao and Dali continued to gripe under their breath. I couldn't make out what they were saying, but after twenty minutes of going up and down hundreds of stairs, no one could spare any energy to complain. Everything had to be saved for the ordeal that lay ahead of us.

After forty minutes I thought I had nothing left. After an hour I was sure that I couldn't go any farther. I had ditched my hat after the first lap and sweat ribboned down my forehead and over my eyebrows and into my eyes. It stung but I had nothing to wipe the sweat away with. My light gray shirt had been turned a shade that was closer to black and it clung to my skin. I doubted there was a dry patch of skin anywhere on my body. My lungs burned and my breath came in gasps and my calves began to cramp. But even though our bodies were beginning to rebel, we kept running, lap after lap around that damn stadium.

Madame Jiang had not moved from her position at the net post. I kept hoping that she would call time at an hour and fifteen minutes. There was a large clock at the end of the courts. I began to stare at the second hand, willing it closer and closer to the top. On the ascents, my legs had begun to feel uncoordinated and even the descents were getting difficult. We were all struggling by this point, all of us except Bowen. He was about to lap us a third time. His face showed no pain, only focus. Bowen would never let anyone, especially Madame Jiang, know. Each time he lapped me he said first in Chinese and then in English, "*Jia you wai guo ren* (Come on, foreigner)."

By the fourth time he lapped us, he didn't say anything, and I caught his eye as he passed, and I saw he was hurting and struggling to finish with the pace he had started. My legs were numb, and I didn't even know where I was putting my feet anymore. Black and yellow smudges floated across my field of vision. Dali and I were lagging, and Madame Jiang clapped her hands again and yelled at us to speed up. 1:50. I watched the minute hand of the clock shudder and then click closer to the number 12. At 2:00 all of us, except Bowen, collapsed. Bowen kept going and then turned and looked behind himself at his fallen teammates. He stopped and walked back to us with as much of a jaunt in his step as he could muster. Little Mao held his side and was sucking in huge gulps of air with his mouth wide open. I bent over and threw up. Bowen stood while all the rest of us had crumpled over on benches or steps. He looked at Madame Jiang, and I was fearful he would challenge her with a statement like, "So what's next," and she would rise to the challenge and make us do something more. But he didn't—whether out of self-preservation or regard for us, I couldn't tell.

Madame Jiang didn't like the fact that she hadn't broken him, but she wasn't going to let us know that. She pointed to the indoor courts and told us to start warming up. Needless to say, practice was without any energy. We were all there physically, but everyone had checked out mentally, even Bowen. At the end of the practice she ordered us to play tiebreakers in a round-robin pattern. Normally tiebreakers were extremely competitive because it was your one chance to beat someone better than you if you had a fast start or got a few lucky breaks and, usually, everyone took a shot at Bowen. But on this day we played points expecting the customary outcome: Bowen was expected to beat us, and Dali would beat everyone except Bowen. Even Little Mao and Hope didn't seem to care. Somehow while we were running up and down those steps the resentment toward Bowen had been transformed into anger at Madame Jiang.

When practice was over, she ordered all the boys to leave except Bowen. He was told to pick up all of the balls and lock them away. She left quickly, and the other boys slotted their tennis rackets back into their bags and, exhausted, walked slowly back to their rooms. There was none of the ribbing or jabbing that often followed them home. I offered to help Bowen, but he said no, he could do it. The balls were spread across three courts, and he walked slowly back to the far side to begin rolling the balls to one side of the courts. I started picking up the balls on the first court, but when Bowen saw me helping, he yelled at me to stop. The frustration in his tone surprised me, and I shrugged and went to pack up my bag. I collected my things and walked out to the parking lot where Victoria and Driver Wu were waiting.

"Where's your hat?" Victoria asked.

I touched my head and checked my bag and then remembered that I'd thrown my hat at my bag during one of the laps. I walked back to the courts and saw Bowen sitting on the bench. He didn't hear me approach; he was slowly peeling his socks off his feet, which were red and dripping in blood. "Bowen!" I exclaimed. He looked up, not acknowledging that I had seen the condition of his feet. "Are you okay?"

"Yeah, it's nothing. Just cheap copies," he replied in Chinese, too tired for English. He pointed at his shoes, and I saw the ghost of a Nike swoosh where the logo had fallen off.

十五

The following day the only sounds at tennis practice were the sounds of tennis balls being hit—no skidding of rubber tennis shoes, no exhalations as someone nailed a serve, no emotional outbursts when a ball didn't go in, no joking around. Madame Jiang may have sensed that she had gone too far, but she also sensed that she had won. We were all sore beyond belief and had blister-ravaged feet, but the thing that hurt the most was the knowledge that we were unable to stand up for ourselves. I knew that the other boys blamed Bowen, but they also hated Madame Jiang for being so unfair and punishing them for something they had not done.

Good tennis coaches are tough, and the best are brutal—they have to push their players beyond the level even the cockiest and most arrogant one thinks he can achieve. And great coaches are never satisfied. They must prepare their players for exhausting physical battles, and more importantly, for taxing mental challenges. Tennis is like a boxing match: you go out on the court and engage in a physical battle to beat the other player—one on one, no one there to help you in a fight that can last over three hours in 100-degree heat.

And how does a coach prepare you for the moment when you choke and dump an easy overhead into the bottom of the net on match point? How does your coach teach you to erase the thought that had you not gotten that bad bounce, or had the net been half an inch higher or lower, or worse, had you not been cheated—you would be walking off the court the winner instead of the loser?

The answer: the coach creates situations on the practice court to replicate those moments, again and again, until you begin to hate losing so much that you teach yourself to block out all the emotions of a match—the joy, the disappointment, the hope, the despair, the guilt, the sense of unfairness, and the anger—until your mind is devoid of everything except a cool, intense focus. It takes a long time, but eventually you get there. Great coaches push you to the point of almost breaking. But they do it to help you, not to punish you.

Madame Jiang was the opposite. She made us run those stadiums because she wanted to punish us, not because she wanted to help us. She made her point. But that day she lost our hearts, because we realized that she had never been on our side.

At the end of practice, Bowen sat down next to me on the bench. He hadn't said a word all practice. We waited while Madame Jiang finished drilling Hope. She was getting irritated that his glasses kept fogging up, and he constantly had to take them off and wipe them. As I leaned down to zip up my tennis bag, I noticed Bowen's white tennis shoes were stained pink around the point where the soles joined the leather.

The following Monday, Bowen didn't appear. I asked Random where he was, and he said, "*Ta sheng bing le* (He's sick)." I asked if he was in the dorms and Random grunted, "*Dui* (Yes)." I asked if I could go and see him. "*Bu keyi* (You can't)," he said. "Guards don't let you in."

With Bowen absent, Madame Jiang started to pick on Hope. Over the past weeks, Hope had seemed to lose focus. He had started coming to practice late, tanking when we played points, and developing a new "injury" every other practice. Even at the age of fourteen, I had been around tennis long enough to recognize the signs of burnout.

I watched Madame Jiang drill Hope on overheads. Start with racket on the net, run back, scissor kick into the air, smash an overhead, sprint back to the net, slap the net with racket, backpedal to hit another overhead, thirty in a row—nonstop. In the middle of the fourth set of this drill, Hope stopped and held out his hand. He took his glasses off and wiped them on his shirt. His hands shook. Random said, "She is supposed to buy contacts for him, but she won't so he has to play with those lousy glasses. They are too big, and they keep slipping."

"Why doesn't she?"

"Where do you think she gets the money to buy those sunglasses?"

We were silenced by another outburst from Madame Jiang. "*Luxi, ni zenme zheneman? Ru guo ni bu jinbu, wo hui song ni hui jia* (Hope, how are you so slow? If you don't improve, I will send you home)."

"Can she do that?" I asked Random.

"*Ta shi. Dang ran laoban* (Of course. She's the boss). She can do what she wants."

When players burn out, their minds and bodies go stale. They stop trying as hard in practice and start losing more matches. And without the joy of winning, they are left only with the anxiety and depression that accompany loss. They spiral further and further down until the sport they once loved becomes a chore they resent or even hate. I had seen burnout among countless players at the academies in Florida, and I could see it happening with Hope.

A wise trainer would notice the signs and see that there was little left and give the player a week or two off. Let the body rest and the mind recharge. But Madame Jiang became harder than ever on Hope. For three days in a row, she spent the entire practice on Hope's court, standing behind him and shouting at him whenever he missed an easy overhead or volley. During a water break I heard Random whisper to Hope, "Just pretend she isn't there." I could see that Hope tried to block her out. He pretended she wasn't there and gazed ahead into nothingness. But I could also see that she made him nervous. He played far worse whenever she was watching. The worse he played, the more she screamed.

So much of my time in China seemed detached from the world I had left behind. Here I was on the other side of the globe, almost seven thousand miles from home, twelve hours ahead, and no one knew where I was or what I was doing. I could disappear, and no one would notice. I could play extremely well or extremely poorly, and no one would care. I wondered how these boys sustained themselves. They had followed the same routine every single day, year after year, since they were seven or eight. I had an escape. I knew that this was only temporary. With each day that passed, I came closer to returning home. And that gave me something to look forward to. But for my teammates, this was it. There was no end in sight for them.

Hope kept himself contained longer than I could have, but Madame Jiang stayed on him, even after Bowen returned, and a couple weeks later he snapped. During a practice set with Random, he missed a put-away overhead right on top of the net on set point. From three courts away Madame Jiang screamed for everyone to stop. She ran over to Hope's court and started shouting at him, telling him what a useless player he was. At first he stood there and took it. As she yelled at him, he kept his eyes focused on the ground. Then without warning, Hope let out a yell and smashed his racket on the ground, breaking it in half. The courts were suddenly silent. Hope walked off the court, leaving the broken racket behind him.

I only saw him again once after that day. A few weeks later as I was leaving practice with Victoria, I saw Hope across the street sitting on the curb staring at the entrance to the sports complex. He removed his glasses and wiped his face with the dirty gray T-shirt he was wearing. When he pulled the shirt away I saw that he had been crying. He put his glasses back on, and we made eye contact for a second. But then he looked away and walked off with his head bowed. That was the last time I ever saw him.

Before coming to Beijing, I had a bad habit of cracking rackets when I wasn't playing well. I wasn't the only one to do it. Most of the kids I played with in the States had broken at least two or three rackets out of frustration. We did it because we thought it looked cool, because we saw players like Marat Safin do it on TV. It was a way of saving face when you were losing. A way of letting everyone know that you should be winning, and that you were losing only because you were playing badly.

After what happened to Hope, I made myself a promise that I

would never again break a racket. I remembered the old beat-up equipment that Hope had to use. What had seemed cool to me before suddenly felt spoiled and entitled. From then on, every time I raised my racket in thoughtless anger, ready to bring it down hard on the cement, I would see that image of Hope sitting on the curb with tears in his eyes. And I never broke another racket.

十六

About a month after we went to see her husband's art studio, Victoria took me to Beijing People's University so that I could see what a Chinese university looked like. First she showed me the original school building, which had been constructed in 1896 by the Methodist Episcopal Church as a seminary to train missionaries and priests. Back then, the school had been known as Beijing Harmony University. The redbrick building with its white windows and small bell tower resembled a classroom building of an Ivy League university. It was an odd thing to find in the middle of Beijing. Surrounded by buildings of Chinese architecture, it looked entirely out of place. Behind the original building was a larger one that had been built with funding from the Nationalist government after Beijing Harmony University had merged with Peking Imperial University in 1917. The building featured a weird blend of European and Chinese architecture styles, with Roman columns supporting a sloped, green-tiled roof that was adorned with gargoyles in the shape of Chinese dragons. Victoria agreed with me that it looked strange and told me that the old Peking Imperial University had a really beautiful campus featuring classical Chinese architecture. She would take me on another day if I wanted to go. We walked a bit farther, and

Victoria showed me a group of four entirely identical buildings that had been built during the 1950s by the Soviets as a gift from Stalin to Mao. The buildings were monstrous four-storied concrete rectangles that had been painted a dull shade of gray. They were buildings that had been designed purely for function with no concern for beauty. Just looking at them made me depressed.

We continued down a road and passed by an athletic facility on our left. Behind two turf soccer fields was a huge concrete playground planted with dozens of basketball hoops. Both soccer fields had pickup games going on, and there were a number of people playing basketball. We kept walking and came to a building that was still under construction. The parts of the building that were finished looked grand and expensive. Victoria told me that this structure was to be the brand-new China Center for a top American university. She said it had become controversial after someone discovered the center had been funded by several wealthy businessmen who used their connections in the government to make it happen. A large grant had been given by the Chinese Ministry of Education and there were rumors that the Minister of Education's grandson had just been accepted to the American university in question. Victoria waved her hand at all the buildings we had seen. "See? It's like a map of one hundred years," she said.

She led me through a parking lot past the university's library to a small one-story building that was set off from the rest of the university buildings in the corner of the campus. She stopped outside the building and examined the entrance. The accumulated layer of grime and soot that covered the walls made it difficult to see that the building was painted a light blue. I could tell from the dusty, broken windows and the graffiti on the front door that the building had been abandoned for some time.

"What is this place?" I asked Victoria.

"Remember how I told you about Gao Fei and Da Ning?"

The names sounded familiar but I couldn't remember what Victoria had said about them. "Who are they again?" I asked.

"The writers!" Victoria said. "I'm going to give you one of Da Ning's books, remember?"

"Oh yeah. I remember now."

"This is where they learned to write," Victoria said. "And Su Tong too. He is another very famous writer."

I looked at the small, run-down building with skepticism. "Here?"

"Yes, this was their school. There was a teacher here who taught all three of them. Now they are China's three best writers."

"What happened to the school?"

Victoria took a few steps in the direction of the front door and stopped and looked around. She motioned for me to follow. Victoria pushed the door open. I heard the sound of glass splintering under her shoes. "Careful," she said.

I followed her through the door and stepped around the broken glass. I looked up and saw that we were in a room I assumed must have been the building's lobby. The room was dark, and the windows were boarded up, and the only light came from the doorway behind us. The floor was scattered with paper, random debris, and fragments of broken glass. The room had been stripped bare and there was no furniture except for a tall reception desk that was pushed up against a wall. I took a step toward the desk and felt something under my foot. I looked down and saw that I had stepped on a dead mouse.

Victoria crouched down on the floor next to several messy

piles of documents. She picked up a loose stack of pages and pulled out her cell phone, holding down a button so that a dim light came from the screen. By the light of her phone, Victoria methodically flipped through the documents.

"What happened to this place?" I asked.

"The government closed it down after *Liu/Si* (6/4)."

"What's that?"

"June fourth. Have you learned about Tiananmen Square?"

"Yes."

Victoria paused her search and assumed the role of questioner. "What do you know about it?"

I shrugged. "My father told me what happened. I Googled it too and read about it on the internet."

"Here you cannot read about it on the internet. The government blocks everything. Nobody really talks about it."

"But why did this place get shut down?"

"After Liu/Si, the universities were in a lot of trouble because most of the protestors were students. The government saw the universities as the cause of the problem. Many professors were arrested. Writers were considered very bad then too because many of the student leaders were writers who were writing very criticizing things about the government. So the university president here closed down the program and pretended like it never existed."

I frowned. I couldn't imagine Harvard or Yale shutting down an entire graduate school because of student protests. "But the protests were over. Why did they have to shut the whole school down?"

"The university president had to. Maybe he would go to prison if he did not close the writing school. I think it is sad though, because maybe many more great writers could have come from this school. I've always wanted to come here."

"Prison? For what?"

"It happened to many people. All the writers like Gao Fei and Da Ning and Dan Xiaolu were expelled and removed from the university records. Their teacher and some of the students were taken away."

"What happened to them after that—after they got out of prison?"

"They didn't get out. I don't know where they are."

Victoria went back to looking through her stack of papers. I had no idea what she was looking for, but whatever it was she clearly didn't find it. She moved on to a second one. Her words unsettled me. I glanced around the dark room. Now that I knew the history of the building, I couldn't help but feel an eeriness and a strange and cruel irony that I hadn't felt before. An institution devoted to writing—the act of recording the past—had become a reminder of how humans often try to remove the unwanted parts of their history. The building stood on the campus, both a dere-lict memorial to what had been and a terrifying reminder of what happened to those who fell out of favor with the government. I thought about the students and teachers who had been here and wondered where they were now. The building's ghostly structure was the only remaining evidence of their history, a history that had been almost entirely deleted from the record. But while the government could remove the physical proof of the past, it could not destroy that past entirely. For it lived on in the memories of the mothers and fathers and children of those students and teachers who had disappeared. The building made me nervous and I wanted to leave.

"Victoria, let's go."

Her head was bent down over a piece of paper, her eyes squint-ing to see it in the dim light. "Chase! Look!"

I crouched down and looked at the paper. It was a page of messy handwritten Chinese characters. I wasn't sure why Victo-ria was so excited by it.

"What is it?"

"I think it's from a story by Da Ning," she said and held it out to me. She pointed to two characters at the top of the page: 大凝. "Look, that's his name there. See? *Da Ning*. He must have writ-ten this when he was a student here."

I tried to share Victoria's enthusiasm, but the piece of paper meant nothing to me. I was nervous that someone was going to find us. The door creaked open. It was only the wind. "Victoria, can we go?"

"Hey! I think I know this one. The character's name is Gui Fu. That's the same as the character of *Dust*." She kept reading. "It's just like the beginning of *Dust*." I had no idea what she was talking about. She was excited and speaking fast in Chinese. I gave her a bewildered look—she laughed when she realized that she had slipped into Chinese by accident.

"Maybe this is the first part of *Dust*. The first story he wrote."

I must not have looked significantly impressed with her dis-covery because she waved the page at me.

"This is very special! Do you understand? This is like . . . Who is the best American writer?"

I thought for a moment. "Maybe Hemingway?"

"Oh, yes, *Hai-Ming-Wei*. Yes, this is like if we found a page that he wrote."

"So it's worth a lot of money," I asked. "Do you think you can sell it?"

Victoria looked up at me and frowned. "Sell it? No, why sell it? This is a treasure. This book, *Dust*, it's a beautiful book. It helped and inspired so many people," she said. She held up the page. "This is where the book came from. This is a treasure of a beautiful moment in our history. The moment when we are not afraid to speak anymore. No money can buy that moment." Victoria put her phone away and got up. She tucked the page into her purse. "I will keep it for my child."

We left the university and went to a nearby bookstore. Victoria wanted to buy Da Ning's book for me so that I would appreciate the importance of what we had just found. I resisted initially. I told her I only read books required by school or fun books like *Harry Potter*, but she insisted.

The bookstore was five stories tall and the entire third floor was devoted to English-language books and translated Western authors. She found a copy of *Dust* in English and reminded me that I had promised to give her *To Kill a Mockingbird*. We found out that *To Kill a Mockingbird* had never been translated into Chinese, but the bookstore did carry an imported copy in English. Victoria was pleased to have it, but she said it might take her a while to read. I looked at the back cover of *Dust* and saw it was about a family's sufferings during the Great Leap Forward and the Cultural Revolution. I wasn't sure it was the kind of book I liked to read. But I thought that maybe my father would be impressed if I told him I was reading it.

Victoria started reading *To Kill a Mockingbird* the day after our trip to the bookstore. She said it was slow progress because she kept having to stop and look up words using the dictionary on her phone, but she read every day during my tennis practices, and she finished the book within the week. She talked to me about it one day after practice. She told me the story surprised her. "I didn't know America had so many scars in its past," she said. "It reminded me of reading about China."

We arrived early to the language school that morning. I passed the time by reading old copies of the *China Daily* left in the student lounge. The *China Daily* had a section called "Around China" that featured two-paragraph news stories from each of China's provinces. Every issue had at least one or two stories that were either really amusing or incredibly bizarre. I remember story headlines like TWO IN GUANGZHOU ARRESTED FOR PLAYING BASE-BALL WITH CHICKENS and MAN PURCHASES 32,000 RMB CAR USING ONLY 1 RMB NOTES and HENAN SCHOOL BANS ROMANCE BETWEEN STUDENTS. Those always made me laugh and made me wish I could tell Tom about them. Not all the stories were funny though. Many of them reminded you how tough life still was for most people in China.

I remember one story about this couple from a rural town who sold their blood to illegal blood banks to pay for their son to go to university. They were paid only twenty dollars for each donation, and every time they donated, the blood banks would take out so much blood that they would pass out and collapse, drenched in sweat. The saddest part about the story was that a doctor had just discovered that this husband and wife both had contracted AIDS. It was a tragedy, not just for the man and his wife, not just for their son who would have to spend the rest of his life with the knowledge that his education cost his parents their lives, but also for all the people who received blood donated by the couple, and for those people's families, too.

During class that day, I told Teacher Lu that we had found a fragment of a manuscript by a Chinese writer over the weekend. She seemed very pleased until I told her that it had been written by Da Ning. She didn't like Da Ning; she said his books were too negative and that he was disrespectful to the government. I asked her why she thought he was disrespectful. I explained that I thought it was good for people to criticize the government when it was wrong. She said that was because I wasn't Chinese and that I needed to understand that for more than five thousand years, China had been a country ruled by an emperor who was seen as a divinely anointed representative of heaven.

"You wouldn't criticize Jesus, would you?" she asked.

"Well, no. That's different though."

"Is it? Do you know what they would call the emperor?"

"*Huangdi*?" I asked.

"That just means emperor. It's like saying *king*. His real title was *Tianzi*. It means 'Son of Heaven.' For Jesus you say 'Son of God,' *dui budui* (true or false)?"

"Okay, but there hasn't been an emperor for almost one hundred years. It's different now."

"One hundred years may seem like a long time to you, but we have five thousand years of history. That history is connected to everything. The way people think, the way parents raise their children, everything. One hundred years is nothing to us. It takes much longer than a hundred years to forget five thousand."

"But—" I protested, still unconvinced.

"Think about it like this," she said. "If you go to England and say rude things about the Queen, English people will be very upset. It's been a long time since the king or queen of England had real power. The Queen is just some lady, she doesn't have power like before. But I think English people would still be very angry at you if you insult her because in their mind—in their culture—you are supposed to be respectful to the Queen. It is the same here, only the title is not Emperor anymore."

She said Chiang Kai-shek, Chairman Mao, and Deng Xiaoping had all been emperors with a different name. I thought about how religion had been eradicated during the Cultural Revolution and Mao's "Little Red Book" had been the only book that people were allowed to read. I saw that she had a point. In a way, that book had been like their New Testament. It was, after all, a book of sayings and teachings from one man, on the correct and proper way to live life.

Teacher Lu explained that China was changing, and now it was more accepted to criticize the government, but it had to be done in a respectful way. She thought Da Ning went too far with his criticism. She considered him rude and disrespectful and told me that I should read other writers.

As I was leaving class I ran into Josh, the businessman I

had met on my first day at the school. I asked him how things were going with his business. He said he had set up a business with his partner importing cheap wines from France and Italy into China, where they sold them for huge markups to Chinese government officials and businessmen. Josh told me they were having trouble keeping up with demand because government officials were buying their wines by the truckload. Apparently it had become a status symbol to serve foreign wines at business dinners. Oftentimes, he said, after the wine had been poured, the waitresses would circle the table and display the bottle label to each guest at the dinner. Nobody cared about how the wine tasted, only how it looked.

Victoria kept asking me if I had finished *Dust*. But I hadn't even started it. Ever since Tom had died I found it really hard to do things that reminded me of him, and nothing reminded me more of Tom than reading. That was his thing. I loved playing tennis. He loved reading stories. When I thought about Tom, I always remembered him reading on the big sofa in his room with his head propped up by a pillow. I had never really been a big reader, but ever since he died, anytime I found myself reading a novel, I had this weird feeling inside as if I was doing something I wasn't supposed to be doing. It's hard to explain, but I felt his presence and I felt as if I was intruding on something that had been special to him. I felt as if I was disrespecting his memory or trying to replace him somehow. For a long while, I had a very hard time doing anything that I considered part of his domain.

十八

As September turned into October, the weather changed notice-
ably. It became very cold and I had to wear a thick jacket whenever
I went outside. Everything started dying too. The leaves seemed
to fall off the trees quicker than they did back home. I wondered
if that was because they didn't get enough sunlight due to the
smog. Soon all of the trees at the tennis center were bare of any
leaves. The grass died as well, and all that remained was the dry,
cracked earth.

On the last Friday in September, Madame Jiang told Victoria
that the following week the team wouldn't be practicing due to
the weeklong national holiday. Most of the boys would go home.
I asked Victoria to ask her if anyone would be around. Madame
Jiang shrugged her shoulders. I mentioned Bowen's name, and
Madame Jiang repeated her shrug and made a face as if she had
tasted something sour. She did little to disguise her dislike of
Bowen. I was never given an explicit reason for her aversion to
Bowen, but I sensed that it was because she knew how little re-
spect Bowen had for her.

At the end of practice on Friday of that week, I sat with Bowen
as we repacked our tennis bags. While I continued to struggle

in my efforts to learn Chinese, Bowen's English had improved. It was in part, I think, due to the fact that I spoke to him almost entirely in English. I knew I should have been practicing my Chinese with him, but it was exhausting living entirely in a language as foreign as Chinese was to me. Not just mentally—physically, too. By the end of the day, my jaw muscles would ache from making sounds I had never before had a reason to make. So when I spoke with Bowen, I would give in and lapse into English.

"So, are you going home tomorrow?" I asked.

"No," he said. I waited for him to continue, but he kept his eyes fixed on the rackets he was slotting one by one back into his bag.

"But Random said everyone's going home." I said the words before I thought of the implication behind them. Despite the fact that we had talked about many things over the past few weeks—about music, about girls, about tennis—Bowen had never once brought up the subject of family. And neither had I. "Because of the holiday," I added.

Bowen shook his head.

"Why?" I asked.

"Too far."

"Where are you from?"

"Tianjin," he said.

"You're from Tianjin?" It made sense, I thought. I had wondered why Bowen didn't speak with the harsh Beijing accent of the other boys, and why they sometimes mocked the way he said things.

"My family is," Bowen said.

"So you're staying here, then?" I asked. "For the whole week?" Bowen nodded again. "And you?"

"I'm staying too. I guess I could have gone somewhere, but I didn't know this week was a holiday."

"So you will be here?"

"Yes."

"We can practice."

"Sure," I said.

We finished packing our bags, and Bowen said, "Wait." He reached behind the tennis bench and picked up my tennis hat. He looked at it before giving it back. "Wimbledon," he said. But the way he said it, it sounded more like *Wim-Bo-Dun*. "You play there?"

"No, I just watched."

"What players?"

"Everybody, really: Federer, Agassi, Sampras, Ivanisevic—lots."

Bowen nodded his head and the corners of his mouth turned down as if he was seriously considering something that required intense concentration.

"We will need to ask for the key."

"What key?" I asked.

"The key to the courts."

"The courts are locked?"

"For holidays, yes," Bowen said. He added, "It is best for you to ask Madame Jiang."

"Me?"

"She will say yes if you ask." Bowen nodded his head as if this matter had been decided. He stood up and lifted his tennis bag over his shoulder. "See you on Monday."

I asked Victoria to speak to Madame Jiang about getting a key to the courts. She was hesitant at first but agreed to do it and walked over to where Madame Jiang was putting away her shopping cart of tennis balls. I sat and watched as they spoke. The conversation took longer than I had assumed it would, and it looked as though Victoria had to do a fair amount of persuading. Finally, after about ten minutes, Madame Jiang looked at me and pulled a ring of keys from her bag. She flipped through them and then twisted one off and handed it to Victoria.

"You should not have asked me to do that," Victoria said when she returned with the key.

"Why not?"

"Because you have asked for a special favor. Madame Jiang is not supposed to give the key to anyone. It is her sole responsibility."

"Then why did she give it to you?"

"Because she is afraid not to. She knows your father must have connections in the government. It's not normal for an American to be allowed to play with the team. She doesn't want to risk making your father's friends angry. If she causes them problems they will replace her."

"But Bowen asked me to get the key so we could play."

"I know," Victoria said. "I am sure Bowen knew exactly what he was doing when he put you up to this. You should be careful. Don't do everything Bowen asks you to do. Not everything is as innocent as it seems." Victoria's comments concerned me. I didn't want my father to hear that I had been asking for special favors.

十九

For the next week, Bowen and I practiced together every morning and afternoon. Each day we took a two-hour lunch break during which Bowen would take me to a different local restaurant in the hutongs around the tennis center. At first I didn't really like the food, but it grew on me. I learned the key was not to ask what we were eating. Usually it all tasted pretty good, but if I asked what it was, I might find out that we were eating duck tongue, or chicken feet, and suddenly lose my appetite. I paid for all of our lunches as I knew Bowen didn't have money to spend on eating out.

I tried to be brave about trying new things, but I did draw the line when Bowen tried to get me to eat fried scorpions. We were walking back to tennis when I stopped and stared at a street vendor who appeared to be selling live scorpions impaled on wooden skewers. Bowen laughed when he saw the expression on my face. He turned to the vendor and ordered two. The vendor took two skewers and dunked them in burning oil, and a minute or two later presented us with two fried scorpion kebabs. It was too much for me, so Bowen ate them both.

At one of our lunches Bowen asked me if I knew the name of my country in Chinese.

I had just learned this with Teacher Lu. "*Mei Guo.*"

"*Dui* (Right)," he said with a nod. "Do you know what it means?"

I shook my head.

"Beautiful country. Mei Guo. That is what we call your country. Mei Guo."

"It's not all beautiful, I mean some of it is, but not all."

"I think it is beautiful," Bowen said.

Bowen asked as much as he could about America. He wanted to know about the movies and the music and what we ate every day. He asked me question after question about the tennis academy in Florida where I had trained. What did it look like? How many courts, did they have indoor and outdoor courts? How many instructors, where did the players come from? Did any professionals train there, too? Did any of the players ever get a chance to play with them? Could you play whenever you wanted? Could you enter any tournament you wanted? Were the rules strict? On and on he went. Bowen would get excited about my answers and switch to Chinese to ask more questions. I did my best to understand his random combination of Chinese and English. Once I asked him to write his question down so I could see if I could understand it. He shook his head and said in Chinese, "No big deal."

I could never understand why Bowen resisted writing anything down. It was not that he did not know how to write. The boys at the center did schooling in the morning. They even studied the English that Bowen was so eager to improve. It was not until I returned to boarding school that I guessed why he was reluctant to show me his writing. Our Chinese teacher handed back the class's first written vocabulary test. Even though most of us had gotten all the characters of the twenty words correct, she had dropped our grades by one full letter because of what she termed bad characters. "In China," she informed us, "how you write your characters, what sort of care you take, shows what kind of person you are. In England, it is your accent that helps to define you, in China it is your writing. It shows the quality of your education." I guessed that Bowen, who had never received much formal schooling, must have been ashamed of the way he wrote his characters and was too proud to let me see them.

On our last day of practice before the holiday ended, I arrived at the tennis center to learn that the indoor courts had been reserved for an official event and were not available to us that day. Heavy rain was forecasted, and it looked unlikely that we would be able to play outdoors.

"We do fitness, then," Bowen said.

I considered Bowen's proposition for a moment.

"Do you want to do fitness with me?" he asked against my silence.

I hated running sprints. "Not really," I said to myself. But aloud I heard my voice say, "*Weishenme bu ne?*"

"Exactly—why not." Bowen translated my words and patted me on the back.

We stretched and loosened up and then started off with suicide sprints. Bowen slaughtered me. We ran ten sets and he won all ten. I asked him if he wanted to run stadiums on the outside running track as a joke, but then he laughed and said, "Why not."

I looked up at the graying sky. "Looks like rain, it could get slippery."

"If the rain becomes too much we stop," he said.

"Okay, but we probably only have time to do one set before it gets too bad."

"Only one?" Bowen asked. "You are slower than I thought!"

We jogged to the stadium and just as we were about to run up the first set of stairs, it began to drizzle lightly. We were halfway through the first set when the rain began to come down hard. We sprinted back to the tennis courts. I grabbed my racket bag and ran to where Victoria and Driver Wu were waiting with the car. The rain was falling heavier now. Bowen took off toward the dorms. Driver Wu slowed as we passed Bowen. I lowered my window and yelled into the rain. "Want a ride?" He kept running and shook his head. "Okay, we'll pick you up at twelve for lunch?" He smiled and gave me a thumbs-up.

There wasn't enough time to go back to the Zhangs', so we waited out the rain at a cafe Victoria liked near the tennis center called Sculpting in Time. When we arrived, I quickly grabbed a menu and began to scan it for amusing translations. We had recently added a new event to the *Translation Olympics* named the CULINARY PENTATHLON. Currently occupying the top spot in that category was a shrimp, noodle, and vegetable dish that had been given the bizarre name "Sludge mixed with family." Equally strange and no more appetizing was something called "Fish head bubble cake." "Very beautiful kelp" had been in poll position for the bronze medal until I came across a tofu dish designed to resemble three miniature pandas with the name "The wet panda skin of tofu." Unfortunately, the Sculpting in Time cafe had no new additions to their menu and the standings of the CULINARY PENTATHLON remained unchanged.

The cafe's name itself had briefly been considered for a medal in the VENDOR & RESTAURANT event of the *Translation Olympics*, but in the end Victoria and I decided that the awkwardly translated name actually suited the cafe quite well. The entire cafe, from the lamps to the furniture to the movie posters and lunch boxes on the walls, was decked out with genuine miscellany from the 1970s and 1980s. Victoria loved going there because it reminded her of her childhood. She always sat at one table in the corner that had four plastic chairs that she said were the same as the chairs she had used in school when she was a young girl.

When we picked him up a few hours later, I told Bowen I wanted to choose the restaurant. I had spotted a McDonald's on one of Driver Wu's drives to the sports center. I figured it was a fifteen-minute walk. He had never been to McDonald's but, as always, he was thrilled by the prospect of discovering something new. The menu was recognizable to me, but pretty much everything had been adapted to local tastes. Instead of chicken nuggets they served chicken wings. We feasted on chicken wings and "shake-shake fries" and Cokes. Bowen chose seaweed-flavored fries and I stuck with salt. We finished our meal off with bean curd ice cream.

As we were getting up to leave I asked him about Madame Jiang. "If she had never been a tennis player, how did she become the coach?"

"Maybe no one knows. She was a volleyball player. But maybe no one knows why she is not coaching volleyball." Bowen could not be drawn into speculation or gossip. It was not that he was resisting, it was just that he was not the least bit interested in her. Over the weeks of tennis practice, I came to understand that it was his total absence of interest and respect for Madame Jiang that infuriated her. There was nothing she could do about it. It was as if she did not exist. The more she tried to goad him, the less visible she became.

It had stopped raining some time before, and after we finished lunch we walked back to the courts. We walked unhurried, perhaps because we both knew that the week, and the freedom we had enjoyed, were coming to an end. As we were walking, I realized that Bowen and I had become close friends. It was fun hanging out with him. It had been a long time since I had hung out with someone my own age who didn't act weird around me because of what happened to my brother. It was also the first time that I wasn't constantly thinking about the friends I had left behind in America. I realized I would miss Bowen when I went back, and I was struck with the sobering thought that I would probably never see or hear from him again after I left.

I wondered if Bowen had ever thought about trying to get a scholarship to an American university. I asked him if he was considering university at all. He shook his head and explained to me that he would never pass the Gao Kao, the university entrance exam. The Gao Kao was made up of four sections that Bowen described as 3 + X. The "3" are Chinese, math, and English. Every single high school student is required to speak English well enough to pass a rigorous English exam. The "X" is an exam that tests a subject that each student feels he or she is the strongest in. Bowen said that every year almost ten million students take the Gao Kao. There was no way he could take it now, having been out of the system for so long. Even the smartest students at the best schools in the country would study from 5 a.m. to midnight every day for an entire year to prepare for the test. Bowen said that the best universities, Tsinghua and Beida, only accepted the top eight students out of every ten thousand who took the exam.

I was quiet for a moment while I thought about what he had just said. The ten million number was simply staggering. The year before when I had almost flunked out of school, my father, in an attempt to make me pick up my grades, had impressed upon me the fact that Yale only accepted a little more than two thousand of the thirty thousand people who applied every year, giving it an acceptance rate of about 7 percent. According to Bowen, Tsinghua accepted twenty-four out of thirty thousand. That acceptance rate was closer to 0.07 percent. Later on during the year, as the Gao Kao got closer, I would read stories in the *China Daily* of parents who had their children prepare for the test by studying and living full-time in hospitals, hooked up to IV drips and oxygen to improve their concentration. Victoria told me that during the two weeks before the Gao Kao, cities all across China became deathly quiet at night as bars and clubs were shut down and special noise ordinances passed so that the students could study in peace. I also read of kids who committed suicide, of elaborate cheating scams that used wireless earphones, camera pens, and signal-emitting watches, and of girls who took hormone injections to delay their periods until after the exam. In America I had heard of students going to the bathroom during the SAT and reading cheat sheets they had stashed in their pockets, but I had never heard of anything as drastic as any of this. To many the Gao Kao was a route out of poverty and there was a competitiveness to every facet of life here that simply didn't exist in America.

The boys on the tennis team had long dropped off the academic track necessary to be eligible even to take those exams. Their futures had been gambled on a game. I thought about Bowen's answer, about how he had absolutely no chance of going to university in China. What if he got injured? A thought came to me. What if over the next few years he prepared for the SAT or TOEFL? As long as he got a semi-decent score, I was sure he could get a tennis scholarship to a school in the States.

"What about an American university? I'm sure you could get into one by using your tennis."

Bowen seemed confused by what I had suggested. "So if I lived in America, I could go to a university?" he asked.

"I'm sure you could get a scholarship for tennis and then play tennis for the university. You wouldn't have to pay anything then. It would be free."

We sat quietly while Bowen considered this revelation.

"But why play for the university? Why not just play professional?"

I shrugged. "You can do both. James Blake played at Harvard, McEnroe went to Stanford. It's good in case you get injured or something. Then you have a backup plan."

"So if you can't play tennis you will go to university?"

"Yeah, I guess. That's what my father wants me to do. I still want to go pro, but it's a good backup option, I guess."

"My father wants me to learn *zenme shuo* (how do you say)," Bowen said. Stuck for a moment, he began imitating the actions of a builder.

"Building?" I asked and pointed at a construction site across the street. "Like that?"

"Uh—maybe, but it's different," Bowen said and gestured at the walls. "He makes the house walls."

"Oh," I said. "Plastering?"

"*Pla-ster-ing*," Bowen said, mouthing the unfamiliar syllables again silently. "Yes, maybe that."

"And not university?"

"He is worried about tennis," Bowen said. "He tells me always people are building in China." He waved a hand toward the window. I looked past the grimy pane of glass and saw construction cranes dotting the distance. "Maybe he is right," Bowen said with a shrug. "But why would I ever stop playing tennis?"

I asked him how he had started tennis. He said he lived near the tennis courts. "There was some old rackets that we could use. I would go with some other kids, and we would hit for hours against the side of the building in the parking lot. I would always stay longer than the other children. I think the director of the facility got tired of the sound of my practicing against the wall. One day he walked out. I thought I was going to get in trouble, or he was going to shoo me away. He said he wanted to talk to my mother about me. I didn't tell her because I was afraid he would say something bad and she would punish me. The next time I went to play, he asked where my mother was. I told him she is working. He asked me if I want to join the tennis classes. He said I have to ask my mother to sign a paper." Bowen bent down to tie his shoe. "How about you?" he asked.

"How did I start playing tennis?" I asked. "I don't know, my brother played. I guess, I always wanted to do whatever he was doing."

"You have a brother? How old is he?"

"I did." The words came slowly. "He died last year."

"Died?" Bowen repeated the word to make sure he understood correctly.

I didn't answer. We sat there for a while and neither of us spoke. I stared at the cracks in the ground. About a month before I left for China I spoke to one of Tom's friends and asked her what had happened that night. I had never heard the full story. My father refused to say anything more than there had been an accident. I found some local newspaper articles online, but those were short and vague. I felt this need to understand exactly what happened, and I knew that Tom's friends were the only ones who could tell me. So I asked a girl he had been close to.

At first she was hesitant. But I pushed her, and then the story tumbled out, fast and disorganized. She told me that a bunch of them had gotten the idea of trying LSD from some movie they saw. They tried to buy it from a senior who sold weed. He didn't have any, but he told them he could get them Ecstasy, so they bought some Ecstasy off him and went to Andrew Green's house, because his parents were out of town, and they got drunk and took the Ecstasy and when Tom started convulsing and throwing up, they panicked and were too scared of getting in trouble to take him to the hospital, so they drove to Dr. Miller's house, carried him to the doorstep, rang the doorbell, and drove off. They hadn't known that Dr. Miller was away for the weekend. Tom died that night in the snow on Dr. Miller's front doorstep. The guy who delivered our newspapers found Tom's body the next morning.

Sometimes the thought—that if only one thing different had happened he could have lived—would hit me like a 120-mile-an-hour wind, and I could do nothing but brace. I was using every muscle in my body to keep it together. I wanted Bowen to leave, but he wouldn't get up. He just sat there, unmoving, unspeaking, and for the first time in a long time I didn't feel completely alone.

Bowen rested a hand on my shoulder.

"*Bie danxin* (Don't worry)," he said. "*Ni hai you yi wei gege* (You still have a brother)."

My father visited Beijing toward the end of October. I hadn't seen him since I left for China in early August. I had been looking forward to his visit for weeks. He was supposed to come over during the middle of September, but something had come up at work and he had to change his plans. I was worried that the same thing might happen again. But one morning at the end of October, I woke up to find an e-mail from my father saying he was about to board his flight to Beijing and would see me later that day. I asked Victoria if we could surprise him by picking him up at the airport. She said of course and e-mailed his secretary to let her know the change of plans. My father wasn't expecting to see me at the airport, but when he did it seemed to make him really happy. That made me feel good.

He had a week of meetings and was staying at the Grand Hyatt. I stayed with him so that we could have dinner every night. Compared to my white shoe-box bedroom at the Zhangs', the Grand Hyatt was almost too grotesque in its opulence. It had been designed by an architect obsessed with waterfalls. The large sitting area to the left of the massive revolving doors was called the Cascade Lounge. Water ran down round columns marking its boundaries. To the right were more sitting areas and, beyond those, the hotel's selection of four restaurants and a cafe. To get around the government-imposed height limit that exists for buildings in Beijing and to maximize the number of floors, the architect had designed several floors underground and had made the ceilings of all the rooms very low. The swimming pool was on the lowest of the three underground floors and was twice the size of an Olympic pool. The architect had given the pool a tropical theme. Its irregular borders were lined with artificial palm trees, and the ceiling had been painted to look like the night sky with glittering lights counterfeiting stars. The sound of whales calling one another was piped in through a hidden speaker system.

The marbled and gilded lobby at the Grand Hyatt was like a cocktail party with people always coming and going. My father and I never walked through without someone stopping him and wanting to meet up later for a drink. Whenever this happened, my father never hesitated to introduce me and explain in detail what I was doing in China. It made me feel like Exhibit A. I wondered if he did it because he felt he had to compensate for Tom. People had heard, I guessed, because no one ever asked us about how Tom was doing.

For the first time in what felt like forever I was surrounded by Westerners. While I had lived at the Zhangs', I would go days without seeing another native English speaker. But the Hyatt was a little bubble of Western culture that had been dropped into the heart of Beijing. Every measure had been taken to replicate the style and feel of a hotel in London or New York. The Starbucks in the lobby, the room-service menu with its Caesar salads and cheeseburgers and French fries, the little boutique that sold the *Wall Street Journal* and the *New York Times*, all comforting reminders of home. While the hotel staff was mostly Chinese, the managers and supervisors had all been imported from the United States or Europe and were tasked with training the Chinese staff in Western manners and customs. At the Hyatt, one could be in Beijing without ever leaving the United States.

I think that was how most Westerners experienced China at that time. Back then Shanghai and Hong Kong were really the only Chinese cities that had truly been internationalized. Once you ventured farther into the mainland, most traces of Western influence disappeared. Even major cities like Tianjin and Xi'an, both roughly the size of New York City, might only have one newly built Sheraton or TGI Fridays. Other than that, everything was alien. The vast majority of Westerners did their best not to venture outside of Shanghai or Hong Kong. Even Beijing was still very much a Chinese city then. There were small pockets of the city where Western influence had been allowed to permeate, and most Westerners I observed back then rarely left that bubble. They stayed in five-star hotels and they dealt only with Chinese or Hong Kong businessmen who spoke excellent English. They saw the country of modernization and "progress," and they ignored the parts of China that didn't fit into that one-dimensional image. The foreignness of the real China disturbed and disoriented them. There was nothing remotely recognizable in the Chinese language. When Westerners saw other Westerners, they would seek them out with a bold desperation and cling to them as if they were childhood friends. Most Westerners stayed in Beijing for less than a week, and for that week they lived at a hotel. They tolerated China; some came because they felt they had to come, some were there because they understood it was the right place to be, but almost all were counting down the days to their departure.

I couldn't help but feel an element of disdain. I found their attitude so hypocritical. They claimed to be interested in China. But in truth they were only interested in the parts of China that felt familiar. They claimed to understand the real China, but they had no interest in even seeing it. There was an arrogance to their attitude. It was like someone coming to America for the first time, spending a week in a hotel on the Upper East Side, and then claiming they knew what life was like for a farmer in Nebraska. I had seen enough of Beijing to know that I understood absolutely nothing of the real China. It was too complex. To understand it would take a lifetime.

On my first night in the Hyatt, we were walking through the lobby on our way to dinner when my father ran into two bankers from Morgan Stanley. He introduced me and they commented on how smart my father was for sending his son to China at such a young age, and my father told them that I was already conversational in Chinese. That was a stretch, but I didn't correct him. After the two bankers' interest in me waned, they spoke to my father for a while about some conference they were in Beijing for. I stood there and tried to follow the conversation for a little while before losing interest and shifting my focus to people watching in the lobby. Fortunately I found entertainment close by in the form of a hugely overweight, cowboy-hat-wearing Texan who was frantically trying to explain to a Chinese bartender how to correctly mix an old-fashioned. Judging from the Texan's growing frustration and the four untouched drinks on the bar, his efforts appeared to be in vain. I watched as the nervous bartender attempted another effort.

"Dammit!" the Texan exclaimed. "I told ya! There's no god-damn vodka in an old-fashioned!" The bartender looked up in confusion, still clutching the bottle of vodka.

"That's the fourth one you've put vodka in! Come on now! I've told you four goddamn times! I'm gonna have to take it away from you, ain't I? Here, gimme that bottle!"

I was reminded of the wrestling match I had watched with David in my first week at the Zhangs'. Just as an alarmed concierge rushed over to resolve the situation, my father tapped me on the shoulder. "Ready to go?" We headed toward the restaurant in the back of the lobby.

"You should look people in the eye when you're talking to them," my father said.

"I do."

"And stand up straighter," he continued. He put his right hand on my left shoulder and pressed his thumb into my shoulder blade, correcting my posture. "Your posture—presence is important. My father used to make me stand in front of the mirror and squeeze my shoulder blades together every night before I went to sleep," he said. "If you look like this, people are going to walk all over you." He slouched and curved his shoulders and pulled his elbows into his body so that he looked like a frail, old person. I pulled my shoulder out from under his hand.

At dinner my father told me that he had just spoken with the Dover headmaster and that he was very impressed with my father's report and said that they looked forward to my coming next year. He asked if I was excited to be going to Dover, and I said that I was very much looking forward to it. I had initially thought that a year off from school would be heaven: no homework, lots of time to concentrate on tennis, no exams, and a way to get away from all the things that reminded me of Tom. But I had found that even by November, I desperately missed the camaraderie of classrooms and sports teams. I had never spent so much time in solitude.

"I like it here," I said. "But I'm looking forward to being around friends again."

"What about the boys you play tennis with here?" It was the first time he had ever asked me about them.

"I've become good friends with one of them. This guy named Bowen. He's the best player on the team. I think he's number one in China in the fourteen-and-under. Most of them don't speak much English though."

My father frowned. "You should be speaking to them in Chinese."

"Well, I try to," I said. "But my Chinese still isn't good enough for me to understand everything they say."

"I thought you said your Chinese lessons were going well?"

"They are. It's just not an easy language. It takes time."

"You really should be making an effort to only use Chinese, Chase. A couple years down the road, you're going to kick yourself if you don't take advantage of your time here."

"I know." I paused and thought about whether to continue. "It just gets kind of lonely sometimes."

"What does?"

"Just being here, by myself. I just get lonely, that's all."

"That's part of life. Everyone's lonely sometimes," he said. "You just have to learn to deal with it."

Our food arrived and we ate in silence. Perhaps trying to compensate for his criticism, my father told me a few stories about pranks he and his friends had pulled back when they were at Dover. I found myself laughing out loud as he told me tales of their bike jousting tournament, which ended with several broken collarbones, and how they had spent two weeks of their senior spring catching squirrels around the campus, collecting them in a pen they built during woodshop, before finally releasing them in different parts of the main school building early one morning. My father wiped away a tear from his eye as he recalled how one of the released squirrels had wreaked havoc on his calculus class when it scurried up his teacher's back and into her thick hair. The teacher, he said, had reacted by sprinting blindly away from her desk only to run straight into the classroom door. Encouraged by his good mood, I told him about the Texan and his desperate attempts to get an old-fashioned. My father found the episode even funnier than I did.

I asked my father what people like the men from Morgan Stanley and the Texan were really doing in Beijing. He said it was hard to know. "There are a lot of people over here chasing deals, but they don't really know what they are chasing. There are a lot of opportunities, but these guys don't really like it over here, and the Chinese have to trust you before they will deal with you. That's what it comes down to, trust. It takes years to earn that trust, and you can lose it in a second. But without that trust you won't get anywhere here. Most Westerners think they can just come over here and beat their chest and say, 'I'm from Goldman' or 'I'm from Citi,' and the red carpets will get rolled out. Even with the best contacts you never really know who you are dealing with." My father paused for a moment before adding, "In some ways, that's the danger, but also the opportunity." My father said it was all about trust, but so many of the relationships I had witnessed in China seemed to be transactional relationships. I do this for you, and you do this for me. Maybe that was why trust was so important. In a society where trust was the scarcest resource, it was also the most valuable.

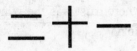

My father went with me to the tennis center the next day but spent the entire car ride on a conference call. As we drove through the gates of the sports center in the black Audi, I spotted Bowen walking in the shadow of the statue. I almost pointed him out to my father, but I didn't when I saw the condition he was in. He looked thin and pale and he walked with a limp. It was strange. I had never seen him look fragile before. I wondered what punishment Madame Jiang had inflicted on him this time. I hoped he was okay.

We started off with the juggling routine. I glanced over at my father to see his reaction to this absurd warm-up, but his attention was wholly focused on his BlackBerry. Madame Jiang fed us forehands for thirty minutes before telling us to practice serves. She walked around the court with a racket under her arms, an old graphite Prince model from the 1980s. It was one of the few times I ever saw her bring a racket to practice; usually she just borrowed one of the boy's rackets when she needed to feed balls. Bowen noticed the racket too, and as we returned to the shopping cart to gather balls for more practice, he said to no one in particular, "What is she going to do with that racket, swat flies?"

For the first hour Madame Jiang walked around the perimeter of the courts watching us, but she also kept her eyes on my father. I noticed that she walked to where Victoria was and chatted with her for longer than usual. Halfway through practice she called us to the net and told us it was time to play sets. She paired Dali with Bowen. During the past week, Madame Jiang had been going after Dali in the same way she did with Hope. She yelled at him for being lazy. She said he was getting worse. I had even heard her warn him that unless he got his act together his place on the team was in danger. I talked to Bowen about it. It worried me. Dali's temperament was not well suited to deal with Madame Jiang. He was losing confidence in his game and he seemed depressed during practice. He was one of the more cheerful, bubbly personalities on the team, but lately he had been despondent and solitary. I wondered why Madame Jiang picked on the players like that. I noticed that she seemed to go through waves of targeting one player, and then would abruptly switch to another. I think it was her way of maintaining control. Her way of reminding them that she was the boss. Maybe it came from the insecurity of knowing less about the sport than the boys she coached. In any case, I hoped that she would move on from Dali before it was too late. I didn't want him to go the way of Hope.

Madame Jiang finished pairing us up, and we headed out to our courts to begin our matches. I was assigned to play Random. He had beaten me quite easily the last time we had played, but I was hitting well that day. I remember glancing in my father's direction after each winner I hit, checking for any sign of approval, or even an acknowledgment that he had seen the point. However, whenever I looked over he was busy sending e-mails on his BlackBerry. It didn't make any sense to me that he wasn't watching to see if I had improved during my time in Beijing. As he continued to ignore my match, I began to have the disconcerting thought that maybe he wasn't watching because it didn't matter to him. Maybe that was why he had never shown any real interest in sending me to Laver in Florida. But it didn't make sense to me that he wouldn't care.

I ended up winning 6-1, 6-2. I was surprised by how well I played. Usually my father's presence made me nervous. The last time he had seen me play had been six months before at the National Clay Court Championships in Fort Lauderdale, Florida, when I drew the number two player in the country in the third round. I lost that match 6-1, 6-1 in less than an hour. Maybe this time I had played better because I knew he wasn't really watching.

I was surprised to hear that Bowen and Dali had split sets and were about to start the third. Madame Jiang was watching the match so intently that she forgot to give us instructions about what to do next, so we sat on the benches and watched too. Bowen had never lost a set to Dali in his life. The only way he would have lost that second set was if he decided to let Dali win. Judging from the few points I had seen, it looked like they were having a very close match. I figured that must be Bowen consciously playing to Dali's strengths. He understood the game so well that he had this ability to raise his opponent's game if he wanted to. Sometimes it felt like he understood your strengths and weaknesses better than you did yourself. Dali looked a changed player from the one I had seen yesterday. He was fired up and full of confidence. It was a big deal for him to take a set off Bowen. It was exactly what he needed to counter all the negativity Madame Jiang had cast on him during the past week of practices.

At 2-2 in the third set, Bowen changed his service motion. Instead of completing a full circle with his left arm, he truncated the arc and brought his racket straight up. He hit his serve flat, and while he still managed to generate some power, Dali did not have trouble controlling and redirecting Bowen's balls. Bowen knew that all Dali had to do to look like a brilliant returner was to punch these flat serves back as if he were volleying. Had Bowen served with heavy topspin, Dali would have been unable to control his return.

Bowen was giving Dali a chance to shine in front of my father. Madame Jiang knew my father had connections in the Chinese system, but she didn't know with whom or how deep. What she did not want to happen was exactly the outcome Bowen was orchestrating. If Dali almost beat Bowen in front of my father, my father might mention to his contact—whoever it was—that he had seen a fine match between Bowen and Dali, the two best boys on the team. Madame Jiang then would not have the courage to throw him off the team. Her threats would lose their bite.

They fought the last set to a tiebreaker at 6-6. Random leaned over to me and whispered, "Bowen had better worry about saving his own skin. If he loses she will go after him." We were all worried for Bowen. Random was right, I knew that much. The system in China was brutal, if you got cut—that was it, there was no one to help you out. I couldn't fathom how these boys dealt with the pressure of such a reality, but they did. I guess somehow they just got used to it, or perhaps it was all they ever knew.

No one understood this better than Bowen. Of all the boys, his place on the team was the most tenuous. He knew as well as any of us that if Madame Jiang could find a way to send him back to Tianjin, she would. Random explained this to me one day. He said it was Bowen's ability that kept him on the team. Madame Jiang's government bosses cared only that the team won. Their promotions depended on the success of the sporting programs they supervised. As long as Bowen was the number one player, and as long as he kept winning matches for Beijing, he was untouchable. According to Random, Madame Jiang had once reported Bowen to her supervisor for disrespect in an attempt to have him kicked off the team. But she was overruled. The team supervisor refused to kick Bowen off the team because he was too good. He didn't want to lose Bowen to a rival team.

Bowen knew all of this. If there was anything consistent about him, it was his subtle defiance of Madame Jiang. Every action was calibrated so as to pull against her. And the calibration had to be careful and exact. One wrong calculation, a piece of bad luck, a bad step, wrong timing, and Bowen could be banished for good. And it scared me for him. He was balancing on a tightrope without anything underneath him.

Never one to confirm our suspicions that he was rigging the match, Bowen gave Dali three match points before finally finishing the tiebreaker eleven to nine. Dali was unable to win the crucial points and in that brief space, I saw the difference between Dali and Bowen, and it made all the difference. Bowen believed in himself so completely that there could be no other outcome for him. Dali got nervous and played tight. I don't know if he understood what his friend was doing for him. And perhaps that made it heavier for Dali because Bowen allowed him to believe that it was all his own doing, that the fate of the match was truly in his hands. But Bowen looked ahead with an infinite confidence in the future. And it was that infinite confidence that allowed him to take risks that none of us would have ever conceived of—let alone dared. But it was all too close for me.

The moment Bowen won, Madame Jiang turned away in disgust and saw us all sitting on the bench. She shooed us back on the court and told us all to do one hundred push-ups, such was her anger at the outcome of Dali and Bowen's match and our taking a break to watch the last set. She told us we did not have time to waste watching a mediocre match. I knew her scolding would have been much worse had my father not been there.

Halfway through the practice my father caught my attention and waved good-bye. He had a meeting scheduled for the late afternoon.

Bowen raised his chin toward my father. "That man, who is he? He is your sponsor?"

"No, he is my father." Bowen looked surprised. He asked me why he had come. I told him that my father wanted to watch me play. Bowen didn't seem to understand this. I asked him if his parents ever came to watch him. "No," he said.

"How about the other boys?" He shook his head. "What about tournaments. Do they come and watch the tournaments?"

"Not really." Bowen went on to explain that they were all paid a salary by the government to play tennis and had been since they were young children. "If you worked in a bank, would your father come and watch you work? It is the same thing."

I suddenly realized in all the time that I practiced with the team, I never once saw a friend or parent come to watch. Bowen was correct: in a way they were already at work. Tennis was their profession, and a certain level of maturity had already developed. Even though the boys' families lived in the Beijing area, they would not have been well off enough to own a car. Using public transportation would have taken a lot of time, and both parents probably worked long hours during the week. At the training centers in America, parents came and visited or, if they lived nearby, drove down to spend an afternoon watching their children practice. In fact, in America, the reverse was true, the academies had to develop policies and rules of behavior to keep the parents from meddling too much.

As we were packing up racket bags at the end of the day's practice, I said to Bowen, "Why do you push her so much?"

"Push?"

"You know." I motioned to Madame Jiang. "Like with Dali. Why'd you give him three match points? You know it drives her insane when she thinks you're messing with her. I don't think it's a good idea to make her mad like that. You're just making life harder for yourself."

Bowen shook his head. "I don't know what you are talking about. I didn't give anything to Dali."

"Come on, Bowen."

He shook his head again, and for a moment I began to wonder. I couldn't be certain whether Bowen really was playing with Madame Jiang's expectation and hopes of match results just to annoy her. I sensed he knew that she could get rid of him anytime and that this was his only permissible act of defiance—through sheer physical and mental talent he could manipulate outcomes and no one watching could quite figure out how. Or perhaps he was indeed injured and was telling it straight. And with Bowen I knew both versions could be true.

After practice, I got back to the hotel and waited for my father. I turned on CNN to watch the news. I caught the beginning of a story about the 2008 Olympics and Chinese violations of human rights. The screen went blank, and five minutes later CNN returned with a story about a hijacker who had been apprehended in Chicago. Later that evening at dinner my father explained that anytime a story came on that the Chinese didn't want on the air, they would censor it by blocking reception for the length of the story. He assumed the censored news story was about people protesting China's having been awarded the 2008 Summer Olympics, given China's human rights record in Tibet.

My father asked me some questions about tennis practice, but he never asked me anything about Bowen or any of the other boys. I guess they didn't interest him. He often asked me about China's young generation. What the "young generation" thought about the Chinese government, about democracy, about America, about censorship and freedom. But he never asked me about my teammates. He wasn't interested in the boys I saw every day. They would never grow up to be entrepreneurs, artists, or political leaders. My teammates were a part of China's young generation, but they were not a part of the young generation who would matter to America.

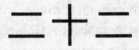

Victoria came to the Hyatt on Friday afternoon to tell us that the Zhangs had invited us to dinner that night. Dreading the prospect of a long, drawn-out dinner at which I would be largely ignored, I asked if we could bring Bowen. Victoria shook her head behind my father's back as if to indicate that it was an inappropriate thing to ask.

"Who?" my father asked.

"Bowen."

"Who is Bowen?"

"My friend from tennis. You know? The one I was telling you about."

My father gave a look that bordered on annoyance. "To this? No, definitely not."

With that dealt with, my father turned back to the papers he had been looking over before Victoria arrived. What made my request so out of the question that it could be dismissed with disgust? For a second I was overcome with a desire to push back, to say that I wasn't going if Bowen couldn't come. But I couldn't bring myself to confront him and I said nothing.

Just before we were about to leave, my father told me that

dinner was going to be at the house of Mrs. Zhang's father, Secretary Su. My father explained to me that Secretary Su was one of the nine members of the Standing Committee. I hadn't known that before. It answered some of my questions about the pictures in the Zhangs' living room. I didn't know a whole lot about the structure of the Chinese government, but I knew that the Standing Committee was the top of the pyramid. The nine men that made up the Standing Committee, which included the president and the premier, were the nine most powerful men in China. As a member of the Standing Committee, I knew that Mrs. Zhang's father would live in Zhongnanhai, the high-security government compound located next to the Forbidden City. It had served as the Beijing residence for all of China's top leaders going back to Mao Zedong and Zhou Enlai and very few outsiders were ever allowed in. It was a modern-day Forbidden City. I would be one of the only Westerners my age to go inside.

The Hyatt had a car waiting for us downstairs. We drove the short distance down Chang'an Avenue to Tiananmen Square. The wide avenue, which had seen tanks roll down it during the student protests, was familiar to me, having walked down it several times for sightseeing trips to the Forbidden City with Victoria. However, this time before reaching the old imperial palace, we turned down a small side street. We were stopped at a security checkpoint and an armed military policeman came up to the driver's window. The driver passed the policeman several papers and indicated to him our business in Zhongnanhai. As the military policeman checked over the documents, two other guards ran mirrors under the car to check for explosives attached to the bottom of the vehicle. The military policeman, satisfied with our documents, motioned for us to get out of the car and then ushered us through a metal detector to the side of the check-point. As I stood there I noticed a screen behind the gate with the words SERVE THE PEOPLE written on it in calligraphy. I smiled to myself. There was some irony to "the servants of the people" taking up residence in the palace of the last emperor. After the driver cleared the metal detector, the three of us got back into the car and drove through the gate.

The interior of Zhongnanhai was quiet and peaceful. A road ran alongside a dark lake that was bordered by trees and grass far greener than anything else I had seen in Beijing. The tranquility of the place was a welcome change from the chaos that defined the streets just on the other side of the wall.

We pulled up outside a smaller walled enclosure. Two soldiers stood guard by the entrance. Before we got out, my father reminded me to be polite and to behave. I hated when he talked down to me, as if I were still a little boy. The large front door swung open, and Mrs. Zhang stood there with David beside her. She greeted my father with a warm smile.

"Tom," she said. "Come in. Come in. You know David, yes?"

"I don't believe we've met," my father said. He extended a hand to David. "How do you do?" he asked in mock seriousness.

David shook his hand. "I'm fine," he said.

"He's very cute," my father said to Mrs. Zhang. She smiled and the two walked down the corridor discussing something, leaving David and me by the door with the two soldiers. David blinked and then pointed at one of the soldiers.

"You see his gun?" David asked. "I'm getting one. For my birthday."

"No, you're not," I said.

"I am."

"You're getting an assault rifle for your birthday?"

"It looks the same. It just doesn't shoot the real bullets," he said.

"What kind of bullets, then?"

"Come on. I'll show you." David ran off down the hallway in the opposite direction of our parents and waved for me to follow. I walked after him, and then broke into a jog in order to keep up. David stopped when he reached the end of the hallway and waited for me.

I caught up with him and we turned the corner, and suddenly to my right was an opening to an expansive courtyard. David kept running down the hallway, but I stopped and looked. The courtyard was simple. The floor of the courtyard was paved with large, smooth, gray stones and the paving was only interrupted in four small areas where trees had been planted. There were bushes around the exterior and potted plants by the small steps that led down to the courtyard. The trees were mostly bare now, giving the courtyard a cold, deserted feel. I imagined it looked quite beautiful in the spring. David had realized that I was no longer following him and stopped.

"Come on," he said. "Let's go."

I waved him off. Something in the far corner of the courtyard had moved and caught my eye. David sighed impatiently and followed as I walked down the wide stone steps and across the flat, gray stone floor toward the far corner of the courtyard. As I got closer I saw that in the corner of the courtyard, between two bushes, was a brown, wooden cage. I peered between the bars of the cage and saw three small, brown furry creatures. They looked like miniature brown monkeys, but without tails. One was hanging down from the top of the cage. The creature was no bigger than a small hamster and looked as though it weighed about a pound at most. It dangled upside down from the bars, hanging on by its two minuscule feet. It stared at me with huge round moon eyes.

"Don't touch them!" David said.

I turned, surprised. "I wasn't going to."

"They're poisonous."

"What?"

"You have to go to the hospital if they bite you." David snapped his teeth and pretended to take a chunk out of his own arm. "I'm just joking. You can touch them if you want. My dad called some-one to take out their teeth. They can't bite people anymore."

"What are they?" I asked.

"What do you mean?"

"What type of animal."

"Oh," David said. "We call them *lan hou,* but I forget how to say it in English."

"Must be some kind of monkey," I said. "Lan hou, doesn't that mean lazy monkey?"

"Yeah, but they're not monkeys. It's called something else in English. I forget. My mom likes them. She thinks they are cute. You can't buy them anymore. There's not many left."

"You mean they're endangered?"

"I guess. Okay, let's go, I have to show you my guns."

Leaving the three lan hou behind, David showed me to a room that his grandfather had given to him for when he came to stay. He opened a closet in the room and showed off an impressive arsenal of airsoft guns. We spent the remainder of the time until dinner sniping toy figurines with David's assortment of military-replica airsoft guns.

Around eight o'clock, David's nanny poked her head around the door to call me for dinner. David, coincidentally, or perhaps not, chose that exact moment to unleash a furious volley of airsoft pellets at a target we had taped to the door. David laughed as the nanny yelped and jumped back behind the door. The two exchanged a few sharp words. David sighed. "Okay! Okay!" he said and dropped his airsoft gun. The nanny poked her head around the door once more and called to me to come with her. I followed her back around the courtyard to the other wing of the house. I asked her why David wasn't coming with us, and she said that he and Lily had eaten dinner earlier, before my father and I arrived. She led me through an elaborate sitting room into the dining room behind it. I came in to find everyone already seated around a large circular table in the center of the dining room.

At the far side of the table my father was seated in between Mr. Zhang and an elderly, serious-looking man dressed in a dark suit with neatly combed jet-black hair that looked as if it had been dyed. I knew that he must be Secretary Su. A young woman who I assumed must be an interpreter sat to Secretary Su's left, then Mrs. Zhang and then her mother to the left of her. Two younger Chinese men sat around the side of the table closest to me. As they were too young to be Secretary Su's deputies, I guessed that they were his aides. I saw that there was an open spot between Mr. Zhang and the younger of the two aides.

The seating of the dinner was no accident. I had attended some of my father's meetings with government officials and seen how seriously seating order was taken in China. Every meeting room was arranged with chairs in a horseshoe shape around the perimeter of the room. The two most important people always occupied the two chairs at the top of the horseshoe, and then people filled out the remaining chairs by order of their seniority. The most junior people would take the chairs at the two ends of the horseshoe. I had once made the mistake of taking the chair directly next to my father—the chair for the third- or fourth-most important person in the meeting. This must have caused quite an awkward situation for the Chinese minister, whose seat I had accidentally taken and who had to sit in a seat that was lower than his position, and yet, at the same time, he would not have wanted to offend my father by appearing to be rude by asking me to move. Just before the meeting began, a staff member came over and told me they had a different seat saved for me.

My father was deep in conversation with Mr. Zhang and Secretary Su and did not see me right away. Uniformed waiters and waitresses stood around the perimeter of the room. I saw the ornately decorated porcelain plates, and the golden napkins and ivory chopsticks, and I knew that this all would have been just as foreign to Bowen as it was to me. I stood there for a moment until the interpreter alerted my father of my presence. He smiled and stood up, pointing to me.

"Ah," my father said. "Secretary Su, this is my son, Chase."

As I walked toward them I could feel the eyes of all the waiters and waitresses watching me, and I wondered what they thought of a fourteen-year-old foreign boy being invited to this dinner.

Secretary Su smiled and extended a hand. I shook it. His hand was soft. He turned to the rest of the table and said something that I didn't understand. The rest of the table laughed at his comment. I smiled awkwardly. The interpreter, a frail young woman with frameless eyeglasses and straight dark hair tied back in a ponytail, leaned toward me. "He says you are a very handsome boy," she said. Secretary Su puffed out his chest and made himself tall. "*Hen qianglie, ah? Xiang yundongyuan yiyang,*" he said.

The interpreter translated. "He says you are strong like . . . uh . . . a sports player?"

My father put his hand on my shoulder. "Tell Secretary Su that Chase is a very good tennis player," he said to the interpreter. He waited while she translated his words. "Tell him he practices with the junior national tennis team, every day."

The interpreter repeated what he said to Secretary Su and waited for his response. "Oh really? he says. Then maybe one day he will be a tennis champion? Like . . ." She turned back to Secretary Su for clarification. "*A-jia-xi-a?*" She looked uncertain and looked to me for confirmation. "You know him?"

My father looked at me. "Who did she say?" he asked. I sounded out the syllables in my head and realized whom she meant.

"Agassi," I said. "Like Andre Agassi."

"Ahh, Agassi." My father smiled. "Well, maybe. Tell Secretary Su that he's also learning Chinese."

She translated and Secretary Su turned to me. "*Ni hui shou Zhongwen ma* (You can speak Chinese)?"

"*Wo hui* (I can)," I said.

He clapped his hands together. "*Tebie hao* (Excellent)!" he said. Then he said something I didn't understand. I wasn't even sure if it had been a statement or a question, and so I just stood there looking at him with an uneasy smile on my face. I could feel the eyes of everyone in the room on me. He laughed and said, "*Mei guanxi* (It doesn't matter)," and we all sat down for dinner.

An army of waiters and waitresses suddenly came upon us, placing trays of steaming vegetables and fish and meat on the table's large turntable centerpiece. A waitress placed a bowl of soup in front of me while another filled my glass with red wine. The waitresses disappeared and were almost immediately replaced by a male waiter who carried a small decanter of clear liquid that he poured into miniature ceramic glasses that looked just like the eggcups I had eaten soft-boiled eggs out of at home. One of the first two waitresses returned with a cup of green tea and asked if I would like anything else to drink. "*Shui* (Water)," I said, hoping to make up for my earlier failure to understand Secretary Su. I had to repeat it twice more before she understood me. A few minutes later she returned with a glass of water. I picked up the glass to take a drink, but put it back down right away. The water was boiling hot.

I turned to my left where Mr. Zhang was slurping down his bowl of soup. He caught my eye and stabbed at the soup with his white spoon. "Very good," he said. "Try some. Shark fin soup. Very expensive." I tasted it. It was very salty. Feeling Mr. Zhang's gaze, I drank a few more spoonfuls and then put down my spoon. On the other side of the table, one of Secretary Su's assistants spun the glass turntable centerpiece, sending dishes of fish and meat and vegetables slowly around the table.

My father spoke with Mr. Zhang and Secretary Su for most of the dinner. I sat there quietly and tried a few of the less exotic dishes as they moved past. The aide I was sitting next to asked me a few questions about my tennis game and told me that he had a son who loved to play basketball. I asked him if he worked for the Secretary and he smiled and said no. He said he was just Secretary Su's "*pengyou*" (friend). I wondered what that really meant. I met a lot of people like that in China that year, people who you could never really figure out who they were or what they did. They always said they were so and so's "friend." I guessed that they must work for the government in some capacity, but I could never figure out who they were.

I tried to listen to the conversation my father was having with Secretary Su and Mr. Zhang. From what I was able to hear I gathered that Secretary Su was due to make a trip to the United States later that year, and he was full of questions about the Bush administration policy and whom the people he should meet with were. My father offered to help him arrange his trip and said that he would make a point of seeing some of the members of the cabinet ahead of time to brief them on Secretary Su's visit. Secretary Su thanked him and told him that his efforts were most appreciated. He said that he had spoken with the U.S. ambassador about his trip, but the ambassador had said nothing of substance, and he wished that my father were the ambassador instead. The three of them toasted to this, and the whole table followed suit by raising their wineglasses and saying, "*Gan bei* (Cheers)." Not wanting to appear rude, but also unsure if I was allowed to drink alcohol, I looked to my father for approval. He lifted his glass at me. Taking this as a sign I should join in, I raised my glass and clinked it with Mr. Zhang and the aide sitting next to me and took a sip of the wine. All of a sudden I felt quite grown up, and the dinner was looking up.

There was a shift in the mood of the room when Mr. Zhang brought up the Dover School to Secretary Su. The side conversations dropped away and everyone became focused on what Mr. Zhang was saying. Although Mr. Zhang was ostensibly speaking to Secretary Su, the interpreter still translated everything for my father's benefit. Mr. Zhang told Secretary Su that my father had assured him that Dover was a very good school and it was known for sending many students to Harvard, Yale, and Stanford every year. Secretary Su nodded his approval and mentioned that the Premier's daughter was currently attending Yale. Mr. Zhang pointed to me and said that I would be attending Dover the following year. Secretary Su spoke a few words to the interpreter and motioned to me with his glass.

"He asks, you are going to this school next year?"

"Yes, I'll be going there next year," I said. "A lot of my friends are there now."

She translated what I had said, and he gave her another question to ask me. "Your friends, what do they think of the school?"

I hadn't spoken to either of the two boys I knew who had gone to Dover in more than a month. I didn't know what their opinions of Dover really were, but I knew what my father would want me to say.

"They love it," I said. "It's demanding. A lot of work. But they say it is preparing them for university very well."

Secretary Su mumbled in agreement as the interpreter conveyed what I had said. "He says that to have a good education is very important. The most important thing," the interpreter said to my father. Mr. Zhang nodded and mumbled his agreement. The interpreter turned back to Secretary Su, who continued speaking.

"He wants to know if you think David will like this school?" the interpreter asked me.

"Well, you know, I think he should visit a few schools and see which one he likes. But yes, I'm sure he will, it's a very good school."

Mr. Zhang cut in. "Tom very good friends with the headmaster," he said to Secretary Su in English.

My father nodded in agreement. "The headmaster is a terrific guy. You'd like him a lot. He was one of my very good friends at Dover and my roommate for one year at Yale—we've stayed very, very close. I saw him just last week, and I told him that he needs to get over to China soon."

Secretary Su waited for the words to be translated. He seemed to approve of what he heard. He looked at my father and began speaking and didn't stop for some time. The interpreter began to translate what he had said, but Mr. Zhang cut her off. "We would like David to go to a university here in China, maybe Tsinghua or Bei Da, but because we used to live in Hong Kong, David is out of the school system in China for too long. We think the best is for him to go to international school and then when he is old enough, to go to school in the United States. And then apply to Princeton or Yale."

"I think that's very smart," my father said.

The conversation moved on to something else that didn't involve me, and once again I was ignored. I tried following it for a while but lost interest and turned back to my food. Just then the waiters brought out small dishes covered by porcelain lids. They lifted the lids to reveal a brown gelatinous glob that looked almost like the body of a slug. Mr. Zhang turned to me and pointed to my plate. "This very good. It's a Chinese delicacy. Very expensive," he said.

"Oh, okay," I said, prodding mine suspiciously. "What is it?"

He thought for a moment. "*Zhe de yingwen mingzi shi shenme* (What's its English name)? From the ocean. It type of shellfish." He frowned and called over one of the waitresses. "*Eh . . . Xiaojie, baoyu . . . yong Yingwen zenme shuo* (Waitress, how do you say *baoyu* in English)?" She looked puzzled but he clicked his fingers and waved her away. "Abalone!" he said. "It's called abalone. Do you know abalone?" I shook my head. "It's very good," he reassured me. "Very expensive. Maybe at a restaurant will be two hundred, three hundred dollars. Try, try."

Dessert consisted of sliced watermelon and dragon fruit. After we had all finished I saw Mr. Zhang motion for a waitress to bring over two bags in the corner. It was a custom in China for the guests and the hosts to exchange gifts at the end of formal dinners. The gifts were almost always presented in beautifully handcrafted wooden boxes. They often looked very expensive, but in my experience the gifts were usually the kind of cheap trinkets one might find in a tourist gift shop.

During my time in China I was given two large scrolls of calligraphy, a silk fan decorated on both sides with a traditional-style landscape painting of a mist-engulfed mountain, a miniature set of painted Peking opera masks, and a calligraphy writing set, complete with two wooden brushes, an inkstone, and an intricately carved stone seal. My father had accumulated hundreds of these gifts over the years and no longer bothered to keep track of them. He told me he thought the Hyatt held them in storage for him, but that he wasn't really sure. My father always gave gifts as well, but he never bought them himself. Instead he had his assistant prepare gifts for every dinner he attended.

He did this because he had heard too many horror stories about Americans who had accidentally given highly offensive gifts to their Chinese hosts. There were all sorts of cultural taboos when it came to gifts. For instance, anything associated with the number 4 was out due to the similarity in pronunciation of the words for 4 (sì) and death (sǐ). Flowers were another risky choice, as white and yellow flowers are highly associated with funerals. My father told me that the owner of the Boston Celtics had once handed out green Celtics jerseys and hats at the end of a dinner in Shanghai, not realizing that in Chinese the idiom "wearing a green hat" refers to a cuckold. In giving a green hat to his host, my father's friend had accidentally implied his host's wife was having an affair. Needless to say, it didn't go over especially well with his host.

At this particular dinner, the Zhangs gave me a copy of Confucius's *Analects* printed on silk paper and gave my father a green jade sculpture of a rooster—the animal of his birth year under the Chinese zodiac system.

There was a darker side to this practice of gift exchanges, for it played a significant role in the shadowy world of corruption. I had heard that at the end of dinners between government officials and businessmen trying to win government contracts, the businessmen would often present the officials with lavish gifts of outrageous monetary value. These bribes might take the form of a piece of art, a case of very expensive European wine, or perhaps even a bag filled with stacks of pink 100 RMB notes. I remembered a story my father had once told me about how he had been invited to dinner at the house of a well-known Chinese entrepreneur who wanted my father's help to open several franchises of a big European supermarket in China. While giving my father a tour of the house, the entrepreneur made a point of showing him a gorgeous vase that dated back to the Ming Dynasty. The vase, the entrepreneur claimed, was worth more than $100,000 and could not legally be taken out of China as it was considered a national artifact. My father had complimented the vase and said how wonderful it must be to own something as special as that. Then they continued the tour and later had dinner. When my father got back to his hotel later that night, the driver went to open the trunk and there, in the trunk of the car, sat the $100,000 vase. My father immediately sent the driver back to return the vase. A year later the entrepreneur's business went under and he was arrested on charges of corruption, fraud, and bribery.

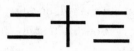

During dinner Mr. Zhang told us that he had arranged a private tour of the areas of the Forbidden City that were off limits to the general public that weekend. However, the next morning, my father informed me that his plans had changed and he had to return to New York immediately. His business partner in New York had called him in the middle of the night—he needed to go back to sort out a problem with a deal they'd been working on—it was complicated—he'd explain when he had more time. He said it was important that I go on the tour so that we did not appear rude to Mr. Zhang. I thought about asking if I could go with him to New York. But I didn't—partly because I knew that he would say no, but mostly because I knew he would be disappointed in me for asking.

At tennis I asked Bowen if he wanted to come on the private tour of the Forbidden City. At first he was extremely hesitant. I hadn't actually asked Mr. Zhang or Victoria, but I saw no problem as the tour had been arranged for three people and my father could no longer come. Bowen had never been to the Forbidden City before. He told me he wanted to come with us, but he didn't think that Madame Jiang would allow him to go. "How about this," I said, "Victoria and I will pick you up by the front gate. Madame Jiang won't say anything if we are the ones who take you out."

"Maybe she won't say anything, but she will be angry."

"*Bie danxin, Bowen* (Don't worry, Bowen)," I said. "It will be fine. I'll just get Victoria to talk to her."

"I don't think I should go," he said.

"Come on man, it will be cool. Mr. Zhang said he would take us to areas that are not open to the public. Plus, I don't want to go by myself. My dad was meant to go, but he had to return to the States for work."

Bowen thought it over. I could see the conflict in his face. After a few moments he smiled. "Okay," he said, "I will go with you."

I spent the next few nights at the Hyatt as my father's secretary had booked the room through Wednesday of the following week, and I wasn't quite ready to give up the Hyatt's seemingly endless room service menu just yet. On Sunday morning, I went down to the hotel's lobby where Victoria was waiting for me. I told her that I had to swing by the tennis center quickly before we went to the Forbidden City. She seemed puzzled by that, but she passed on my request to Driver Wu. When we arrived, Bowen was waiting by the gate, dressed in a warm-up suit and tennis shoes.

"Oh, look, there's Bowen," Victoria said. She waved to him, but the windows were tinted too dark for him to see her. I rolled down my window and waved him over. Victoria frowned when she saw him walking toward the car. "Bowen's coming with us," I said.

Victoria turned in her seat and looked at me. "Does Mr. Zhang know about this?"

"No," I said. "But I mean it's fine. It doesn't matter, right?"

"You should have asked him," Victoria said. She pulled out her pink cell phone. "This was arranged for your father. I hope Mr. Zhang won't be mad. I should call his assistant. Tell Bowen to wait while I ask."

"Victoria, it's fine. He's coming with us. It won't be a big deal."

Just then Bowen reached the car. I opened the car door and slid over and he climbed in. Victoria shrugged and put away her phone and told the driver to take us to the Forbidden City. We arrived with half an hour to spare. The driver dropped us off by Tiananmen Square and went to find a place to park and wait for us. We walked the short distance down Chang'an Avenue to the huge square where an enormous crowd was massed. All around the square were security cameras. Ahead of us, a group of American teachers held up a flag bearing the name of their school and posed for a photograph. Within moments two policemen arrived and confiscated their camera and emptied the film out onto the pavement. Before I could even ask, Victoria whispered to me that the policemen destroyed all photos with banners because Tiananmen was such a politically sensitive area. The policemen were fearful that any sign they didn't recognize or understand might be the slogan of a protest group or something referencing 6/4, and they couldn't risk that picture getting on the internet.

Victoria changed the topic and asked us if we wanted to get a hot chocolate.

"Where?" I asked.

"Follow me." She made her way through the crowd of tourists to the Meridian Gate, the large main outer gate that led to the courtyard where tickets and souvenirs were sold. Above the gate hung a massive portrait of Chairman Mao. I was astonished to see a Starbucks sign—the same size and color as in the States—on top of the doorway of one of the buildings.

"Starbucks?" I asked. "How is there a Starbucks here?"

Victoria turned and looked at me, puzzled. It was clear that she didn't understand my question.

"How did Starbucks get here?"

"They just came," Victoria said.

"No, I mean how did they get permission to put a big American chain in an ancient building of the Forbidden City?"

"Oh," she said. "The officials invited Starbucks. They needed to raise money to restore parts of the Forbidden City."

"But isn't this an original building?"

"Yes," Victoria said. "It's from Qing Dynasty."

Victoria was not bothered by the presence of Starbucks. She obviously understood it as a practical solution to a funding problem and not as an affront to Chinese culture. "In fact, the Qing Dynasty was ruled by the Manchu." Victoria pointed to a small blue plaque with a red-and-gold-edged frame on the side of the building. Next she pointed out two columns of three characters each. The first column was Chinese characters that read, "Please come in." I did not recognize the characters in the second column. They were less elaborate than the Chinese and almost looked like Arabic. Victoria answered my question before I could ask it. "That's the Manchu language," she said, pointing to the Arabic-looking characters. "It says please come in."

"You can read Manchu?" I asked. The Manchu people were one of China's fifty-four ethnic minority groups. I had learned about them from Teacher Lu. As their name indicated, they had originally come from Manchuria.

"Only a small amount. My father's family is Manchu, so he taught me how to read very basic words."

"So are you half Manchu?" I asked.

"Yes, but I am registered as a Han," Victoria said.

"Why?"

"I was born during the Cultural Revolution and my parents feared that being different might bring unwanted attention. Almost everyone changed their official ethnicity to Han during those years. Ninety percent of China is Han now."

"I am Han too," Bowen added.

I had read about the Han Dynasty, which had lasted over four hundred years from about 200 BC to 200 AD. I knew that during the Han Dynasty the Chinese had come to rival the Roman Empire in wealth and power and geographic reach. But I didn't really understand what it meant to be Han. It seemed like such an umbrella term that included so many dissimilar people. Perhaps tracing one's lineage to what was considered the high point in Chinese civilization was why it was so important. My father had often told me how Chinese civilization had been at the forefront of human culture and technological advances for most of the past five thousand years and how it had been humiliating for many Chinese when they fell behind the Europeans and became seen as a second- or third-tier nation in the nineteenth and twentieth centuries. At times like that, people needed to cling to links from a glorious past to feel pride for their country.

Victoria ordered us two hot chocolates and got a latte for herself. We walked outside with our drinks and a small Chinese woman came up to us waving books of Mao's quotations and paper Chinese flags. She didn't understand English but had mastered a few simple phrases like, "Look, look, very cheap." Bowen waved her off, but I stopped walking and looked at what she was selling. As I was about to learn, if you showed the slightest interest in purchasing something, these street vendors would harass you for half a mile. It didn't matter how many times I waved her away, the woman continued to follow me for another few minutes, periodically jumping in front of me, pushing her trinkets toward my face. Several other vendors, seeing that this woman had found a prospective customer, started following us as well. Victoria turned and snapped at them in Chinese and they fell back.

Victoria said, "Keep moving. If we stop, the beggars will come."

The beggars clawed meekly at the edges of the tourist groups. They were dirty, and most were physically disabled. A boy a few years older than I hobbled up to me on crutches. He tapped me on the arm and stood and looked straight at me, holding his hand out. His right foot was missing. His leg ended at his knee in a dirty ball of gauze. He was pale and weak and he was missing most of his teeth. His face was dirty and clothes were ragged, and his eyes looked past me. I reached in my pockets and pulled out the change from Starbucks and a crumpled U.S. bill. I unfolded the thin bill, which must have been left in my jeans when they were last washed. I handed the worn-out image of Abraham Lincoln to him. "*Xie xie nin* (Thank you)," he whispered.

I felt someone grab my arm. I turned and saw that it was Bowen. "Let's go," he said. "You can't help them all."

Mr. Zhang called and gave Victoria instructions on where to meet him. We followed Victoria back through the Meridian Gate to a side street on the west side of Tiananmen Square. We were there only a few moments when two big Audi SUVs with darkened windows came roaring up. A driver hopped out of the second Audi and opened the doors for us to get in. We drove off down the side street and came to a heavily guarded checkpoint where five soldiers stood guard. The driver of the first Audi rolled down his window and spoke with the soldiers who seemed to be expecting us because they waved us right through. We passed through the checkpoint and entered the city through a gate and came to a small parking lot where several dozen cars were parked. I noticed their license plates were all military or government plates. We got out and I saw that our Audi also had military plates.

Mr. Zhang and a second man exited the first of the two Audis. Mr. Zhang greeted Victoria and me and introduced his companion as his "friend, Mr. Chen." He frowned when he realized my father was not with us.

"Your father? Where is he?"

"Oh, he had to go back to New York," I said. "He said it was urgent. Did his office not tell you?"

"No," Mr. Zhang said. "Nobody told me." I could tell that he was irritated. He turned to Victoria and demanded answers for why he hadn't been informed.

"I brought my friend Bowen instead though," I said, not wanting Mr. Zhang to think that my father's place on the tour had been wasted. Mr. Zhang abruptly stopped speaking. His attention shifted to me. He looked at Bowen and then turned back to me. He grunted his acknowledgment of Bowen's presence and then walked back toward the SUV, dialing a number on his phone. Victoria, Bowen, and I stood in silence with Mr. Chen while Mr. Zhang finished his phone call. After a few minutes he hung up and walked back to us.

"Okay, no matter," he said. He gestured to Mr. Chen. "Chen Jie will take you for tour. I have to go to a meeting. I will see you after." With that, he got back on his cell phone and turned back to his SUV where the driver was waiting with the door open. His actions confused me because I had thought he was meant to go on the tour with us. But Mr. Chen motioned for us to go with him, and we followed him into the second SUV. The gates opened, and we drove inside and crossed a wide moat. Victoria turned to me and explained we were now in the Inner Court where the emperors lived with their extended family. Mr. Chen was met by a man who worked in the Forbidden City and would be our guide. The guide led us down a long, narrow alley enclosed on each side by stuccoed walls twenty feet high. The only sounds came from our footsteps as we walked single file down the alley, which felt more like a crevasse. The contrast between where we were now and where we had just been was disorienting. Occasionally we passed huge wooden gates that were locked by thick chains and padlocks.

We must have gone four or five city blocks before we stopped in front of one of the gates. The guide pulled out a large ring of keys and flipped through it, selected one, and opened the lock. He pushed one side of the gate open and asked us to step across a raised wooden transom into an expansive walled courtyard. Set in the middle of the courtyard was a decaying temple nestled in scraggly grass. Broken branches lay around two old and desiccated trees. I could see that the temple had once been painted bright colors of red, gold, yellow, and blue, which were now faded and dulled. Paint had chipped off in large patches and some of the wood appeared charred as if there had been a fire. Roof tiles and pieces of an elaborate cornice lay on the ground.

The guide led us to the door of the temple. The door wasn't locked, but it was jammed shut and he struggled to open it. He spoke in Chinese, and Victoria translated for me. "This is a very special tour. No one has been in here for many years." He beat his body against the door several times and freed it open. He motioned for us to step inside. It was dark. The only light came from the doorway, and it was hard to see anything farther than five feet into the building. A statue of Buddha greeted us at the entrance. The Buddha along with everything else was covered in dust, almost as if this building had been sitting at the foot of a volcano and ash had settled on top of everything. I glanced at Bowen and saw the fascination on his face—it was the look of someone seeing something that they never knew even existed. I turned to Mr. Chen and asked him when was the last time someone had been in this temple. "Probably not since 1924. When the last emperor was expelled." He said that most of the Forbidden City was like this. "Only one-third is open for public. More than one hundred twenty acres is closed and is like this."

It was hard to see much of anything beyond five or six feet from the door opening. Furniture was stacked on the sides so there was no room to move around except in the little rectangle of open space at the entrance. My eyes began to adjust to the dark and shapes gradually emerged from the darkness. We walked deeper into the building. A thin beam of light came through a small hole in the roof, and a colony of tiny dust particles, disturbed by our presence, seemed to celebrate. The air was thick and smelled faintly of incense. I felt as if I were breathing the dust of departed souls.

A hundred years ago the Forbidden City would have been filled with thousands of ministers, servants, courtiers, and concubines—people whose behavior and freedom were determined by where they fit into a stratified structure. Now, except for the spaces that were open to the public, it was deserted. Perhaps more than any country, China's history was scarred with hardship and violent change. I was reminded of Victoria's comparing the past to a wound that had not completely healed. Some things were so powerful they could not be remembered. It was as if sentimentality didn't have a place in their culture. They just got on with it.

Our guide led us out of the courtyard back to the alleyway. He paused to push the large padlock shut and then went around us to regain the lead.

I asked Victoria why we were allowed to be in this area that had been closed off to the public for so long. "Maybe Mr. Zhang asked an official to do him a favor," she said.

"He can do that?"

"Sure."

"But why would the official agree to it?"

"That's how it works in China," Victoria said. "Maybe before Mr. Zhang did something to help the official."

"Like what?"

"I don't know, it could be anything. Maybe Mr. Zhang helped him get his job, or maybe he arranged for some money to be donated to the Forbidden City to repair damaged buildings. Something like that. Now, it is the official's turn to help Mr. Zhang."

We followed the guide down the alleyway and around a corner to another gate that appeared identical to the one we had just passed through—same size, same color, same chain, same lock. It opened into a courtyard house that had been the home of the Imperial Noble Consort, the Emperor's favorite concubine. The guide said we couldn't go in because the roof was falling down, but he led us around the building. In front of the building was one of the biggest trees I have ever seen. The trunk must have had a circumference of at least twenty feet and the tree's thick limbs canopied out above us, restrained only by the thick tendrils that stretched down to the ground like taut cables holding a hot air balloon in place. The guide pointed to the tree. "The same tree under which the first Buddha was buried," he said. Victoria gasped when she heard this and raised her eyebrows. "*Zhende ma* (Really)?" she asked. The guide nodded, and Victoria dropped to her knees and began collecting seeds. The guide followed her lead. I asked Victoria what she was doing. She explained to me that they were the seeds of a holy tree and if you planted these seeds and they grew, you would have good fortune. "This tree is one thousand years old. These are valuable seeds!" She said, "Chase, you can sell these for a lot of money."

Bowen looked at Victoria in surprise. "A lot of money?"

Victoria laughed. "Maybe. I'm joking," she said. "It is better to keep them though."

I followed their example and knelt down and pocketed a few seeds. I noticed that Bowen wasn't joining in. "You should take some seeds," I said. "Who knows? Might help in a tennis match someday."

He smiled wanly and looked down at his feet and waved both of his hands in protest. "No, no," he said. "These are not for me. For you. I am only the guest."

Our guide tucked his handful of seeds in his pocket, stood up, and spoke to Mr. Chen and then to Victoria. We followed him out of the courtyard. He went to lock the door to the temple, but the rusty lock jammed and the key became stuck. The guide frowned and applied all his strength to the key but still it would not turn. He shrugged and said that this happened sometimes and that someone would fix the lock later. He led us down another long high-walled alley. The walls were so high and buildings relatively low that I don't know how anyone could find their way around this maze. Everything looked the same, and there were no numbers or signs to tell you where you were.

At some point we turned down a side alley and walked a hundred yards or so before the guide stopped in front of a door and fit a key into the lock. He opened the door and stepped aside with his arm extended and nodded for us to step in front of him. A small, seemingly perfectly restored courtyard house sat in the middle of a large square of land. The lawns had been meticulously groomed.

Our guide said something to Mr. Chen, and Victoria translated for me. "This is where our Premier has spent many hours with the President of America when he came to Beijing." We walked inside the courtyard house. The first room was sparsely furnished with simple Chinese furniture. Along the wall, glass cases displayed Chinese ceramics. Bowen and Victoria walked around the room admiring the pieces on display. The guide stood in the middle of the room with his hands folded in front of him. He led us into an adjoining room that must have been the dining room. This room was sparsely furnished, too, with only a round dining table with eight chairs. Mr. Chen became quite excited when he saw the dining table and chairs. "It is rare to find a matching table and set of chairs dating back to the Ming Dynasty. Much of the furniture was destroyed in the Cultural Revolution. Very few sets exist."

"How did this manage to survive? I thought most of the furniture in the Forbidden City was burned?" I asked Mr. Chen. He turned to the guide and asked him my question. He said he did not know, but I wondered if he did and did not want to say.

Mr. Chen led us to one more room, which was lined with glass cases filled with bowls and vases. He led us around the room pointing out the pieces from various periods. As our guide explained, each emperor had his own kiln and on his death, he had the kiln destroyed. Each emperor emphasized different techniques and styles. One cared that the china be "the color of the sky after rain," another wanted the china to be a pale cream and so thin that light could pass through it, another prided himself on the faux finishes his craftsmen could master. Our guide showed us one bowl that looked as if it were brass, another that looked as if it were enamel, and a third that looked as if it were gold.

Mr. Chen and the guide began to get into an in-depth conversation about the history behind the golden bowl and the emperor who had commissioned it. I wandered about the room on my own, checking out the various display cases. I came across a bowl with an interior decorated with a classical painting of an old man with long white hair and fierce eyebrows, wearing long, flowing robes. He was sitting on the ground, by a small fire, next to the stump of a tree. I could tell from his appearance and the tone of the painting that the man was most likely an ancient sage or philosopher. For some reason his face looked oddly familiar to me. I looked closer before I suddenly realized and almost burst out laughing. The philosopher bore an uncanny resemblance to our teammate Little Mao. I knew that Bowen would find this hilarious, and I turned to call him over.

It was then that I noticed that Bowen wasn't with us anymore. The only people in the room were Mr. Chen, Victoria, our guide, and myself. I slipped back into the room we had just left to see if he was lagging behind. He wasn't there and so I went through the front door to the courtyard outside. Just as I stepped outside, I saw the courtyard's door crack open. The doorway was dark and hidden in the shadow of the overhang but I was able to make out a thin, shaggy-haired silhouette slipping past into the courtyard.

Instantly I recognized the figure as Bowen. He had his back turned to me and did not see me watch him as he pressed the door shut against the wall. I wondered why he had left and where he had gone. I was struck with the urge to hide so that he would not know that I had seen him. He turned and stepped out from the shadows and into the light and saw me before I could make a decision either way. For a fraction of a second I saw panic in his eyes—but it vanished and made me doubt what I had seen. He smiled and waved at me. "*Wo zhaobudao weishengjian* (I can't find the bathroom)."

The guide had pointed to the bathroom, which was inside to the right of the door. "It's inside," I said and lifted my chin in the direction of the house. Why had he panicked? Why was he lying to me about where he had been? He smiled and walked toward me with his customary bounce of confidence in his step. As he got closer I saw that his tennis shoes were dirty and his tracksuit pants dusty and marked with dirt at the knees, and I realized that he must have gone back to the ancient tree to collect seeds for himself. He walked past me and into the house.

We rejoined the others in the last room of the house. Mr. Chen and the guide were still going on about the bowls, but Victoria had realized that we were missing and was walking through the doorway to look for us as we came into the room. "We were looking for the bathroom," I mumbled to Victoria and walked past her to Mr. Chen and the guide.

As our guide led us out of the house, he turned and said that many important state meetings take place in this house. We followed the guide and Mr. Chen down a long passageway to a side gate where the drivers were waiting with the cars. Mr. Zhang was on his cell phone by the SUVs. As we neared the cars, he paused his conversation. "The Forbidden City goes on and on," Mr. Zhang said to me. "I will now take you to a place for you to tell your father about."

As we left the Forbidden City behind, I could not get one thought out of my head. Why had Bowen lied to me?

二十四

We traveled straight north from the center of Beijing. After over an hour we arrived at a large area that had recently been cleared of all buildings. It was at least the size of Tiananmen Square. It felt like a graveyard without headstones. Mr. Zhang got out and pointed to the northern part of the land. "The Olympic Stadium will be there." He turned and looked behind him. "This is mine. I am going to build five apartment buildings with courtyard houses on top. There is already a waiting list for them. They will be in the shape of a dragon. So when you are at the Olympics and look at my buildings you will see a dragon."

No one knew what to say. Finally I asked, "How long will it take to build?"

Mr. Zhang held his fingers in the shape of a peace sign.

"Eleven years?"

"Two," he said. "At the top of the dragon building I will have a luxury hotel." His cell phone rang, he answered. He asked the listener to wait and lowered his cell phone and held it open against his pant leg. "You will now go and look at my houses." He raised his cell phone to his ear and returned to his call.

Mr. Chen turned and offered me a fat folder of brochures.

I took a handful and then held out the folder for Victoria and Bowen to take some. Mr. Chen shook his head. "No, those are for you," he said.

I shuffled through the brochures. There was a combination of apartments in high-rises and detached houses in suburban-like settings. The high-rises had names like *La Forêt* or *Upper East Side* or *Park Avenue*; the suburban "villas" had names like *Yosemite, Ascot, Beijing Riviera*, and *Grand Hills*.

We were back in the car heading to the eastern part of the city to view some of Mr. Zhang's "showcase" developments. The first one we came to was called Grand Hills. Bizarrely the landscapers had shaped mounds of earth to create a rolling hill effect around a large drainage ditch that was masquerading as a lake. The water level was far too low. It needed at least another three feet of water to cover the brown sludge of its slopes. The brochure noted that the interiors ranged from "tasteful to rather opulent." The driver brought us to Number 10 Grand Hills. It was a two-story house with a double-height portico with spindly columns. The house clearly had never been touched by an architect with any knowledge. Its symmetrical facade was marred by the placement of a disproportionately large garage that had been attached to the front of the house in the area generally reserved for the front lawn.

As soon as we pulled up, a real estate agent opened the door. She was young and wore spike heels and held out a silver tray of champagne flutes. I was struck how this agent carried on in the face of this incongruous appearance of two teenage boys and a twenty-something Chinese woman wearing jeans and Converse sneakers. The tour of the houses went from silly to absurd. We were asked to admire the white marble floors and a bathtub with a cascading water feature.

After Grand Hills we went to Beijing Riviera a few miles away. I have no idea how they landed on the name Beijing Riviera as it certainly wasn't on the coast. There was no water anywhere except for a small fountain with a statue of three cherubs that sat somewhat incongruously behind the entry gate. Beijing Riviera was just another subdivision of houses that all pretty much looked the same. There was nothing French about them. They were cheaply made. The walls were so thin we could hear everything from any room. All were painted white, and as far as I could tell, all the furnishings were white, too. Despite the suburban setting, no one seemed to have moved in. There were no cars or children on bikes or soccer balls left on lawns. It looked like a hastily constructed movie set. The estate agent kept emphasizing how wonderful these houses were for entertaining. After the tour of three suburban developments we went to one high-rise, La Forêt. There all of the furnishings were Lucite, even the bed. The dining room of the apartment had what appeared to be a structural support column placed off center, making it impossible to accommodate a traditional dining room table.

Mr. Zhang's firm had obviously appropriated all the American and French names they thought evoked a level of quality and exclusivity, and they did so without much knowledge or discrimination. The idea that anyone would buy a landlocked house in a subdivision called Beijing Riviera or think that a high-rise called La Forêt with Lucite furniture was worth going to see seemed so naive it was almost charming.

The real estate agent led us into a kitchen stocked with brand-new appliances. Victoria asked her a question about the size of the bedrooms and the agent beckoned for Victoria to follow so that she could show them to her. Bowen and I were left alone in the kitchen. When the real estate agent was safely out of earshot, I joked with Bowen about the names of the developments. But he failed to see the irony of the names. I tried to explain it to him, but he didn't seem to care. He ran a hand over the plastered walls and shook his head. The lack of craftsmanship seemed to agitate him.

"No good," he said. "My father should be working here. He is known for work that is very high quality. His work in Tianjin is a waste. They make him use plaster that has very bad quality. Very bad . . ." he struggled to find a word. "I don't know how to say but it's like *kongqi wuran* (air pollution). He has to wear mask."

"Fumes?"

"Fumes. Yes, maybe fumes. The fumes are for five days or more. They make him sick. And his salary is very small. Very, very small. To pay for one ticket to Mei Guo he would have to work for more than one year. Maybe two years. Here they get paid more than two times more." He pointed to the walls. "And their work is no good."

"Why doesn't he find a job in Beijing?"

"It is not so easy. He's from Tianjin, not from Beijing. He has no Beijing *hukou* (work permit), so to find work here is not so easy. The risk is too big. If he goes to Beijing, and there's no work, and so he wants to come home but maybe someone takes his job in Tianjin. In Tianjin no care about quality. Anybody will do."

"I could ask Mr. Zhang about it for him."

Bowen raised his hand. "No. Maybe that would be not so good. In China if you ask favor, you must be able to give something back. My family has nothing. Maybe he thinks we are try to cheat him."

"You sure?" I asked. "It seems like such a simple thing . . ."

Bowen pulsed the palm of his hand down like a traffic cop signaling cars to slow down.

Victoria couldn't stop talking about all of the houses. She thought each development more beautiful than the last. She kept saying how they would be such lovely places for children to grow up in. She said it was very difficult to find a good place for children in Beijing. Here they had space to run around and play games outside, and it was safe, too. The real estate agent happily agreed with Victoria and said that they had already pre-sold a lot of units to young families. The agent said that these houses were perfect for young professional couples who wanted an elegant home that was ideal for entertaining guests. I noticed that this was probably the fifth time I had heard the agent talk about hosting parties. When the agent was out of earshot, I asked Victoria why she kept emphasizing entertaining. "Most people who live in Beijing, their apartments are so small that they are embarrassed to have people over. Most people don't entertain at home. They always go out to restaurants with friends. To have a home like this and to be able to invite guests over is rare. A real symbol."

"Really?"

"Yes! Because at home there is no room to do it. Ask your father if he has ever been a guest at someone's home." Victoria pointed to the picture of Number 10 Grand Hills. She said she would now dream of living in one of them. She doubted they would ever be able to afford one, but she said she still liked to dream. I said to her that if she and her husband combined their salaries and saved they might be able to afford one in the future. Victoria shook her head. She explained that they both sent money—half of what they made—back home to their parents. "They still work, but they do not make enough money. They rely on us now. It is our responsibility."

二十五

Victoria spent the car ride home looking through the brochures, pointing out things that she liked to us. From her purse she took out a pair of small scissors and a glue stick and a book that she said was her journal, and then she cut out things from the brochures and glued them into her journal. She did this for a while, cutting out pictures of refrigerators and bathtubs and televisions. I watched from the backseat, pretending to be asleep. As she went through the journal, I saw that the pages of the book were filled with rooms that Victoria had designed from clippings taken from home furnishing catalogues. There were several pages of kitchens and several pages of bedrooms and a few dedicated to living and dining rooms. Then she flipped to the back of the book and I saw that she had ten or fifteen pages dedicated to bedrooms for children. There was a lot of pink in those pages and most of the rooms looked as though they had been designed for a girl.

When I returned to the Zhangs' apartment, I showed one of the maids my handful of seeds and asked for a plastic cup. She thought I wanted her to cook them. I shook my head and dropped to the ground as if I were planting the seeds in imaginary soil.

She instinctively dropped down to her knees and improved on my gestures. She nodded, straightened up, and disappeared. She returned with a paper cup. "*Keyi yong zhege beizi* (You can plant them in this cup)."

"Thank you," I said. I put the seeds in the cup and placed it on my windowsill. I wondered what Bowen did with the ones he took.

The next day my father called from New York. I told him about the tour he had missed. I asked him how Mr. Zhang had gotten the rights to own the land next to the Olympic site. "I'm not really sure," he said. "Either he bought the land a long time ago when no one knew the Olympics were coming to China, and he was unusually lucky—theoretically possible, but very unlikely—or someone told him where the stadiums were going to be built before it was announced. That's more likely. Everything in China works off deep personal relationships of trust. He probably did someone a favor years ago and they repaid him."

"That seems so capitalist," I said. "Isn't that a contradiction?"

"Yes, of course in theory, but not in practice. Mr. Zhang is not, however, a member of the Communist Party, but he could be. Only about seventy-five million Chinese are members of the Party. The Communist Party is only for the elite who are chosen by teachers and professors at an early age. They are meant to be the most outstanding members of society. Until recently, essentially all ambitious young people would try and join the Party. But it's changing. Mr. Zhang is a member of one of the eight lesser parties, probably the party for businessmen. I think it is called something like China National Democratic Construction Association."

"Why would he join that?"

"The lesser parties are small. Most have only about a hundred thousand members, so you have a chance of having an important position. The government usually saves a position for non–Communist Party members in governments. For example, in a city government they usually have one mayor and seven vice-mayors. Usually one of the vice-mayors is a non–Communist Party member. So if you haven't been invited to join the Communist Party, or even if you have, joining another party could provide a path to a position of some influence."

"Oh, by the way, I brought Bowen with us to the Forbidden City. He had never been before. Isn't that crazy?"

"What?"

"I said that Bowen had never been to the Forbidden City before."

"You brought him on the tour?" My father's voice was terse. It was more of a statement than a question.

"Well, you couldn't go," I said. "And, you know . . . he had never been before."

"Did you ask Mr. Zhang if that was okay?"

"I didn't think it would be a big deal. I mean you couldn't go, and Bowen had never been so I thought it would be nice for him to go."

"What did Mr. Zhang say when you came with Bowen?"

"He didn't really say anything," I said. "I think he was more surprised that you weren't with us."

"What do you mean?"

"It seemed like he really wanted you to go on the tour. And then when he found out that you weren't there he went back to the car and called someone. So he didn't really say anything about Bowen."

"But he already knew that I wasn't going to be there," my father said.

"I don't think he did."

"Goddamn it," my father said. "Victoria didn't tell him? I reminded her three times. And then she brought along your tennis friend? What the hell is she thinking?"

"It wasn't her fault. She didn't know about Bowen," I said quietly. "That was me. I told the driver to pick him up on the way."

There was a long pause. "Chase," he said. "Can you do me a favor and use your brain just once in a while? You're not a kid anymore. Don't you see how that is just totally unacceptable? You think Mr. Zhang has time to take a morning off work to give your tennis team a tour of the Forbidden City?"

"It wasn't my tennis team," I said with an edge of resentment. "It was Bowen. He's been the nicest to me of all the boys."

"Christ," my father said. "I'm going to have to call him tomorrow. You do now realize he thinks I totally blew this off and sent my son and his tennis team instead? I'm going to have to get off. I've got a GE board call in five minutes."

I had trouble sleeping that night. I couldn't stop thinking about the conversation I had with my father. I didn't understand why what I had done was so bad. Why couldn't I bring a friend with me? Why did I always have to be alone? The worst part was that I had no one to talk to about it. I missed being at home. I missed Tom, and I hated the feeling of being powerless to change my situation. I was on the other side of the world. And besides, I wasn't even able to leave the apartment without my hosts' permission.

二十六

After three and a half months of Chinese lessons, I hit a wall. As I learned new characters, I forgot the ones I'd learned previously. I could still recognize them and read them, but if I needed to write something, I could only think of the pinyin, the phonetic spelling of the characters. It was as if my brain had become fully saturated. I brought this up with Teacher Lu, who said that as long as I could recognize the characters it was all right. There were so many that even she needed to look them up in a dictionary from time to time. Besides, she said, so much of writing nowadays was done on the computer where you only needed to know the pinyin, that writing was not as important as it used to be. But Chinese wasn't like learning French or Spanish, where you could guess what words meant because they were spelled similarly to words in English. With Chinese, if you hadn't learned a word you had no way of guessing what it meant other than by the context. Even if I understood 75 percent of a sentence, if I hadn't learned two or three key words in that sentence, I had no idea what the meaning of the sentence was.

My routine at the language institute remained the same every day. I would arrive shortly before nine and climb the rickety fire escape up to the fifth floor and wait for Teacher Lu to arrive. She had told me that she lived far away and that she had to get up at five o'clock to make it in by nine. The traffic had become so bad in Beijing that the government had started restricting the use of private cars in the city. Unfortunately it didn't seem to make a difference. The only thing that changed about the school was the people who came to take lessons. It had been some time since I had seen Josh at the school but over the course of the fall, the number of Western businessmen showing up for lessons at the Taiwanese Language Institute had increased. And like Josh, they would show up every day for two to three weeks and then disappear. Whether they had picked up enough Chinese for their purposes, or whether they had given up after realizing that no matter how many mornings they showed up at the institute, they would never be good enough at the language—I don't know. I suspect that after two weeks of feeling as if each lesson was a repeat of the prior day's because nothing had been retained, they gave up.

There were a few regular attendees at the school that fall. The one I got to know the best was Tao, the guy who had dropped out of Texas A&M to come to Beijing. We both took classes in the mornings, so I saw quite a lot of him, and we became pretty good friends. Tao was often at the school even when he didn't have classes. He would sit in the student lounge and work through textbooks on his own and try to read Chinese newspapers and would chat in Chinese to whoever came into the lounge. He was much older, so we didn't hang out outside of the school, but I would always chat with him whenever we ran into each other.

He had a girlfriend he mentioned a lot who was still enrolled at Texas A&M who thought he was crazy for dropping out to come to China.

The city's smog had a way of wearing you down. During the winter months, it often built up over the course of seven or even ten days before a wind came and carried it away. Everything was covered in a layer of soot and the bleak, gray sky felt like it stretched on forever. The air was grimy and it made your skin feel all dirty when you went outside. The smog would block out the sun completely, and sometimes it would last for so long that I would forget when the last time I had seen the sun was. It affected your sense of time. Without the sun, there was no changing of light, no passage of shadows on the ground. Time seemed suspended in the absence of shadows to mark and measure the earth's rotation and the passing of the day.

The novelty of learning Chinese had worn off and the lessons became a grind. Most days, my brain was dead by the third hour of one-on-one instruction. I began to slack off. I started coming to class without having done my homework, and I would ask to take frequent breaks. Other days I would pretend to have slept through my alarm so that we were late in leaving the house. We'd get caught in the bad rush hour traffic, and I'd usually miss the first hour of class. This continued for a few weeks. I knew it was juvenile, but I didn't really care.

After an unrewarding morning one day, Teacher Lu decided to give me a thirty-minute break in the hope that I would be focused for the last part of class. When I heard that I had thirty minutes off, I went straight to the student lounge and found a spot on the sofa and flipped through a magazine that was lying on the table. A few minutes later, Tao came into the room. I put the magazine down and waved to him and asked him how he was doing. He didn't sit down but just stood there looking at me. He seemed pretty upset about something.

"What are you doing?" he asked.

"Oh, my teacher just gave me a quick break."

"Dude, I just talked to Ai Lu. She told me she had to give you a break because she didn't know what else to do with you. She said you're screwing around in all your lessons and wasting her time. Dude, if you don't want your lessons then give them to me. I'll take them. I'm scrounging so I can afford to stay here another month. Get it together, man."

His words stung because I knew he was right. I put my book away and got up and walked back to my classroom. I knocked on the door and apologized to Teacher Lu and asked if we could begin again. She nodded and said that she wanted to tell me a folktale. She told me a story about a man and his three sons. The man, a great fisherman, was known as the "Fisher of the World." His sons, however, were poor fishermen, and their father was frustrated. One day he met a philosopher who asked him three questions:

> "When did your sons start to learn fishing?"
>
> The father replied, "As early as in their childhood. They have grown up in my fishing boat."
>
> The philosopher asked a second question: "Who taught your sons fishing?"
>
> The father answered, "I did. I taught them every experience and every skill, even the top secret of the fishing profession."
>
> The philosopher asked his third and final question: "Where did they practice your teaching?"

And the father replied that his sons had learned everything in his boat, that he had watched over every detail to make sure that they would not do anything wrong.

The philosopher had his answer. "The tragedy of your sons is that you have arranged everything in your sons' lives. What your sons got in their life are all your experience, but what they lacked in life are the lessons of fishing from difficulty and failure. They never left you to try on their own. You taught them everything, but all your valuable experiences are only indirect experience to them."

I wasn't really sure what the relevance of Teacher Lu's folktale was, but I used it as an opportunity to ask her if we could veer off from following the table of contents of my Chinese lesson book, which was much more geared for businessmen. I didn't need to know words for conducting negotiations or ordering at restaurants. I really needed to focus on words and phrases that would help me with the boys at tennis—words and phrases I could use each afternoon because without some reinforcement, there was almost no hope of my remembering anything from one day to the next. My progress was jump-started with this new tactic, and from that point on Teacher Lu would tell me a fable whenever I seemed to be lagging. Over the course of my time with Teacher Lu I heard stories about eagles and donkeys and oxen and goats and fishermen and farmers. I never knew whether these stories were Teacher Lu's attempt to impart advice and wisdom to me or whether they were a creative strategy to tailor the teaching material to a fourteen-year-old.

Sometimes Teacher Lu was late, but I never complained or asked for a cut in fees as Victoria urged. I was more than happy to have five or ten minutes subtracted from a three-hour, mind-punishing marathon of Chinese. When I would arrive, I would go to my classroom and sit by the window and look out at the street. People—walking or riding bikes or walking bikes laden with cargo—moved with a sense of purpose. There was no doubt in my mind that they all had a specific destination.

One morning I heard what sounded like an old dump truck without any suspension system banging slowly down the street, and then I saw a rusted old truck that bumped up onto the sidewalk and parked. Piled high on the flatbed were five thick tree trunks. They were about two and a half feet in diameter and stretched the length of the bed of the truck. At first I couldn't tell why this truck was stopping. Almost before it pulled up, two men and one woman jumped out of the cab of the truck and started unfastening the chains that held the trunks down. They were dressed in dark, worn clothes, and I guessed they were peasants from the countryside. They pulled two sturdily built sawhorses from the truck and hoisted one of the trunks across the sawhorses. Cars were slipping around them, and horns were going off, and drivers were shaking their fists at them, but they were oblivious to it all.

When class was over, I looked out the window and saw that this truck and the three people were still there. Their work had progressed. They were removing the bark on one of the trunks with what looked like an antique saw. The two men moved it back and forth in an even and measured rhythm almost as if they were two mechanical figures.

The next morning when I arrived they were still there. The woman and one of the men were working on the fourth trunk. The other man was asleep in the cab of the truck. I assumed they had worked all night and had taken turns sleeping. After my lesson, I looked out of the window again. The sleeping man had now taken the woman's position. She was squatting down and seemed to be cooking something over a portable gas stove.

On the third day they had started sawing the trunks into planks. On the way to tennis practice I described this scene to Victoria and asked her what she thought these three people were doing with the newly sawn timber.

"They are most likely for one of the courtyard houses. The planks are made in the traditional way."

I could not understand why they were sawn on the street— why they weren't sawn before they were brought into the city.

Victoria didn't know either. "Perhaps they wanted to make certain the measurements were exact, perhaps it had to do with bad luck," she said. "Chinese can be extremely superstitious. After your lesson tomorrow, we can go ask them."

Tom would not have needed to ask. Like all those times in the car rides when he entertained me with stories and intrigues of all the people in the cars, he would have enjoyed coming up with multiple stories of what these workers were doing, and each story would be more fantastic than the next.

But the next morning the workers were gone. Tom would have had a story for that, too.

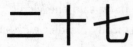

二十七

At the beginning of practice the following week, Madame Jiang announced that the team would begin practicing for the National Championships. They would be held in two weeks in Tianjin in the last week of November. She said that she had not decided yet which players would go to Tianjin to represent Beijing and that everyone should practice hard if they wanted to go. Even though my Chinese had gotten quite a bit better, I still had a hard time understanding her thick Beijing accent from time to time. Bowen listened to her intently and then quickly, under his breath, translated for me. When he translated Madame Jiang's words, that she wasn't sure whom she would take, Bowen added, "No way, she has to take everybody."

Madame Jiang's threats, which were meant to unsettle everyone into not being complacent and working as hard as possible, served to undercut her authority. If she could have denied Bowen a spot, she would have, but the security of her position would have been threatened. As much as she disliked Bowen, she wasn't going to lose her job over him.

Bowen practiced unusually hard that week. He did everything Madame Jiang said and spoke in deferential tones. He asked that if he was selected for the team, could he go by his home to see a doctor. He wanted to get something for his shoulder. It had been hurting for some time. It would help him play better for the National Championships. Madame Jiang said she would consider his request. Bowen uncharacteristically pleaded with her to let him go. She told him to go to the gym to do exercises to help his shoulder. She didn't even ask him what his problem was or try to examine his shoulder. I wanted to tell Bowen that if he had a shoulder injury, he should be careful about doing exercises. Exercises could make his shoulder worse.

It was then that I understood the depth of her hatred. It went back so many years that she could not see through it to have any sympathy for this young boy who was standing in front of her begging. It had pushed her sense of compassion to some undiscoverable corner of her heart.

The following week passed quickly. All of the boys were energetic and positive. Even Little Mao played as if he were expecting something good to happen. Bowen worked hard and went to the gym every day after practice to do shoulder exercises. I warned him there was nothing to be gained by "playing through injury." I had cautioned him about worsening his shoulder through exercise, but he smiled and exuded the same confidence in his ability to look after his body that he did in his game. As always, Bowen worked harder than the other boys. If one of them raised his work ethic a notch, Bowen raised his, too. In all of my practices with Bowen, I don't think he ever hit a ball on the second bounce. If a shot hit the net cord, he sprinted to touch it before it bounced a second time. No matter how good the put-away shot, he always tried to put his racket on the ball. Most of the time he succeeded.

It was during that week that Bowen came over to me one day

before practice as I was getting my rackets out of my bag and said, "I thought of a name for you."

"Okay?"

"Yu," he said.

"Yu?"

"Yes. Yu, like Yu the Great."

"Who's that?"

"He lived more than four hundred—" Bowen paused and frowned. "No, four thousand years ago. He is a great man. He is never giving up."

"Okay. I'll think about it."

"There is nothing to think about. It is a good name for you," Bowen said, smiling. "Now you have to give me a name."

"Okay," I said. "Let me think."

Madame Jiang left the courts fifteen minutes before practice ended. She told us to practice our serves for the rest of the practice. Bowen and I shared a basket. As we returned to the basket for more balls, he asked me questions. Ever since I had mentioned that one of my friends had gotten a sponsorship contract with Lacoste after getting to the semifinals of the Orange Bowl, Bowen was always asking me about the tournament. I think he saw it as his way to get out of the Chinese system, to get funding and sponsorships, a pathway to make it to the pros. He asked me how I did when I played it the year before. I told him I won three rounds of qualifying, but to be in the main draw you had to win four rounds.

"Only qualifying?" he asked me.

"It's a really tough tournament," I said.

"But you are very good."

"Not good enough."

He thought about this and didn't say anything for a while. "So you are not able to get in the real draw."

"No, I missed it by one match. The best kids in the world play the Orange Bowl. The main draw is only one hundred twenty-eight, so it's really tough to get in the main draw."

As I was packing my bag after practice, I said to Bowen, "I brought you a T-shirt." I reached into my tennis bag and tossed Bowen a long-sleeved white shirt that had the logo of the Orange Bowl on the front. He caught the T-shirt and studied it.

"I can't take your shirt," he said, "you earned this. It's yours."

"No, don't worry, they were giving them out free, everyone got one. I have one from last year. Really, here." I handed it back to him. "Take it, I have lots of shirts like this."

"*Xie xie, Yu* (Thank you, Yu)." Bowen bowed his head as if I had given him something precious.

"Hey, how's your shoulder?"

Bowen offered no answer. I took his silence to mean that it was still injured. We picked up our bags and slung them over our shoulders and walked down the avenue of trees to the dormitories. I walked with him to the end of the avenue where he turned right to walk back to his room. I turned back and found Driver Wu and Victoria waiting with the car.

That evening after dinner I Googled "Yu the Great." I found a short biography of him on the internet:

During China's Great Flood, Yu's father, Gun, was assigned by the King to tame the raging waters. Gun built earthen dikes all over the land in the hope of containing the waters. But the earthen dikes collapsed everywhere and the project failed miserably. Gun was executed. The king then recruited Yu to succeed where his father had failed. Instead of building more dikes, Yu began to dredge new river channels, to serve both as outlets for the torrential waters, and as irrigation conduits to distant farmlands. Yu spent a backbreaking fourteen years at this task, with the help of some twenty thousand workers.

"Passing his own door three times" is a tale of Yu's dedication. It is said that when Yu was given the task of fighting the flood, he had been married only five days. He then said goodbye to his wife, saying that he did not know when he would return. His wife then asked him what name to give if a son were born. Yu replied, Qi, a character meaning "five days" in ancient Chinese. Then in his thirteen years of fighting the flood, Yu passed by his own family doorstep three times. The first time he passed by, he heard his wife's cries of pain as she bore their first child. The second time he passed by, his wife was holding their child's hand as he learned his first steps. The third time he passed by, his son greeted him and implored him to come in for rest. Each time, Yu refused to go in the door, saying that the flood was rendering countless people homeless, he could not rest in his own.

I could see why Bowen admired Yu the Great. Like Yu, Bowen knew what he had to do to succeed, and he refused to give up no matter how antagonizing or cruel Madame Jiang was. But I wondered why he picked that name for me. It seemed a name better fit for him. He was the one who had saved me during the trial in the beginning of the year, and he was also the one who had saved me from my loneliness. I didn't know it then, but the moment when Bowen would need my help was fast approaching.

二十八

The following week Madame Jiang insisted that we play practice matches. Five days of grueling matches to determine the
lineup even though we all knew what the order would be. I think
we all felt it was Madame Jiang's desire to make Bowen prove
himself yet again. This kind of match play was not in the best
interest of the team. Most coaches who knew anything would
have their players, in preparation for a tournament, drill, work on
technique, practice different patterns, work on their serves and
return of serves. Playing a week's worth of matches before the
tournament would almost ensure that the Beijing team would
not perform at their best. Because there was an odd number of
boys, I was slotted in to play whoever wasn't paired against a
teammate.

Bowen won all of his matches, but not as easily as usual. He
was serving with only 50 percent of his usual pace. Now I began
to see things differently. Bowen served at half speed not because
he was torturing Madame Jiang but because his shoulder was
hurting. The other boys assumed Bowen was doing it to irritate
Madame Jiang, and they were not happy about it because they
knew that when she got mad at Bowen, she punished them all.

At the end of the week, I spoke to him as he sat next to me on the bench.

"I've got some Advil. It could help your shoulder." I held up the bottle of Advil I always carried in my tennis bag. Bowen rested his elbows on his knees and looked at the ground. He shook his head. Without bothering to look at me, he added, "No thanks."

"You should see a doctor."

"If I can just get home . . . there is a medicine man near my house. He will give me something to fix this."

"Why not see a doctor here in Beijing?"

Bowen shook his head. "Doctors in Beijing too expensive. Madame Jiang will not pay for medicine."

"Really? That's ridiculous."

"She told me to go to the gym. She said that if I was doing the weight training properly it would get better. I did what she said. I went to the gym early in the morning and after dinner and tried to do more weight training so it did not hurt anymore. But yesterday I have to stop because when I wake up, my shoulder is . . . not good. Hurts very bad to move it, even just to move it a small amount."

"The weights are probably making it worse," I said. "You need to see a doctor. I can't believe she won't let you see one. You should rest and ice it. No more weight training."

"She thinks I'm serving this way just to show to her that my shoulder is not good."

We sat in silence for a bit.

"Are you excited for the championships?" I asked.

"I hope my shoulder is good so that I play well."

At that moment I was about to say that he needed some sort

of good luck charm and then I thought about those seeds we had taken from the Forbidden City. "You know those seeds? The lucky ones from that old tree in *Gugong* (the Forbidden City). Do you want mine?"

Bowen shook his head and gave a tired smile. "Thank you, but no. You keep them. Your friend, Victoria, she was wrong. You can't sell them for much money. Not enough to buy medicine."

"Sell them?" I asked, surprised. "Oh, I meant if you plant them then maybe they will bring you good luck for the championships."

"Maybe," Bowen said. "But maybe I am not the good luck person."

I pulled out the bottle of Advil from my bag and held it out to him.

He looked at it briefly and shook his head. "If Madame Jiang knows, she will be angry. Not just angry at me. Angry at you, too."

Bowen straightened his back and went to throw away something in the garbage can by the door. While his back was turned, I dropped my bottle of Advil into his tennis bag. I don't know if the Advil helped his shoulder, or if he even used it. He never acknowledged receiving it, but I never expected him to.

The National Championships in Tianjin were the following week, and the team would be gone for three to five days. I would have no one to practice with, so Victoria suggested we go to Tianjin, too. "You can try out your Chinese and see how you do. It will be good practice. We can take the train and stay with my aunt. It will be good for you to see what an average family is like and how they live. You have seen China from the top, now you should see China here." Victoria held her hand high and then dropped it to chest level. "I will show you around Tianjin, and if the team does well, we can go and watch them play."

Two days later, we took the afternoon train to Tianjin. We arrived at the packed train station at about 1:30 p.m. There must have been several hundred people queued in half a dozen ill-defined lines. Victoria sent me to buy our tickets as a way to test my Chinese. I stood at the back of the first line and waited. As I advanced in line, I heard a series of depressing announcements. The first said that all the trains before 3:45 p.m. were sold out. Then about three minutes later they said the 3:45 train was also sold out. Just as we approached the window to buy our tickets, the announcer added that all the sitting tickets for the 4 p.m. were sold out, but standing tickets were still available. I bought two standing tickets that together cost less than 40 RMB, the equivalent of about five U.S. dollars.

Two hours later it was time to board. We pushed and shoved our way onto the platform and then into the standing-only car. The car was poorly ventilated, but we managed to squeeze into a corner near a window. The train squeaked and groaned its way out of the station. Victoria took the new silver cell phone she had just bought out of her handbag and checked her text messages. A group of five men, wearing cheap, loosely buttoned blue cotton shirts and dirty cotton trousers tied at the waist, pushed their way back-to-back and stationed themselves next to us in our corner. Many of their teeth were missing, and those that weren't missing had turned grimy shades of brown and yellow. All five were smoking and occasionally spitting on the ground. As more and more people crammed into the train car, the men pressed us farther and farther into the corner with absolutely no regard for our space. By the time the train doors closed, I was firmly pressed between two of the men, their faces only inches from mine. They continued talking past me, blowing smoke in my face, laughing loudly and shouting at times to be heard over the noise of the train. The man on my left had a habit of spraying me with spittle every few minutes. Lukas had taught me not to complain about such things by calling me a princess anytime I objected to poor conditions. Victoria, on the other hand, had other ideas. After ten minutes of intense texting, she looked up from her phone and saw one of the men blowing cigarette smoke in my face. "Hey!" she shouted. "*Ni zai gan shenme? Ni de limao zai nar* (What the hell are you doing? Where are your manners)?" The two men grumbled and shifted in the carriage so that their backs were turned to me.

The city didn't have plush suburbs in the way that American cities did. Instead the thick metropolis gradually fell away and was replaced by sparse countryside. The land was flat and dry, and it reminded me of the China you would see when you watched films set during the Great Leap Forward.

In contrast to the denseness of the city, life in the countryside seemed as if it would be very isolated. We would pass a cinderblock farmhouse or two with a few chickens running around or a cow tied to a post. I would see people out in the fields. Sometimes a small child worked alongside an adult. I didn't see any tractors or modern farm equipment other than an occasional truck. The farmers worked their fields with the help of oxen. Most of the roads were dirt. Even when we were well outside of Beijing, the impenetrable smog still filled the sky. I wondered how crops survived with such an absence of natural sunlight. The whole landscape served as a reminder that for the majority of China, life was still a cruel and hard existence. For all the talk of modernization and progress, there were still hundreds of millions living on a dollar a day in a world that the West had long since left behind, far in the past.

For the first part of the journey I worked with Victoria on vocabulary words that would help me talk with Bowen when we had lunch together, but soon the strain of balancing body against body against the bumps and changes in acceleration exhausted me. Seeing that I was struggling, Victoria subtly pushed against the people in front of us and edged out enough room for the two of us to sit down on the floor with our backs against the car wall. She rubbed the top of my head. "Almost there," she said cheerfully. "Only one hour to go." I leaned my head back and closed my eyes.

An hour later, I was awakened by the stop-start jolting of the train as it stuttered into the station. As soon as the train stopped, everyone pushed their way to the exit. There was no order—none of the Western courtesies of letting old people or women with children go first. Some passengers were actively pushing people out of their way without apology.

We spewed out of the train station into a vast concrete square and dispersed in different directions. I imagined that from above we looked like the particles in the science experiments on osmosis and diffusion I had done in school. The air outside was humid and almost as hot and stale as the air in the packed train car. The boundaries of the square were framed by large low-rise buildings that replicated for miles in all directions. I did not know what I was expecting, but I had not realized how large Tianjin was. Victoria said it was over half the size of Beijing, its population over ten million. It was the fourth-largest city in China, southeast of Beijing along the Hai He River, and had a large port along the

Bohai Sea in the Pacific Ocean. She said its name meant "the place where the Emperor crossed the river."

At the train station we caught a taxi, and Victoria asked the driver to go through the area of the foreign concessions. Like Shanghai, Tianjin had foreign districts, or concessions, at the turn of the twentieth century and each small neighborhood area revealed the nationality of its former inhabitants by the design of its villas. Victoria asked me to name each concession as we passed through—"English," "French," "Russian." Victoria clapped with delight. "Chase, maybe you will become an architect." I wasn't certain I was correct, and I knew Victoria did not know either, but I had come to see how she liked to give the appearance of knowing where she was going, both physically and metaphorically. The only concession that I could identify with certainty was the English Concession—all the buildings, especially the row of terraced houses, looked like the Victorian houses I had seen in London when my father had taken Tom and me to Wimbledon that one year. They looked like those houses except that they all had a diluted, impure look about them, as if they had been designed by an architect with a faulty memory. We arrived in the eastern part of the city where massive apartment buildings stood at least twenty-five stories high, many of which were still under construction.

"My aunt lives in one of these," Victoria said proudly. The buildings were all identical—a platoon of off-white skyscrapers against the gray sky, a city within a city. Between the buildings were concrete paths lined with rather sickly-looking grass. There were a few shops located at the base of the buildings.

Victoria's aunt lived in Building Eleven. We arrived a few minutes before six just as she was returning home from work. Her name was Zhang Hui, but when she introduced herself to me, she told me her English name was Cinderella. She worked for a multinational company as a bookkeeper. As she fished her key from her bag, Cinderella explained that she owned two apartments in the building. She interrupted herself to unlock the building's door and usher us into the elevator. I noticed that the elevator's number panel was missing the number 4. This was because the Chinese word for 4 and the Chinese word for death are both pronounced with the same sound and tone. Their number 4 was equivalent to our number 13.

Once we were on our way up to floor five, which was really floor four, she continued telling us about her apartments. One was a three-bedroom apartment, the other just a one-bedroom. Cinderella's mother, husband, and son all lived with her in the bigger apartment, and she usually rented out the other one. It was just down the hall. The former tenants had just moved out, and I could stay there. She unlocked the door and showed me around. In addition to a small bedroom, the apartment had a living room, a tiny kitchen, and a bathroom. The apartment was simple with just the bare necessities—one table and sofa in the living room, an air-conditioning unit, one bed, one closet, a stove, and a refrigerator. The walls were white with nothing on them. No pictures, no carpets, no potted plants. In the bathroom was a washing machine, a toilet, a sink, and a showerhead that protruded from the wall. There were two buckets on the ground beneath the showerhead. There was no shower enclosure, just the showerhead. The water went onto the tile floor of the bathroom into a drain next to the washing machine.

Cinderella wanted me to meet her son. She said his English teacher had given him the English name Chris, but recently he had decided to change it to Dwyane after some basketball player.

"He loves to play basketball," she said with an eager smile. "Basketball his number one favorite sport. Every day he plays with his friends. He has many basketball shoes. So many! Is basketball your favorite sport?"

"I prefer tennis."

"Oh, tennis. Yes. Good, maybe you can play basketball, too."

We walked down the hall to her apartment. Chris or Dwyane, I wasn't sure what to call him, was in his room playing video games. He was tall—about six foot two—and was rather chubby. He spoke very little English. I asked him who his favorite basketball player was. "Allen Iverson," he said. His answer surprised me. I guess I had expected him to say Dwyane Wade or maybe Yao Ming.

Cinderella invited us to share her dinner—rice with vegetables and a little chicken. As we ate, she complained to Victoria that her husband's sister was after her to give their son, Cinderella's nephew, her small apartment. He was planning to get married, and his parents were worried he would not be able to get married if he didn't have an apartment. "It's difficult," she explained. "Many more men than women now. Very difficult for man to find wife." Cinderella added that she could not let her sister-in-law know the apartment had just lost its tenant. She looked at me and said, "In China families are pushy. They think whatever is yours is theirs, too."

After dinner, Dwyane invited me to go downstairs to play basketball. Across the street from the apartment complex was a community sports center. There was an outdoor volleyball court, an area for tai chi, and a concrete basketball court. When we got there, we each had to pay a 2-RMB entrance fee. It was the U.S. equivalent of a quarter. There were two four-on-four half-court games going on. Another twenty guys watched from the sidelines, waiting for their chance to play. I sensed that most were regulars. Dwayne went about recruiting a team and putting us down for a game.

The rules were simple: first to seven points, winning team stayed on to face the next challenger. Our team consisted of Dwyane, myself, and two other guys that Dwyane had recruited. The first was tall but overweight and was wearing a counterfeit L.A. Lakers jersey. Whoever had manufactured his jersey had taken a fair amount of creative license with it, not only changing the spelling of "Lakers" to "LeKars," but also determining that "MIKEJORDAN" (all one word) was a player on the L.A. Lakers. The second of Dwyane's two recruits was a thin, wiry man who was no more than five foot six. In the five minutes that we had been teammates I had seen them each finish two cigarettes. Needless to say, this wasn't exactly the Dream Team.

After we lost, we walked off the side of the court. Dwyane pulled out a pack of cigarettes and offered everyone a smoke. We debated waiting for another game, but more players had shown up, and Dwyane said that it could be forty minutes until we played again. Our two teammates both decided that they had had enough basketball for one day. After finishing his second cigarette, Dwyane said that we should leave, too.

As we walked back to the apartments, I got a text message from Random that the Beijing team had won its first two matches and just beaten the Nanjing team easily in the semifinals. They would be playing the Tianjin team in the finals of the tournament tomorrow afternoon.

I told Victoria the good news. She said she would give me a quick tour of the city tomorrow morning, and then we could head over to the sports complex after lunch. I remembered Bowen telling me that there was a very good traditional Chinese medicine clinic near his home. I doubted that Madame Jiang would have allowed Bowen to visit the clinic, but I figured that we could go pick something up for him. I was a bit skeptical about traditional Chinese medicine, but both Bowen and Victoria seemed to put a lot of faith in it. I asked Victoria if she knew of a good traditional Chinese medicine shop. She said the best one in Tianjin was in the old part of the city. "Famous all over China," she said. "Owned by the same family for over three hundred years." We agreed we would go the next morning.

二十九

The medicine shop was located just past the outskirts of the French Concession. We passed through what I sensed were the slums of the city—run-down buildings overrun with families, laundry hanging everywhere like flags of surrender, birds' nests of illegal electrical wires.

"This used to be an okay area to live," Victoria said. "But now everyone wants to live in the new part. So this is where a lot of the peasants who come in from the country or the laborers live. The shop is just around the corner."

The shop was a traditional stucco one-story building that had managed to stay intact amid the squalor that surrounded it. No one was inside. The shop was small and dark and quiet. The walls were lined with wooden drawers, all about the size of a book. They reached almost five feet high. Victoria pointed to the drawers.

"Count how many there are," she said. "And then count everything else. There is a special number."

I counted the drawers. There were seven of them. I looked around the shop for other objects. On top of the drawers sat two more shelves holding identical ginger jars on top, three on the top shelf, four on the bottom, seven in total. There was a counter that ran the length of the wall and in the middle of the counter was a small table with a stack of what appeared to be mixing bowls. I counted the bowls. Again there were seven.

"Seven," I said. "What is it about seven?"

"Seven is considered spiritual or ghostly. The seventh month of the Chinese calendar is also called the 'Ghost Month,' when the gates of hell are said to be open. Seven is often linked with fate or destiny."

"What is the luckiest number?" I asked her.

"Eight, of course. And the word for eight?" Victoria asked, reversing the questioning.

"Bā," I said.

"And the word for prosperous?"

"Fā?"

She nodded. "See, very close in sound." She pulled out a pen and a piece of paper from her satchel. "There is also a resemblance between the two digits '88,' and the *shuang xi* (double happiness) and," she said, "to show you how truly superstitious the Chinese are, the Olympics in 2008 are scheduled to open on 8/8/08 at 8:08:08 p.m." Victoria leaned over the counter and looked down a passageway.

"I don't think there is anyone here," I said.

"Don't worry, Doctor Song will be out soon."

I asked Victoria what was in all the jars.

"Different ingredients for medicine."

"What kind of ingredients?"

"There are many ingredients. In China we believe that everything is medicine. Tea, parts of animals, herbs, all can be medicine."

"But what's an example of those ingredients?"

"Maybe the roots from trees," she said. "Here, look." She moved behind the counter and pointed to jars arranged neatly on the shelves below it. "Things taken from animals. Sometimes they use parts of turtles, snakes, lizards, sharks, even bats." She pointed to a jar that had a complete iguana and some sorts of plants submerged in a liquid. "Sometimes the doctor makes a mixture and lets it . . . how do you say, become like wine?"

"Ferment."

"Maybe, yes. Ferment."

We heard a door shut and the shuffling sound of someone walking slowly in slippers on a stone floor. When Doctor Song, an elderly man with a heavy brow that almost closed his eyes, appeared, Victoria began speaking with animation. She tapped her shoulder and mimicked a service motion. She asked him for something for a bad shoulder. Doctor Song must have asked her who it was for. Victoria said it was for a friend who could not come. Doctor Song shook his head several times and said something I could not understand. Victoria tried again. "Okay, can you help him with his elbow?" she said, referring to me. She swung her arm out as if hitting a tennis ball.

"I don't want anything," I whispered to her in English. Victoria held her hand up as if to signal me to stop.

Doctor Song shuffled around the counter and put his hand on my elbow and then on the top of my head.

"He is feeling for the temperature to see if he needs to deal with cold or heat," Victoria explained. I looked at her impatiently. She nodded her head and raised her index finger and whispered, "After." Doctor Song nodded and grunted and then shuffled back around the counter. He turned around and took a few jars off the shelves and placed them on the center table. He then bent down and pulled out several more jars from the drawers behind the counter. He shook them and placed them on the table next to the other ones. Then he shuffled down the long row of drawers and opened three other drawers and took out three glass vials containing crushed-up powder. He tapped pinches of each into the bowl and then added ingredients from the jars on the table. We watched silently as he finished mixing the ingredients. He took out a heavy stone pestle and ground up all the ingredients until the bowl was filled with a fine yellow powder and then reached under the table and took out a glass jar. He funneled the yellow powder into the jar and screwed the top on tight and handed it to Victoria. I asked her what it was, and she said it would help my elbow.

"Can you ask him again to make something for Bowen's shoulder?"

"I'll try, but he has already said no." Victoria turned to the doctor and spoke to him. Doctor Song answered in a low mumble I could not understand. Again she mimicked a tennis serve with her right arm. He seemed to repeat what he had just said. "He says he cannot make something for someone without seeing them. He says Bowen will have to come."

"Can't I just show him where it hurts on me?"

"I tried to show him on me, but he says he has to feel for heat and cold on Bowen."

I paid for the medicine the doctor had mixed for me but I knew I would never open it. Victoria and I had incorrectly assumed that if I bought something for myself, Doctor Song might be more willing to mix up something for Bowen.

"Sorry," said Victoria. "Maybe Bowen can come here. It's only fifteen minutes from the tennis center." I nodded but said nothing. I could tell by the way she said it that Victoria didn't really believe Madame Jiang would let Bowen do that. At least he had the Advil I had given him. I hoped that would help.

We arrived at the Tianjin Tennis Center just as the boys were starting the finals. Madame Jiang was standing with her back to us. She was speaking with the Tianjin coach. Victoria and I took a seat in the bleachers behind them. They were watching Bowen play on the first court. The acoustics in the building were such that we could overhear most of their conversation. The Tianjin coach asked, "Is he injured? He looks injured."

"No, there is nothing wrong," she said. "He does this to be difficult."

She continued, saying that Bowen was trouble. "No discipline," she said, "he causes so many problems for the team." She stabbed the cold air with her words. She added that Bowen lied and that she often caught him disobeying her. The Tianjin coach said that Bowen should win this match easily. Madame Jiang agreed. "He is losing to try and make me look bad," she said. The Tianjin coach watched Bowen double-fault and agreed that Bowen wasn't trying.

Had Bowen not told me that his shoulder hurt so much that he could hardly hit the ball, I would have assumed that his behavior was just another case of his making the game more evenly matched or perhaps toying with his opponent. But now I understood his situation differently so I found myself watching another kind of high-wire act in which Bowen never left a margin of error—not because he was playing with people's expectations but because it was all he could do. I had been looking at one thing and thinking about it in a certain way, and now I was looking at the same thing and understanding it completely differently. China itself was a lot like that, I had learned. You could never assume you understood something unless you knew it inside and out and even then you still couldn't be certain.

Bowen's match against the number one player from Tianjin seesawed back and forth. With his injured shoulder, Bowen could not serve as hard as he usually did and had to rely on his wits and clever play to win points. He had to use surprise to throw his opponent off balance. By the time the other boys had finished, Bowen had just won a hard-fought first set in a tiebreaker. Hope and Dali had won their matches, Random and Little Mao had lost. Bowen's match was crucial. They all came to watch Bowen. I could tell that they thought he was consciously making the match close in order to torture Madame Jiang or to seek revenge for the way she had treated him. Little Mao turned to Random and said something about "Bowen showing off again." He resented what he thought Bowen had put them through. Random told him to shut up.

"Look at the way he's hitting forehand," Random said. "There is something wrong with his shoulder."

I watched the next few forehands that Bowen hit and saw that he wasn't extending his arm on the backswing and his motion was stiff and truncated. The second set was not going well for Bowen. With his opponent up 3-2, Bowen played a terrible service game, double-faulting three times. I could tell that he was in agonizing pain every time he hit a serve. He lost his serve at love. I looked around at the people watching the match to see if there was anyone who might be Bowen's parents. Most all the spectators were players and coaches. In the next game Bowen began running around his forehand to hit backhands on the forehand side of the court. In the men's game, players often run around their backhand to hit forehands as the forehand is almost always the stronger and more offensive shot. But it is almost unheard of for a player to run around his forehand to play his weaker backhand. It was obvious to me that Bowen would only be doing this if he was in too much pain to hit his forehand properly. But Madame Jiang had a different reaction. She turned to the Tianjin coach and said, "See how he clowns around? He insults your player and your team by not taking the match seriously." A few minutes later Bowen lost the second set 6-3.

Bowen walked to his chair with his head down and his left arm limp by his side. He held his racket loosely in his right hand. Madame Jiang stormed over and gave him a furious dressing down in front of everyone. I felt sick. I didn't think he was going to be able to finish another set, let alone win one. But when the break between the sets was over, Bowen walked to the baseline, his head held high, and I hoped he had a new plan. With the exception of Random, the other boys on the team thought Bowen would make certain he would win the third set. The National Championships for them felt secure, but Random and I knew otherwise.

In the opening games of the third set, Bowen raised his game and unleashed his full talent. He pulled off impossible angles, inch-perfect drop shots, slice serves that dragged his opponent onto the next court, and topspin lobs that traced a precise trajectory just over the top of his opponent's racket and landed within half a foot of the baseline. Bowen must have realized that he couldn't win the match by beating his opponent with power, so he exhausted every single ounce of his talent to find victory through finesse.

Despite some of the miraculous shots that Bowen was pulling off, his opponent had managed to edge a slight lead through stubborn grinding. He stood on the baseline and ran down every shot Bowen hit and just put the ball back in play, knowing that eventually Bowen's shoulder was likely to fail him. The player's two styles could not have been more different. After forty-five captivating minutes of play, Bowen's opponent led him by five games to four. Luckily, it was Bowen's turn to serve, in theory giving him the upper hand in the game.

Bowen started the game strong and went up 30-love. But his opponent retaliated with two immense return winners to level the score. At 30-30, Bowen hit a slice serve that curved into his opponent's body, jamming him and causing his opponent to send a wild return long past the baseline. At 40-30 Bowen took a gamble and went for a huge first serve out wide. The gamble almost paid off. His serve cracked through the air at upward of 115 mph and skidded off the slick court and flew past his opponent, thumping into the curtain behind. About half of the spectators assumed Bowen had aced his opponent and started cheering. But Bowen's opponent held up his racket and indicated that the serve had landed just out, and the umpire agreed. The supporters that Bowen had won over to his side cried out, appealing the decision, but Bowen waved them down because he knew that the decision had been correct and he had missed the serve.

When the commotion died down, Bowen returned to the baseline and bounced the ball seven times. His face looked calm. He
tossed the ball and as he went up for his second serve, he winced
and exhaled in pain. He must have damaged his shoulder further with that big first serve. The second serve limped through
the air and meekly landed at the bottom of the net. The score was
now deuce and his opponent was only two points from victory. I
will never forget what happened next.

The atmosphere in the indoor arena was tense as Bowen prepared to serve the deuce point. He bounced the ball seven times
and then tossed the ball up like he was going to serve normally.
The toss was wild and too far to the left. Bowen acted as if he was
going to let the ball drop and catch it so he could re-toss. He put
his right hand out to catch the ball, but at the last second, just
before the ball fell into his hand, Bowen flicked his racket out
and hit an underhand slice serve. It was a trick shot that I had
seen him hit in practice. The ball curved through the air and
landed just on the other side of the net, before the tremendous
backspin that Bowen put on the ball caused the ball to bounce
backward toward his side of the court. His opponent stood frozen
to the spot and watched with confused horror as the trick shot
spun backward over the net and landed back on the same side
that Bowen had served it from. It was Bowen's point. His opponent hadn't touched the ball, and the serve counted as an ace.

There was silence in the indoor arena as the spectators tried
to comprehend what had just happened. The ball bounced twice,
rolled past the service line, and stopped near the baseline. Bowen
wordlessly walked to the ball and picked it up and prepared to
serve the next point. Still nobody clapped. Random, who was sit-

ting next to me, whispered, "Wow." I looked around at the other spectators and everywhere I looked I saw stunned faces.

Madame Jiang shattered the silence.

"Hey! Come here!" she screamed at him. She had stormed onto the court from her position beside the umpire chair and was walking toward Bowen at the baseline. She looked angrier than I had ever seen her before. "You think this is a joke? This is not a joke! Treat your opponent with respect! Serve properly! Replay the point!"

I couldn't believe it. Bowen had just hit one of the more incredible shots I had ever seen, at a crucial time in the match that would decide the final, and Madame Jiang wanted him to replay the point? I would have been livid if I were in Bowen's shoes, but he just stood there and looked back at her with clear, glassy eyes and showed no reaction. He nodded. "Okay," he said quietly. I turned to Random and gave him a look of incredulity. He just shrugged. Bowen was back at the baseline and readied himself to serve again. "Forty-forty," he called the score loud, as if to ensure that everyone in the arena understood that Madame Jiang had ordered him to replay the point. He bent his knees and raised his right arm, tossing the ball high into the air. His body was coiled, but still loose, like a whip before it strikes. The ball toss reached its apex and the ball hung in the air and Bowen released his service motion. His racket whipped through the air and connected with the ball, sending it rocketing toward the other side of the court. The serve was wild and off target. The ball screamed through the air and smacked against the tall umpire chair, ricocheting back off the hard wood at a slight angle and hitting Madame Jiang square in the side of the face.

Bowen rushed over and made a show of being extremely concerned for Madame Jiang's well-being. She didn't acknowledge him. Even when the ball had struck her she had hardly moved. She just stared straight ahead with hate all over her face. The umpire determined that Madame Jiang was fine and waved Bowen on to continue playing. People in the crowd were split on whether it had been an accident or an act of retribution and a few low hisses rang out as Bowen walked back to the baseline.

Bowen was finished. He looked as though he could barely hold the racket. He served his second serve underhand and watched powerlessly as his opponent rocked a forehand return into the corner for a winner. On match point, Bowen managed to get an overhand serve in, and a long, grinding baseline rally ensued. Bowen was too hurt to do anything more than to loop the ball high over the net, and as Bowen's opponent was unwilling or too nervous to go for a big shot, the rally seemed to last for an eternity. Unable to continue the rally any longer, Bowen took a gamble and went for a slice drop shot, hoping to catch the other boy out of position. It was a hopeless shot. His aim was off and the shot landed too short, dancing off the net cord up into the air where it hung for a second before falling back down onto Bowen's side of the court. It was the kind of shot that he had been pulling off all match. But he finally reached the point where either his talent or his luck ran out.

His opponent sank to his knees and raised his arms. The other Tianjin players cheered and stormed the court, enveloping their victorious teammate and lifting him on their shoulders. I looked to Random and my other teammates. They were already packing up their things silently with heads bowed. Madame Jiang left the courts without a word.

Bowen sat on the court behind the baseline with his knees bent and his back against the wall. He rested his forehead on his crossed arms. I went over to him. He lifted his head and saw me approaching and got to his feet before I could offer him a hand. Where he had been sitting was now a dark patch of sweat. He had truly left everything on the court. I went to say something to him but he waved me off. I understood though. Sometimes it's better to be alone.

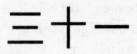

The team was given the week after the championships off to rest. When we returned to practice, Bowen wasn't there. At first I assumed that he had been given extra time off to rehabilitate his shoulder, but as the days passed without even a mention of Bowen, I began to worry. When he didn't appear at the start of the second week, I asked Random if he knew where Bowen was. He simply shrugged. I asked Dali and Little Mao the same question. They replied in identical fashion. At the end of Friday's practice I finally summoned up the courage to ask Madame Jiang directly.

"*Ta hui jia le* (He went home)," she said.

"Where?" I said.

"Tianjin."

"Did he change teams?"

"*Bu zhidao* (I don't know)," she said without looking at me. With that she walked off.

The next day I asked Random if he thought Bowen had rejoined the Tianjin team. The addition of Bowen to the Tianjin team would almost ensure that Tianjin would win the national championships again next year.

Random shook his head and said he didn't know but doubted it.

"Why?"

"He came to Beijing because he was expelled from the Tianjin team."

"He was? Why?"

"His mother angered the Tianjin head coach because he thought she went around him and tried to get a sponsor for Bowen from an academy in America."

"What happened?"

"Bowen told me that she did nothing wrong. She was approached by an American coach who was visiting Tianjin. Bowen was very, very good when he was twelve, definitely the best player in China. The coach spoke to Bowen's mother about whether she would consider letting him come to America to train. When the Tianjin head coach heard about it, he blamed Bowen's mother. Bowen told me that she was very ashamed. She did nothing wrong, but she was told that she could not come back to the tennis center. After that, Bowen was so disruptive that he got kicked off the team. I think the team director used Bowen to send a message to the other parents and players. It would make them look very bad if they lost any of their good players to America."

"So how did he end up in Beijing?"

"The coach before Madame Jiang took him. He had been a badminton player and knew something about tennis. I guess he figured if he could get Bowen, his team could be number one, but he was sent to coach the woman's professional team in Shanghai two months after Bowen arrived."

"But then why did Bowen go back to Tianjin if he doesn't have a chance of getting on the team?"

Random shook his head. "He never belonged here."

I sensed there was more to know, but Random wasn't telling.

When I awoke the following morning, Beijing was cloaked in a ghostly light, and the sky was gray. A sandstorm had blown in overnight. I had been told about the dangerous sandstorms that plagued Beijing each year. As the sun rose the sky turned from a gray to a yellow to an orange. When Victoria and Driver Wu arrived, I sprinted from the lobby of the apartment building to the car. The sand stung my face and stuck to my lips.

"This is your first sandstorm. You will be tasting sand for days," Victoria teased and then went on to remind me how much of China was desert. "Over a quarter," she said. "The sand comes from the deserts to the north of Beijing and is blown into the city by high winds. The deserts are growing and moving, and the government needs to plant trees and grass, but it will take time and money. The Gobi Desert is now less than one hundred fifty miles from Beijing."

Driver Wu grumbled the entire car ride to the language school. There was a film of fine orange dust covering everything. Driver Wu was worried the sand would get inside the engine of the car and cause damage. Despite the sandstorm, the traffic was still bad. There were fewer cars, but they moved even more slowly, and a few had broken down and been pushed halfway onto the sidewalks. I wondered, perhaps even hoped, that Teacher Lu might be late, or might not show up at all—sort of like praying for rain on a summer day in Florida when you didn't feel like another five-hour tennis practice. Teacher Lu was there when I arrived with more energy than she normally had.

During a break between classes I ran into Josh in the student lounge. It was the first time I had seen him in over two months, and I asked him how his wine importation business was going. He shook his head and said that everything had been going great until there had been a cyclical crackdown on corruption in the government. All of a sudden, officials could no longer afford to be seen holding elaborate banquets and drinking expensive European wines and the demand for Josh's business had disappeared completely. He didn't seem too worried about it though. He told me that his business partner had assured him that this was only temporary and that these crackdowns happened every now and then to keep people in line and to give the appearance that something was being done to combat corruption. In the meantime, Josh and his partner were setting up a bottled sparkling water company. Josh said that his business partner's uncle was party secretary of Harbin, a major industrial city in the northeast where they had natural hot springs—a perfect source of free sparkling water. At that moment, Josh was incorporating a bottled water company in Europe for two reasons: one, because it was easier to get the money out of China if it was a foreign company, and two, because they wanted to give the water a fancy-sounding European name to make it seem high-class. He said they had liked the name Mont Blanc but were afraid it would get confused with the pen company, so they were thinking about the name Courcheval. I wanted to ask him more, but at that moment the bell rang, and I returned to class with Teacher Lu.

After class as I ran to the car where Driver Wu and Victoria were waiting, the force of the winds, which had been building all morning, felt out of control. A half-block sprint to the car and already the sand was in my hair, clothes, eyes, and mouth. I felt as if I were being attacked with hundreds of needles on all the exposed areas of my skin and it was difficult to breathe. As we drove to tennis, I saw many people with makeshift remedies. Some people walked around with plastic bags over their heads. Others wore surgical masks while some covered their whole head with scarves. I saw one man riding a bike with his head covered by a sheer blue scarf. A woman with a similar red scarf half jogged, half ran a few meters behind him.

By the start of tennis practice, the winds had died down, and the air was beginning to clear as the sand settled. Even though we practiced indoors, my throat still felt scratchy, and my eyes burned. On the drive home, people began emerging from apartment buildings and storefronts and alleyways with makeshift brooms and shovels to push and sweep the orange sand into piles.

I skipped dinner that night—my throat was sore and my head hurt and I didn't feel like eating. I lay down on my bed and stared out the window into the dusty orange haze. Wherever he was, I hoped that Bowen would be all right.

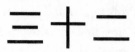

A few weeks went by and life went on largely as it had before. Madame Jiang continued to lead practices as before, and a new player, Sun Li, was added to the team. But it wasn't the same without Bowen. A crucial component that had kept us together as a team was now gone. When professionals came through, there was no one to give them a run for their money the way Bowen could. The truth was that no one enjoyed tennis the way Bowen did. He played with such joy and intensity that he always seemed to want the ball to come back to his side of the court. He was disappointed when his opponent didn't return his shot.

We could have all been lost in a desert, but Bowen would have convinced us that he knew exactly where the path to water was and that the condition we found ourselves in was nothing out of the ordinary. Nothing to worry about. No one wanted to talk about Bowen, and as many times as I tried, I never could get any of the boys to give me more than a sliver of information. It was almost as if he had never existed. But without Bowen, the boys were listless, and Madame Jiang had turned even more irascible. Even Victoria, who sat at most practices and played with her phone and sent text messages, did not bother to pull her phone from her purse. Maybe it was the early dark winter days, the cold, smog-filled air that never seemed to let up, or maybe it was just that we all had relied on Bowen's presence to give us energy, to push us forward, to give us a sense of purpose. I used to look forward to seeing Bowen; now I had begun to dread practices.

Christmas was approaching and, with it, the promise of a trip back home. When we had first discussed my spending a year in China, my father had told me that I could return for a few weeks around Christmas when my friends would be on their winter breaks.

Somewhat surprisingly for an institution in China, the language school had a two-week winter recess on either side of Christmas. In my last week I kept track of the number of steps I would have to take up and down the rickety staircase of the Beijing Women's Publishing House—840, 672, 504, 336, 168, 84. I handed Teacher Lu a special package of fermented tea leaves that Victoria said she would like. I thanked her for all of her perseverance with me. When our lesson ended, Teacher Lu told me she had one more tale for me. She told me a story of a young eagle who was raised among a group of young chickens. The young eagle believed that he was a chicken so he didn't try to fly. "The owner was mad at the eagle's identifying himself as a chick. 'What was the sense of raising an eagle?' he demanded." Madame Lu stood up and raised her fist in anger as if acting the part of the owner. "He threw the eagle down a cliff." She mimicked throwing something down. "The eagle fell down the cliff straightly and at the moment he was nearly to the ground to hit himself, he suddenly can use his wings and fly, thus living as an eagle ever since." Teacher Lu reached up and patted me on my shoulder. Once again, I wasn't clear what she was trying to tell me, but I smiled and thanked her.

Madame Jiang had given us a rare day off from practice, so I had the afternoon free. As I trotted down the last steps of the fire escape, I was struck with that rare sense of freedom that one always gets on the last day of school. I rehearsed in my mind conversations that I would have with friends when I returned home. "So what was it like?" they would ask. I smiled to myself when I thought about the reactions they would have to my telling them about the draconian Madame Jiang, about eating sea snails and duck heads, about the sandstorms. I knew they would laugh when I showed them the fake DVDs with their brutally spelled titles and blurbs stolen from the covers of totally unrelated films. Or share with them the winners in the different categories of the *Translation Olympics*. The girls would be impressed, I thought, when I told them about how I had practiced with the national team every day, with boys who would be playing professional tennis in the future and how my best friend, Bowen, was the best player in China and probably one of the best players in the world and how he . . . I stopped. How would I tell them about Bowen? How would I explain what had happened to him, when I still did not understand? Even if I did know what had happened to him, how could I make them understand how unfair it all was? How could I make them care? I walked down the last ten steps and doubted that I would ever be able to make any of them understand the complexities.

Victoria and Driver Wu were waiting for me in the car. In the space of those last eighty-four steps my mood had turned, but Victoria was determined to change that. When I got in the car she handed me a wrapped present.

"It's for Christmas," Victoria said. "Don't open it yet! I was going to wait until Christmas to give it to you but then you told me you might go back to America for two weeks."

"Yeah," I said. "It'll be great. Where are we going now?" Driver Wu had turned down a different street than the one we usually took.

"I'm taking you to a market," Victoria said. "So you can get presents for your friends back home."

Most markets in Beijing are now housed in large, several-story buildings that resemble malls filled with hundreds of individual stalls. But at the time there were still quite a few traditional open-air markets. Victoria told me she was taking me to the Panjiayuan Flea Market. She referred to it as the dirt market. She told me it was the oldest and the largest of the markets. Located just off the eastern Third Ring Road, it was not too far from the Zhangs' apartment, but it took us some time to get there. The market was vast with rows and rows of covered stalls.

"This way," she said. She led me around the back of the entrance. There, spread out on dirty, worn, irregular pieces of cloth, was a wide collection of goods—china, pottery, bits of leather, ox bells, flint wallets, even old wooden washboards.

"Lots of fakes, but sometimes you can find good things."

Most of the vendors were squatting, but if we paused, they stood up and pushed some trinket at us and said, "Very very good price" as if it were one word. Victoria shooed them away. She pointed to one washboard, a rectangular piece of wood with worn ridges carved across the face. "One of Z's partners came here and bought twenty-four washboards and did an installation with them. An American collector bought it for a lot of money."

I saw three young boys playing together. I gathered that their parents were selling things in the market. The three boys whom I guessed to be eight or nine years old were playing some version of rock-paper-scissors. They were standing facing each other and stamping their feet and shouting three words and then swinging their fists downward. They danced around in a loose circle. I watched for a few minutes, mesmerized by the intensity with which they were playing this game. I asked Victoria why the kids weren't in school. She said that they were probably the children of the "illegal immigrants" of the city, people from the countryside or other cities who had migrated to Beijing to find work but did not have Beijing residency cards and therefore could not send their children to school. Victoria said that after staying here for a few years, the immigrants would probably take the money that they had saved up and return to their home village. One of the shopkeepers shouted something at the boys, and they laughed and ran off together, pretending they were being chased, and looking as if they were being blown by the wind.

We walked down row after row of stalls. Other potential customers stalked the market alongside us. Everyone had their eyes on the ground, scanning blankets filled with trinkets and jewelry. Eyes watching eyes to discern with precision exactly what object was being considered. Victoria stopped in front of a stall that had a set of small dishes of different shapes that fit together to form a circle. They were painted with dark pink peonies and light green leaves and were displayed in a worn velvet box. As Victoria looked over the plates, the vendor handed me a small brass pot engraved with circular markings on the side. It was similar to one that my father used as a pen holder in his office in New York. He could use this one in his study at home. I nodded to Victoria. The vendor understood that I had chosen this piece, and he was a tough negotiator. I ended up paying 200 RMB or about thirty dollars. Victoria thought it was far too much, but I was pleased with my purchase. "Next time walk away," she said. "He would have dropped the price. You could have gotten it for seventy RMB."

After looking at several rows of offered goods, the goods began to develop a sense of sameness, and anything unusual stood out. "Don't act interested," Victoria said in English. "But did you see the fighter pilot's helmet?"

Laid out on a blanket to our right with trinkets and chipped pieces of pottery was a green helmet with a red star on the side. There was also a large pair of binoculars.

"Those are some serious binoculars," I said to Victoria. The man squatting behind the blanket stood up and handed them to me. They had red lenses and were heavy. I wondered what they had been used to sight. It was still too dark to see how well they worked. I handed them back. He watched me look at the helmet and picked it up and thrust it at me. "You like. Good price." I turned the helmet over in my hands. It was heavy and looked authentic to me. "*Kan yi kan* (Take a look)," he said and mimed putting it on himself. It had a sun visor. I pushed it up and then lifted the helmet onto my head. It was cool, I thought. It was the kind of thing I would have gotten Tom as a present. It would have pleased him, and he would have found a reason to wear it. I put the helmet down.

Just as I started to walk away, the vendor tugged my shirt and motioned for me to wait. He lifted the top of a large crate and searched vigorously through it until he found what he was looking for. He pulled out a small red cardboard box wrapped closed with string. He took his time untying the knot. Inside the box were four medals. He took one from the box and handed it to me. The red ribbon was dirty and crumpled and stained. The metal's luster was gone. But for some reason that made me like it more. It felt real. Not like the spotless medals you see pinned onto starched uniforms in films. This medal was scratched and imperfect, heavy in my hand.

I asked him, "*Zhe shi ni de ma* (Are these yours)?"

"*Dui* (Yes)," he said. He pointed a stubby finger at the medals. "*Wo baba de* (My father's)."

The first price he asked I accepted. It felt immoral to haggle with a man reduced to selling the medals that his father had won during a war. As I walked away, Victoria told me that I had paid three times too much.

I didn't like bargaining. The people had a lot less than I had and were doing whatever they had just to get by. It felt wrong to haggle and try to save a few dollars at their expense. Victoria treated this bargaining as if it was a game and maybe it was to her, but to the vendors it was survival. Did it matter if I had paid double for something? It mattered to that man, it might have helped him get through a day when no one was buying. Victoria laughed. "Chase, you have a soft heart, it is good, but in China that's a luxury we cannot afford."

Once we had completed a circuit of the outer stalls, Victoria led the way inside the covered area. The vendors inside were different from the peasants who squatted behind their blankets on the perimeter of the market. These vendors presided over a chaotic paradise of counterfeit goods. They were pros, and there was a rhythm to the negotiation that everyone understood. They spoke relatively good English, and they told you whatever you wanted to hear. Doubts were answered with confirmations. "Is this real gold?"—"Yes." "Is this old?"—"Very old." "Does this work?"—"Work very good." The conversations took on a kind of gospel-music-verse-and-repeated-chorus rhythm. They waited by their stall and pretended to be a customer examining the goods until you came and looked, and then they would give you advice on what to buy. They set the prices high so that they could give up a lot of value in the negotiation and still get the price they wanted.

I picked up a New England Patriots jersey for one of my friends back home who was a huge fan. When the shopkeeper handed over the jersey I was surprised by the garment's quality. It felt and looked exactly like an authentic one. I showed it to Victoria.

"It could be a real one," she said.

"But I only paid eighty-five RMB for it," I said. "I saw a real one in a store by the Hyatt. It was nine hundred RMB."

Victoria shrugged. "It could be stolen from the factory where they make the real ones. Sometimes the truck drivers 'lose' a delivery."

I bought a few other small things for friends back home and also bought a counterfeit DVD set of the first season of *Mr. Bean*. We ended up in front of a stall selling shoes. Victoria had found a pair of Gucci tennis shoes for her husband. Victoria said 100 RMB and when the vendor said no, she motioned for me to walk away with her. He then instantly lowered the price, to 80 RMB. Victoria said 100 for two pair of shoes. He handed her the matching pair of his and her Gucci tennis shoes, and she handed him 100 RMB.

"Don't you want to look around a little more?" Victoria asked.

I didn't, but I could tell Victoria did. She pointed to a pair of

Chanel sunglasses. "Those are good copies. The Cs are the right size, not like those of Madame Jiang's. Her Cs are too big. You should give her something when you leave."

I was surprised. I had absolutely no interest in buying a gift for a woman I considered unreasonable and cruel. "After the way she treated Bowen?" I asked. "No way."

"Okay," Victoria said. "You should understand, though, that in a Chinese way, sometimes Bowen acted very disrespectful."

"Yeah, you're right," I said. I could not conceal my antagonism and my voice was heavy with sarcasm. "Maybe if I give her some new Chanel sunglasses or some fancy white gloves she won't have to steal money from the team to buy them herself."

"It's not that simple!" Victoria snapped at me. "You see everything as good guys and bad guys. Madame Jiang bad, Bowen good, Chairman Mao bad. Nothing is that simple, Chase."

Her anger subsided and her voice turned soft and sad. "Bowen is not the only one who has been badly treated," she said. "Madame Jiang wears those gloves because she is ashamed of her hands. When she was a child, her hands were broken badly by the Red Guard. Now her hands are deformed. She is ashamed of them, so she wears gloves."

"What do you mean?" I asked, confused. "Her hands are broken?"

"Haven't you noticed that she can't hold a racket properly?" Victoria asked.

I had noticed that, but I had always assumed that it was just because she didn't know anything about tennis. "Random said she used to be a great player on China's Olympic volleyball team. How could she be a volleyball player with bad hands?"

"In volleyball you don't use your fingers so much, you use the butt of your hands and your wrists." Victoria demonstrated hitting an imaginary ball.

"Do you know what happened?"

"Her father was a senior executive at a company in Shanghai. They lived in a large house across from the factory. During the Cultural Revolution the Red Guard came in and taped up all the rooms in her house. Her family could only live in one room. Madame Jiang loved to play the piano, but the Red Guard put tape across the piano. They were afraid to go into the rooms with the tape because if they were discovered they would be beaten. One day, Madame Jiang took the tape off the piano to play, and one of her neighbors reported her. The Red Guard came and made her sit on the piano stool and tied her hands to the keyboard and slammed the cover down on her hands, many times, breaking many bones. She wears the gloves to hide her deformed hands. The bones were never reset. They look like claws. She told me she still cries when she hears a piano make music that is beautiful."

I was stunned and struck by this odd sense of pity and guilt. It made me feel conflicted, because I still disliked her, but I also felt horrible for the times that Bowen and I had made fun of the way she held her racket.

"How do you know all of this?" I asked.

"One day when the team was running laps on the track, she was adjusting the tennis net and the crank came loose and pinched her hand and it started bleeding. I was at the courts waiting for you so I helped her. She took her glove off to wrap her hand. That is when I saw her hand, and she explained what had happened. It turns out my grandfather had worked for the same company as her father."

"Why didn't you tell me?" I asked.

"This is not my story to tell," she said. "I would never tell anyone this story. I only told you now because you needed to hear it to understand properly."

I now saw what Victoria had been doing all year. All of her hanging around the courts, texting on her phone, waiting for a moment in which she could assist Madame Jiang, all were just pretexts to get to know Madame Jiang, to understand who she was. It was part of her job as my guide, but it was also part of the Chinese character to understand things in context. A few weeks earlier my father had e-mailed me an article about an experiment a psychologist had conducted at an American university with an equal number of American and Asian students. The students were recruited to look at a succession of images on a computer screen. One by one, at three-second intervals, a series of pictures appeared on the screen. All had a large object set against a complex background such as a tiger in a forest or a horse in a field of flowers. The Americans all had excellent recall of the specific object, while the Chinese honed in on the background. The psychologist's conclusion was that Americans are naturally inclined toward a "me first" view of life, while the Chinese understood things by way of context. Understanding context was ingrained into their daily lives even at the language level. As I had learned, the only way to understand the multiple meanings of certain words, or to decipher the skewed tones of strong regional dialects, was through understanding the context of what was being said.

Victoria did not assess Madame Jiang's behavior against an absolute standard as I had done, but against a standard that took into account the context of her background. She understood that what could be seen on the surface was only that—the surface—and that to see a full picture one must go beyond. When I had come to China I viewed the world in sharply defined spheres of black and white. Now I was beginning to see that my perspective had been incomplete at best.

It reminded me of a boy I had played against at the national championships in the States. His name was Dennis Tikomirov and he was the son of Russian immigrants. He was top ten in the country and he had a reputation for being a ruthless cheat. When I played against him, any shot that was within four inches of the line he called out. I had never seen such shameless cheating ever before in my life. By the end of the match, I was so frustrated and angry that I gave up trying to win, and just focused on trying to hit the ball as hard as I could at his face anytime he came up to the net. After that match, I hated Dennis Tikomirov with a passion. But my attitude toward him changed after I saw what his father would do when he lost.

At the Winter Nationals, Dennis was upset in the second round by a lower-ranked player. They had barely finished shaking hands when Dennis's father burst onto the court, swearing at his son in Russian. He yanked him off the court by the collar and dragged him out to the parking lot. In full view of everyone at the tournament he shoved Dennis against their car and started yelling at him in Russian at the top of his lungs, pausing occasionally to smack his son in the face. I was shocked by how hard he hit him. Dennis was a small kid, and the last slap knocked him to the ground. His father stared at him in disgust, called him a loser, and got into the car. Dennis got up and tried to get into the car, but the doors were locked. His father rolled down the window and told him to find his own way back to the hotel.

He didn't drive losers. Watching that sobbing kid chase after his father's car as he drove away was probably the saddest, most pathetic thing I had ever seen.

Victoria saw the troubled look on my face. "Don't be sad," she said. "There was no way for you to know those things. Come on, let's go." She smiled, and the cheerful Victoria who always seemed happy returned. That was the surface that Victoria chose to display to the world, and that was all I had seen when I had met her in the airport that day in early August. "I have a surprise for you," she said.

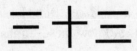

I followed Victoria down the narrow alleyways that snaked through the mazelike labyrinth of hutongs outside the boundaries of the market. I asked her where we were going but she wouldn't tell me. It was a surprise, she said. We eventually stopped at a small restaurant. I recognized it as a Guizhou restaurant where Victoria said she had eaten every day during her first month in Beijing because she was so homesick. I remembered that we had gone there with Bowen during the week of the national holiday.

The restaurant was no more than a small, dimly lit room with four or five tables and a kitchen in an adjoining room. It had no front door, just a curtain of clear plastic strips that hung from the ceiling. In the corner of the restaurant, sipping tea, sat Bowen. Victoria broke the stunned silence as I stared. "Look, Chase, it's Bowen! I found his phone number from the tennis center in Tianjin and got him to come visit."

We went over to the table and sat down. Bowen had cut his hair short, but there was something else that was different about him. I couldn't quite place it. I searched for something to say.

When neither of us spoke, Victoria laughed and pointed at me. "You should see him," she said to Bowen. "He's so mopey at tennis now."

I tried to make a joke about Madame Jiang. "She's *even crazier* now . . . you're lucky you got out, man." Bowen did not smile back.

"Lucky?" He shook his head. "No, you're the lucky one."

"Sorry," I muttered, "stupid joke."

"*Mei guanxi* (No matter)," Bowen said.

"So what happened, man?" I asked earnestly. "Where have you been?"

"Tianjin."

"Are you playing on the team there?"

"I'm working with my father."

"Why?"

Bowen shrugged. "What else would I do?"

"No, I mean why did you leave? What happened?"

"Madame Jiang expelled me from the team."

"What?" Victoria asked, surprised. "She told me that your parents wanted you to go home."

"She can't do that, can she?" I asked. I felt a sense of outrage and frustration. It was all so unfair.

"No," Bowen said. "She talked to the Beijing team director and the Beijing Minister of Sport, and they make the decision."

"Because you lost?"

Bowen nodded. "She told me I decide to lose the match because I want her to lose her job. I told her she is wrong, that my shoulder is not good. But she said I am lying."

"That's so outrageous," I said. "How is your shoulder now?"

"Okay," he said. "Sometimes still hurts."

"But they can't expel you just because you lose a match!" Victoria said.

"No," Bowen said, shaking his head. "That's not why they say. When Madame Jiang speak with the director she tells him that I say I am fourteen years but I am sixteen years. She says I lie. But it's not true! I no lie! Madame Jiang lie and say she has proof I am sixteen. The director and the minister are worried about . . . *choushi* (scandal) . . . you know, choushi? Before the *Aoyunhui* (Olympics). The Aoyunhui is very important for their job. So they don't want trouble. They know that maybe Madame Jiang will give her proof to a newspaper. And then there is big *choushi* about Chinese sport players' real age." He shrugged. "They don't want trouble so they expel me from the team."

I looked him straight in the eyes. "How old are you actually?"

"Fourteen years," he said.

"But if you're fourteen then Madame Jiang has no proof, so there can be no scandal."

"It doesn't matter," Bowen said. "I can't do anything. I am just a tennis player. I have no power."

I had an idea. "What if my father talks to the Minister of Sport?"

When I said this, Victoria cut in, "Chase . . ."

Bowen lowered his eyes. "I don't know," he mumbled. "I don't think they will let me join the team again."

"There must be some way we can help," I said.

"What about America?"

"America?" The question caught me off guard.

"You will go back there after one year, yes?" Bowen asked. "Maybe your father can help me find a sponsor? You said the academy where you practice is very good, maybe I could practice there with you. We will play doubles together. Brother-brother team, we win Wimbledon, like the Bryan brothers."

He had clearly thought this all out. We would need to get him a visa, talk to the head of the Laver Academy, find him a place to live, and either find a sponsor or sponsor him ourselves. It was all certainly possible, but it would come down to whether or not I could convince my father to do it. In any case, I guessed that at a minimum it would take several months or maybe even a year to arrange everything. The first step should be to try to get Bowen back on the Beijing team.

"You will help me, yes?"

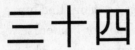

三十四

My father was scheduled to arrive in Beijing that night. Driver Wu took me back to the Zhangs' to pack up some things to take to the Hyatt while Victoria dropped Bowen off at the train station. Victoria had seemed upset when we had left the restaurant. I could not tell if learning what actually happened to Bowen had made her upset, or whether she was uneasy about what I had suggested. In any event her buoyant mood disappeared and she did not speak to me after lunch. Not even to wave good-bye. I showed Driver Wu the medal. He nodded his head in approval. He explained that it was an award for courage in the old Chinese nationalist army, the army that had fought Mao and his Red Army. He held the medal and gently turned it over. He lifted his hand several times. He then said something in Chinese that I could not quite make out. I asked him to repeat it.

"Take good care of this," he said. "It is covered in courage."

Traffic was light that night and Driver Wu dropped me off at the Hyatt an hour before my father's flight got in. As usual there was a room key waiting for me in an envelope at the concierge desk. I went up to the room on the seventeenth floor. The door lock flashed green and I entered. I was surprised to see Victoria perched on the sofa in the living room. I dropped my bag by the door.

"Victoria?" I said.

"We need to talk about Bowen," she said.

"What about him?"

"I made a mistake arranging his visit. You need to understand what he's asking you to do."

"He's not asking me anything," I said. "I offered."

"He's lying, Chase. He's not fourteen. You know that too. He is asking you something. He's asking you to lie to your father for him."

"How do you know?"

"I just do."

"He told me he's fourteen. I believe him," I said.

"None of those boys are fourteen. They're all fifteen or sixteen. That's how it is here."

"Well then why does it matter how old he is?" I asked.

"Of course it matters," Victoria said. "The boys get away with it here because nobody asks questions. The team officials just pretend they don't know. But if Madame Jiang officially reported Bowen for lying about his age, they can't ignore it. It could be a huge scandal. Ten years ago some Chinese athletes were caught using drugs to make them run faster. It was very embarrassing for China. The coach who was giving them the drugs was fired and sent away. It is the same with lying about the ages."

"Bowen wouldn't lie to me," I said.

"If you don't help him, his dream is finished. Don't you see that? Completely finished. He will say anything to make you help him. He lies, Chase. You can't trust someone like that."

Her words touched on a truth that I didn't want to hear. "It doesn't matter if he's fourteen or fifty-five. If he's lying about his age, it's because he doesn't have any other choice."

Victoria was silent.

"Look," I said. "He's had to fight every possible obstacle to get to where he is. I haven't. I've been given everything. It's not the worst thing in the world if I take one risk to help him. You were the one who lectured me about Madame Jiang, about having to understand her whole story. Not just what you see. How is Bowen any different?"

"How old he is does matter," she said. "It's not you taking the risk. It's your father. You will have to ask your father to risk his name, his friendships, his reputation, everything he has here to help a boy he doesn't know."

"I'll explain that to my father," I said. "He'll understand. He'll listen to me."

"Will you?"

"Yes, I'll explain it to him."

She was silent for a moment. "Good," she said. "That is who matters most. Friends like Bowen will come and go, but no one in the world cares for you like your father does."

She got up and left.

A few hours later my father arrived. He was in a good mood. Things had progressed well with the deal that he had been working on and he expected it to be wrapped up soon. It was still early so he suggested we walk down to Tiananmen Square.

It was a clear night in Beijing, one of the rare times that you could see stars over the city, and the night air felt cool and fresh. My father told me that he had been getting good reports about me from Victoria and the Zhangs and that he was very proud of me for what I was doing. I told him that my Chinese was now good enough for me to understand even Madame Jiang's rapid-fire Beijing dialect. He seemed happy to hear that. We reached Tiananmen Square, the red walls of the Forbidden City on our right. I had never seen it at night before. Uncluttered by people, we could hear our feet strike the pavement. I thought about bringing up Bowen to my father, but I decided against it. He was in such a good mood, and I was afraid I would ruin it.

The portrait of Chairman Mao that hung above the Meridian Gate of the Forbidden City was illuminated and Mao's bright eyes stared out into the dark night. We turned around and headed back in the direction from which we came. I looked at the Hyatt and the tall modern office buildings that surrounded it. We passed a Nike billboard that had been put up on one of the outer walls of the Forbidden City and it reminded me of the Starbucks within the gates of the ancient palace. I wondered what Mao would have thought of all of this.

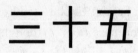

三十五

I ended up spending Christmas day in the Hyatt with my father. The morning after my father arrived in Beijing, I asked him when we were planning to leave, and he gave me a surprised look and asked, "Leave for what?" I reminded him how he had said I could go home for Christmas and he brushed me off and said that we didn't need to figure that out right away. Several days passed and still there was no mention of when we would return to America, so I asked again.

"I think we're just going to stay here for Christmas."

"Wait, why?" All of my happiness of the previous days had been borrowed from my return home.

"I've got a number of meetings the week after that I can't miss. I don't think it makes any sense to go back for just a couple days."

I knew he was right, I knew it made sense to stay here. But at the same time I didn't care. I had been so close to going home.

"Look, you don't have to stay, if you don't want to," my father said. "You can go home for Christmas if that's more important."

"I would like to see my friends."

He seemed disappointed. He told me that he had come to China early so that he could spend Christmas with me. I went into my room and lay down on the bed for a while thinking about it all. His reaction surprised me. We'd never been the kind of family that placed a lot of importance on formal celebrations. We never celebrated Father's Day, we had eaten most of our Thanksgiving dinners at the Fireside Tavern in town, and I had yet to have an Easter lunch. There was only one day out of the whole year that I can remember us having any sort of family tradition and that was February thirteenth, the day before Valentine's Day, the anniversary of the day my father and my mother met. Every year on February twelfth, Tom and I would accompany my father to the quiet cemetery behind St. Mary's and would wait as he placed a bouquet of poinsettias on that plot of land in the far corner of the cemetery where my mother lay. There was something particularly tragic about that day, especially when my father had to discard the cheesy Hallmark card the florist included complimentarily with all Valentine's Day orders. I've always wondered why my father chose that day out of all the days in the year to remember my mother. He could have chosen any number of other days, their wedding anniversary, or her birthday, or even the day she died. But he didn't. He chose that day.

I thought it over for a while. It began to occur to me that maybe my father just didn't want to spend Christmas by himself. It was our first Christmas without Tom. I began to dread the idea of spending Christmas alone in our big house in Connecticut. I went back into the living room and told my father that he was right and that I should stay.

I woke up early on that Christmas morning in Beijing and went into the living room of our suite and saw that my father had arranged for a small artificial Christmas tree to be brought in. The tree was about four feet tall, and the plastic branches and needles were all white with pre-attached ornaments and multi-colored lights. My father was already awake and showered and sitting at the desk in the corner of the room on the phone with someone. When he saw me come in he waved and indicated that he was wrapping up the call.

I remembered the present Victoria had given me a few weeks before and went into my room to dig up the gray wrapped present. I found it in my backpack with my schoolbooks, untouched since the last day of class. I pulled off the wrapping paper. She had given me a framed picture of the two of us at the tennis center. I remembered the picture. She had asked one of the guards at the tennis center to take it a few weeks before. Clipped to the back of the frame was my yearbook photo from the year before. In the corner of the picture my name and phone number were written in my father's handwriting just like on the one my father had given me of Victoria before I had left for China.

My father hung up the phone and went to his suitcase and took out a bundle of wrapped gifts. I opened them and inside I found the Nike tennis shirts I had asked for. He also gave me his old Yale varsity tennis team jacket. He told me that he hoped I would be wearing my own in a few years. I put on the Yale jacket and then went into my room to get the *Mr. Bean* box set and the ceramic pot I had bought for him at the dirt market. As I was leaving my room I saw the old army medal lying on my beside table. I had originally planned to keep it for myself, but at that moment I changed my mind and decided to give it to my father along with the other two presents. My father thanked me for the gifts but didn't seem too interested in them, so I told him what Driver Wu had said about the medal. He told me that I should keep the medal as a reminder of how quickly fortunes can change.

We had breakfast in the seventeenth-floor lounge. I still hadn't brought up Bowen. I knew that I needed to ask at the right time if I wanted him to say yes. After breakfast we went back to the room and I asked him if he wanted to start watching *Mr. Bean*. He said that first he had to take a couple calls and then meet Mr. Zhang for lunch.

"On Christmas?" I asked.

"Well, they don't celebrate here," he said.

The phone rang and he answered it at his desk in the living room. It sounded as though it was going to be a long call. I decided that I might as well watch a few episodes by myself. The only television with a DVD player was in the living room, but it was on the opposite side of the room from his desk so I figured it would be all right to watch it there as long as I kept the volume low. I was about five minutes into an episode when my father put down the phone and walked to the door.

"I'll take it in the lounge," he said, pointing to the phone. "I'm just having trouble hearing in here."

"Oh," I said. "I'm sorry. I'll turn the volume lower."

"No, no," he said. "You're fine. Watch your movie, I'll be back in a few hours."

I heard from someone once that the reason they put laugh tracks in sitcoms is because laughter is contagious. People find things funnier when they have other people to laugh with. I had seen the episode I'd put on before, and this time, sitting alone in that hotel room on Christmas, the jokes felt stale. I turned it off and opened my computer and turned on AOL Instant Messenger to see if any of my friends were online to chat with, but it was nearly 11 p.m. on Christmas Eve in the States, and they were all either asleep or with their families.

About twenty minutes later my father returned.

"You finish up your call?" I asked.

"Nah, I just told my secretary to reschedule everything," he said.

"What about Mr. Zhang?"

"I told him I had to move lunch to tomorrow," he said. He saw my surprised expression. "It's Christmas." He shook his head. "Sorry, Chase. It's like I have blinders on sometimes. What happened to that TV show you wanted to watch?" As I had predicted, my father found the show hilarious. We watched five episodes straight.

Around two we called room service and ordered two cheeseburgers with fries for lunch. I knew that this was as good a chance as I would ever have to ask about Bowen.

"I feel like my tennis has improved a lot over here," I said. "I'm winning matches against some of the guys on the team who used to beat me easily."

"That's great."

"I was thinking that this summer I should play some of those men's open tournaments they have at Yale."

"Men's opens? Are you old enough for that?"

"They're open to anyone. And I've got nothing to lose, really. I know that some of the Yale guys usually play them to get practice matches during the summer. It would probably go a long way with the coach if I had a good result against one of them."

"Sure, but you just want to make sure that you're ready for this. It wouldn't be great to get wiped off the court by one of his weaker players. First impressions are important." He thought for a second. "You know, I might shoot the Yale coach an e-mail just so that he's aware of you and what you're doing. It can't hurt to get you on his radar."

"That'd be great. I'll be ready. I've gotten a lot better. Remember how I told you about my friend Bowen? He was number one in China last year. I was hitting with him every day for a while. He really helped me improve."

"You should keep that up. I've always found that the best way to get better was to play with better players."

"I wanted to, but he isn't on the team anymore."

"Oh?"

"The coach kicked him off."

"She kicked him off? Wasn't he the best player?"

"He lost the deciding match in the finals of nationals, and she said he lost the match on purpose to embarrass her, to make her look bad."

"Did he?"

"No, he was injured but she made him play anyway. I think he tore something in his shoulder, he could barely serve. She wouldn't even let him see the doctor."

"What? Why?"

"She just didn't, she thought he was faking," I said. "Anyway, he won his first four matches, but then in the final he was up a set in the deciding match when his arm totally gave out. He was serving underhand and running around his forehand. He kept fighting though, the third set was six-four. Pretty amazing."

"He was serving underhand?"

"She made something up to the head of the tennis center about how Bowen is lying about his age, about how he is really sixteen but lies and says he is fourteen."

"Didn't you say that a lot of that goes on here?"

"I think some of them are a year older than they say. But Bowen's fourteen."

"You know that for sure?"

I had thought this over for a while, and I knew what I needed to say. I didn't know if Bowen was actually fourteen or not. I knew there was a chance that he wasn't fourteen, but I wanted to believe him. I knew he had lied to me before, at the Forbidden City, but I think that's because he had been embarrassed and had not wanted to lose face in front of me. This was different. Even if he wasn't fourteen, who cared? All the boys on the team lied about their age. It wasn't fair for him to be kicked off the team for that. As I had learned during the past few months, the world didn't exist in black and white, but in shades of gray. He had been there for me and helped me when I had needed a friend, and now he had asked the same from me. It was my duty to help him, and I knew what I needed to say. That didn't make it any easier though. I looked away, down at the ground and felt my throat tighten even more, but slowly the words forced themselves out.

"He showed me his birth certificate," I said.

"Why didn't he show it to the tennis director?"

I shrugged. "Bowen can't do anything. No one is going to listen to him. He's just a fourteen-year-old from Tianjin."

"This coach sounds like a real piece of work. She hasn't given you any trouble like this, has she?"

I shook my head. "The worst part is that without tennis Bowen has nothing. He's in Tianjin now, doing construction. For fifty cents an hour."

My father sighed and took off his glasses. I had hoped that the injustice of the situation would infuriate my father, and he would fix this situation. He polished the lenses on his sweater and placed them back on his nose.

"That's too bad," he said.

The words stunned me. That was it? That was all he had to say? "Can't we do something to help him?"

"Look, Chase, in all likelihood that was where he was always going to end up."

"What is?"

"Where he is now."

"No," I said. "He would have turned pro."

"In the best-case scenario. But then what? He plays a couple years on the pro tour, barely breaks even. If he's lucky, maybe he'll get to play in a grand slam once or twice? That road ends with him twenty-five or twenty-six years old, no money, no education. From there it's either teach tennis or do whatever he's doing now."

"No. With the right coaching he'd be a great player. I think he could be top ten in the world. That's his dream. He wakes up thinking about it and doesn't stop thinking about it until he falls asleep. He told me that."

"There's a reason they're called dreams, Chase, not plans."

I was silent and thought for a minute. The frankness of his words stunned me. I had thought that he genuinely believed in my chances of becoming a professional player. Since we were little, my father had encouraged my brother and me in our dreams of becoming world-famous tennis players. He had started us in tennis clinics early, taken us to the U.S. Open every year since I was old enough to remember. He even arranged for us to get passes to the players' lounge and meet our favorite players. He had joked with the players about how Tom and I would be nipping at their heels soon. For my eleventh birthday he had arranged for his secretary to go to a sports memorabilia auction and buy one of Pete Sampras's actual rackets, signed by Sampras himself. At that age, I idolized Sampras. I had a five-foot poster of him on the wall in my room and insisted on using the same model racket even though he used the heaviest racket on the pro tour. The night of my eleventh birthday, I went to sleep holding that autographed Sampras racket, as if I were terrified that it would slip away during the night, and I dreamed of serves and volleys on the green grass of Centre Court.

I had seen these trips and presents as his way of encouraging our dream of becoming professional tennis stars. But I realized now that my father did not deal in dreams, only plans. He had merely been implementing the first step of his plan for Tom and me to be recruited to Yale for tennis. Now that I was older he was shifting my focus from playing professional tennis to playing for college. I thought about how much of myself I had put into trying to be good enough to play professionally eventually. How many hours on the court I had spent hitting forehand after forehand, serve after serve, how many times I had thrown up after running suicide drills. With an offhand remark, my father had crushed my dream entirely, and I felt a mixture of resentment and denial about what he had said. "Well, Lukas always said that he would take the player who puts everything he has into chasing his dream and fails, than the player who settles for less because he is scared to fail." The unsubtle dig at my father hung listlessly in the air.

"That's just naive."

When I didn't respond, he asked, "What's really going on here? What's this all about?"

"You never listen to me. You never ask me what I think, or what I want to do. I never wanted to come here. It's so lonely. I had one friend, and now he's gone. You didn't care about what I wanted, and you didn't care about what Tom wanted either. Maybe if you had, he would still be here."

Before he could respond I sprinted to my room and locked the door and buried my head in the pillow on my bed, making it damp with my tears.

I must have fallen asleep because it was late in the afternoon when I opened my eyes. I unlocked the door and walked out into the living room, hoping that my father would not be there, but he was sitting on the sofa in the same place he had been earlier.

"Come here," he said.

I joined him on the sofa.

"I'm sorry," he said. "I'm sorry, Chase. I can do better. It's not that I don't care about you. Of course I do. You're my son and I love you and I loved your brother, more than anything. Your mother was always much better at this."

I was quiet for a moment. "Sorry," I said. "I didn't mean what I said."

"You were right. I should have thought more about what it's like for you to be over here by yourself. I thought I would be over here more this year. I thought I'd get to spend more time with you. But I haven't made time for you and I'm sorry for that."

"It's okay."

"I'm going to try and help your friend."

His words caught me off guard. I lifted my head so that I could study his face. "You mean it?"

"I'll talk to Mr. Zhang about him. I'm sure his buddy, the sports minister, can sort this out."

"Really?"

My father smiled. "Sure. It's the least we can do for this kid. You're sure that he's actually fourteen, right? I don't want to ask these guys to stick their necks out unless we're positive that this kid is the age he says he is. You said that you saw his birth certificate?"

I had no choice but to say yes.

"Okay. Write down his name for me and the name of that coach, and I'll make some calls."

That afternoon, my father called Mr. Zhang and explained Bowen's situation. I was filled with hope when Mr. Zhang said that he would be happy to do my father this favor and ask his friend the sports minister to have Bowen reinstated to the team and to deal with Madame Jiang. I didn't allow myself to think one step further than that.

三十六

Several days passed before we heard anything back from Mr. Zhang. On the third day I asked my father to call Mr. Zhang again. Mr. Zhang said that he had spoken with the Minister of Sport who had agreed to look into it for us. Another few days passed, and still there was no word from either Mr. Zhang or the Minister of Sport.

My father's efforts for Bowen more than made up for my not being able to go home for Christmas. I enjoyed time off from my normal Beijing routine, and Victoria and I explored some parts of the city that I had not yet been to. On the day that my father finally heard back from Mr. Zhang, Victoria and I had taken a day trip to a small village about an hour and a half outside of Beijing that had been an important site of resistance against the Japanese occupation of China during World War II. Victoria had visited it once during her first few years in Beijing when she had held a research job for a local news channel, and she had stayed in touch with the woman who had shown her around.

We left the Hyatt at eight in the morning. There had been no wind over the past week and as a result, the pollution had been steadily building up throughout the week. The sky was bleak gray and the smog hung above the city like a great cloud of volcanic ash, blocking the sun from view. That morning, buildings only a block or two away had disappeared from view. Driver Wu pulled up and I saw that the normally pristine black Audi was caked in a layer of grime. I thought about Victoria's comment that the Chinese were buried up to their neck in pollution.

As we headed off, I felt carsick and opened a window, but Victoria and Driver Wu protested and told me that the air would only make me feel worse. Driver Wu rummaged around his glove compartment and pulled out a stack of paper surgical masks and handed them to Victoria and me. I looked at the mask skeptically, wondering how this flimsy paper mask could possibly help, but it did, and my headache began to subside.

As we drove farther from the city, the smog began to lift, the air began to clear, and gradually all recognizable signs of Western capitalism disappeared. The expensive new Audis, the signs written in both Chinese and English, the Nike advertisements, and the American fast-food restaurants that had sprouted up in Beijing were nowhere to be seen in the rural countryside.

An hour and a half later we arrived at the village. The people were dressed in homespun garments and lived in small, one- or two-room shacks and cottages. I saw only two automobiles in the village, and both were blue, three-wheeled vehicles composed of a small cab and a pickup truck–type bed. Each must have been at least twenty-five years old and looked as though they had come out of a Soviet factory. As I looked around the village, I was struck by how untouched it was by the forces of modernization. Judging from our surroundings, it could have been 1975. Here we were, just seventy miles from Beijing, but thirty years in the past.

We parked behind the schoolhouse. Victoria had arranged to meet the woman who had given her the tour back when she was a newscaster.

"She said she would be waiting here," Victoria said.

"Can you call her?" I asked.

"She doesn't have a phone," Victoria said.

I took another glance at the surrounding village and felt stupid for asking the question. "Let's go, we will find her," Victoria said. "The village is not big."

As we walked down the village's dusty main road, almost every villager we passed stopped and stared at us. I asked Victoria why everyone was staring at us.

"Most of them have probably never seen a white person before," she said. "Not in real life anyway."

A voice called out to Victoria, who turned and waved at an elderly woman standing in the open doorway of a house to our left. "That's her," Victoria said. "Let's go, she will show you the tunnels the Red Army soldiers used to hide from the Japanese."

Just then Victoria's phone rang. "*Wei* (Hello)? Oh—Mr. Robertson. Hi. Yes, he is here with me. We are at that village I told you abo—" She abruptly stopped speaking and listened. Her face showed confusion. "Right now? Okay. We will go back now." She hung up the phone.

"What was that about?"

"Your father says we have to go back to Beijing, right now."

"Why?"

"He just said we need to go back right now. He needs to speak with you."

"Did he sound angry?" I asked Victoria, but Victoria was busy apologizing and explaining to the old woman that we were very sorry but there was an emergency, and we had to return to Beijing immediately.

On the car ride back to the Hyatt, I couldn't help but worry that this had something to do with Bowen. Victoria came up to the room with me and we found my father sitting at his desk in the living room sending an e-mail on his BlackBerry. He looked up from his phone when we walked in, but then immediately turned his attention back to the e-mail he was composing. Victoria said that she would be leaving, but my father held up his hand. "One second," he said without looking up from the keyboard. He finished and put the BlackBerry down on the desk and turned his attention to us.

"You're going to move out of the Zhangs' today," he said to me.

"Move out? Why?"

"I made a mistake sending you here. You're too young. I thought you'd be able to handle it."

I had assumed that my father had called me back to talk about Bowen. But the Zhangs? Had I said something to them or done something wrong?

"That kid Bowen has caused a real shit storm, let me tell you," my father said.

"What are you talking about?"

"The coach was right. He's been lying about his age this whole time."

"No, he hasn't. Madame Jiang is just saying that because she hates him."

"The sports minister called the team director at the training center and put pressure on him to dismiss your coach, which he did. The coach appealed her dismissal, but the sports minister said no go. They were going to call Bowen back to the team, but your coach then leaked all of this to some reporter. Told him the whole story, gave him your friend's real birth certificate, told him about you, about me, told him that she was getting fired because some corrupt official had taken a bribe from an American businessman to do it."

"But that's not true!"

"So then last night the reporter publishes this all on his blog, and it starts to spread around the internet. Luckily Zhang and his friends noticed it and jumped on it quickly and had it all shut down by this morning. But the damage is done, Zhang said that rumors have been flying around. You can't practice with the Beijing team anymore and Zhang can't risk getting dragged into this by having you live with them."

"I don't understand. Why?"

"Chase, this kid played you. I should have warned you, but you've got to watch out for people like this. The world is full of people who will try to take advantage of you. I'm not mad at you, it's my fault. I should have seen this."

"No, Bowen wouldn't do that."

"You have to face the facts."

I was silent for a moment. "So what happens now?"

"Now? Victoria will take you to the Zhangs' so you can pack up your stuff, and I'll get my office to work on getting you a flight home."

"No," I said. "I mean what happens to Bowen?"

"I have no idea, and frankly I really don't care what happens to him. You know that deal I've been working on with Zhang? That's finished. You think anybody wants to risk associating themselves with someone accused of corrupting officials? No chance. This is over, Chase. You're going home."

My father turned back to his BlackBerry and began firing off more e-mails. I had known there was the possibility that Bowen might have been lying about his age, but I had never imagined that the consequences of helping him could be anything this drastic. I looked at Victoria, who offered nothing. She was calculating the consequences for herself. I thought about all the hours and energy that my father had put into the deal he had been working on with Mr. Zhang.

"I'm sorry about your business deal. I'm really sorry. I just—I didn't realize . . ."

My father sighed. "I'm not mad at you, Chase." He paused. "The thing I don't get though, is how we didn't realize that this kid was lying. I thought he showed you his birth certificate. Did you read it wrong or something? Victoria, do you know this kid?"

Victoria nodded, her lips pursed tight. My shock was replaced by the horrible realization that Victoria was going to tell my father that Bowen had never shown us any birth certificate, and that she had warned me that Bowen was lying.

"And?" my father asked.

"Yes, I know him," she said. "I told Chase that many sports players in China are lying about their age, many of the tennis players on Chase's team too, they are lying about how old they are. Chase knows this. With Bowen, it could be the same thing. But I always think that Bowen was fourteen, like Chase thinks. Not sixteen."

I could barely believe what I was hearing.

"And the birth certificate? Did he show that to you too?"

"Yes," she said. "It looked just like my one. It says he is fourteen. Maybe it is fake, but very good quality fake, or maybe he buy a new one from a hospital. I don't know. Sometimes people do this in China, for work permits too. It is difficult to tell."

My father turned back to his BlackBerry. "There's nothing we can do about it now." In that moment he looked old and defeated, and his voice sounded tired. "Victoria, can you take Chase to get his things at the Zhangs'?"

"I have to go to my husband's gallery and help prepare for an exhibit. Driver Wu can take him." Victoria had lied for me, but she blamed me for it, and right now she didn't want to have anything more to do with me.

Driver Wu took me to the Zhangs' apartment and waited for me to get my things. I looked out my little window down at the street below and wondered how many more Bowens were out there. It was strange, but I didn't feel any bitterness toward Bowen. Maybe part of me had always suspected, maybe even known, that he was lying. I just never wanted to accept it. It hurt that he had lied to me, but I couldn't hold it against him. He did what he had to do. I'm sure the lie ate away at him the same way the lies I told my father about Bowen continue to eat away at me. Secrets are heavy things to carry.

I picked up the small cup of seeds on my windowsill and briefly thought about asking Driver Wu to stop by the training center on the way home so that I could give them to my teammates. But I realized I probably would not be allowed back at the center, and I doubted if I would ever see any of them again. Dali, Sun Li, and Little Mao would remain where they were— playing tennis. When they didn't make it in the pros, they would be placed by the state system to run a tennis training center and slowly, over time, the tennis level in China would improve. Only Random had a chance to do something else. For them, my leaving was as if I were walking out into the sea. I could go anywhere. They could never even comprehend the wide array of choices that awaited me back home. I decided to take the seeds home with me. I considered giving them to my father for a brief second, but I knew he would dismiss them as silly and superstitious and probably leave them in the ashtray of a room at the Hyatt.

By the time I returned to the hotel, my father had already left for the airport to fly to Shanghai for a meeting with his business partner to try to salvage the Zhang deal. He left me a note on my bed that said a car would pick me up in the morning to take me to the airport. I was on the 11 a.m. flight to Newark.

Victoria was waiting for me by the car the next morning. I started to thank her for lying to cover for me, but before I could get the words out she held up a hand and shook her head. "We all make mistakes," she said. She gave me a hug and said that she was sad that I was leaving and that I must send her e-mails from America. I said I would as long as she promised to send me funny pictures of any mistranslated signs or notices she came across. It hit me then that I was leaving for good. I realized that I would probably never again see Victoria or Bowen or Teacher Lu or any of the other people I had become close to during my time in Beijing. There were so many times that I had longed to leave, yearned to return home. I had never thought that when I actually did leave, I would be sad—but there I was, about to get in a car for the airport, and part of me didn't want to leave any of this behind.

Victoria took a white package out of her bag and handed it to me. "You can open it," she said.

I opened it and saw that it was the page she had found lying in the dust at the abandoned writing school. "For me?" I asked.

Victoria nodded. "I want you to have it to remember your time here."

I shook my head and pressed it back into her hands. "No, Victoria. You should keep this. Give it to your kids, like you said."

"I don't think we're going to have children," Victoria said.

"What? Why not?" I looked at her, surprised.

"It's too much money. We have to look after our parents."

"But—"

"We're their only children. If we don't do it then who will? We can't afford to do both."

I tried to think of something to say, a solution to offer, but I came up with nothing.

"Here, it's for you," she said. She held out the page. I couldn't take it. I shook my head again. "Keep it," I said. "You'll find a way to make it work. I know you will."

I said good-bye and got in the car before she had a chance to change her mind. The driver took me to the airport, and I got on the flight to Newark.

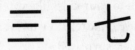

When I returned to America, I felt as if I had crossed into a Technicolor world. I returned to our home where the grass was green, the sky was blue, and the clouds were white. I had never noticed how sweet the country air smelled. My father was still in China, so it was only our housekeeper and me at home. It was strange being at home at first. I was worried about how it would feel when I walked into Tom's room. Would his clothes still be there? Would they still smell like Tom?

Somewhere in my heart I could hear Tom encourage me just as he had that summer in Italy when I was afraid to follow him into the dank, frog-infested tunnel that connected the main house to the kitchen house. And I knew Tom would have been proud of me for "venturing forth." Sometimes even now, as I did then, I have to believe that Tom is alive just so I can tell him things.

My friends from school were still on winter break when I returned, and I met up with a bunch of them at the Brunswick Country Club where we often played pickup ice hockey. We ordered cheeseburgers and Cokes from the snack bar and then sat on the bleachers outside and watched one of the club hockey games. Most of my friends had been away at boarding schools like Dover and the talk ranged from complaints about their workload to chatting about which school had the prettiest girls. We drifted into the pro shop and looked at the latest hockey equipment. These boys thought nothing about charging whatever they wanted to their parents' accounts.

Some of them asked me about China. I tried telling them, but I found it hard to convey what it was like over there. Most of my friends weren't really that interested anyway. A few of the know-it-alls in my class asked me about Beijing as an excuse to lecture me on what they had read about China in *Time* magazine. Though they had never been there, they expressed opinions on China that I assumed were more their fathers' than their own. They talked about how there was no freedom or democracy and how no country could succeed without both. I thought of the stories I had read in the *China Daily* about how the Chinese government had experimented with democracy with local elections in rural areas and found that almost half the electorate had sold their votes for next to nothing. To those farmers, a kilo of rice held more value than vague ideals.

I didn't even know how to respond to some of the things they said. There was no point in even trying. I wouldn't have known where to start. Having lived for months with Bowen, Hope, Little Mao, Random, and Dali, it now felt as though my American friends were the ones speaking a foreign language. Home seemed farther away than when I left.

I spent a week at home and then traveled down to the Laver Tennis Academy in Florida where I trained until I went to Dover in the fall. The hot humid air felt good and clean in my lungs. The hacking cough I had developed from the pollution in Beijing began slowly to disappear. Being back with old coaches and a mixed collection of students felt comfortable and familiar. Good players would come and go for three- to four-week periods. It was a relief not to know too much about anyone's circumstances. I could focus on myself and not wonder or worry about anything else. The five-mile fitness runs on the beach that I used to dread were nothing compared to that day in Beijing running stairs. Now I almost always finished first.

I spent the spring and summer working with Lukas and playing on the national tennis circuit. While in China I had lost some of my technique. I had to work hard to get it back, but the work didn't feel so hard anymore. What had once been a chore was now almost a pleasure, an opportunity I was happy to have.

As I was packing my bag for school I came across the seeds I had taken from the Forbidden City but had completely forgotten to plant on returning to America. That afternoon I biked to the local florist and bought a packet of poinsettia seeds and biked home and planted them, along with the seeds from the Forbidden City, in a patch of earth in the back of our garden. It seems silly now, but at the time I really believed those seeds might bring our family luck.

That September, my father drove me the hour and a half from our house to Dover and helped me move into my small room in Brinkley Dormitory—the very same dorm in which he had lived during his first year at Dover.

I enjoyed Dover even though many of my classmates felt immature to me when I compared them with my teammates in Beijing. My speaking ability was strong enough for me to go into third- or fourth-year Chinese, but because of my sloppy characters, the Chinese teacher placed me in second-year Chinese. The companionship of my classmates—going to the snack bar after class with a friend and talking about a movie or listening to someone's favorite song on their iPod—made everything seem almost too easy.

From time to time I thought about the five boys I had played with in Beijing. I wondered how they were getting on. I especially wondered about Bowen. At first Victoria and I e-mailed each other about once every other week, but slowly the things we had to talk about thinned, and our e-mails became less and less frequent. The boys on the Beijing team didn't have access to e-mail so there was no way to get in touch with them. I once thought about asking Victoria to take the train to Tianjin and see if she could find Bowen, but in the end I decided not to because I knew she would refuse.

三十八

Almost a year after I left Beijing, I ran into Bowen in America, his Mei Guo, his beautiful country.

I had continued playing tennis after going to Dover. The intense academic schedule meant that I had much less time to practice and compete in tournaments, but I still improved at a steady rate. Just before the end of the first term, I left to go down to Florida to play the Orange Bowl with Lukas. I had moved up to the Boys sixteen-and-under and had gotten into the qualifying tournament. The draws for the Boys sixteens and eighteens were more international than the Boys fourteens. The main draw of the Boys sixteens and eighteens tended to have many of the top players in the world. Not that many boys from the States made it into the main draw. National teams from Europe and South America traveled to Florida to play a monthlong group of tournaments—the Prince Cup, Eddie Herr, the Orange Bowl. There were no weak players, and by the time these boys reached the sixteens and eighteens, many of them had decided tennis would be their career. In fact, they wouldn't have been there had that not been the case. They dropped out of school, took a few courses on the internet, and fought for survival in each match.

I played my first match against a boy from Argentina. Most South American players grow up on clay courts. They have great ground strokes and generally put a lot of topspin on the ball. They tend to be retrievers and patiently wait for an opening to make a shot. They are prepared to hit the ball thirty times in one rally if they have to. In the warm-up, my opponent proved to be no exception. I figured I would have to take control of the match early to win. I started off playing well. I had nothing to lose and found myself in a 4-1 lead, but then I began to doubt myself. How was I beating a member of the Argentinean national squad so easily? Because I was leading, I became more cautious and tight and didn't go for as many winners. I eked the first set out 7-5. I knew I was going to have trouble in the second set, and I did. My opponent made very few errors, forcing me to beat him with winners and unreturnable shots. The second set lasted for over an hour. Grinding and grinding. I lost 6-4.

I heard Lukas clap his hands several times and say, "Come on, let's go," as a way to encourage me. The third set was a test of will. The Argentinean had reduced his game to sprinting all over the court to retrieve shots. He edged ahead three games to two. At the changeover, his Argentinean teammates handed him a racket through the fence. It was odd, my opponent had not broken any strings. He examined something on the plastic-covered racket, but he didn't bother to unwrap the racket from the plastic bag. Then I got it. The coach of the Argentinean team was passing a message to my opponent under the guise of his needing a new racket. I forgot my exhaustion, and for the next three games I played as if my life were on the line. I forgot to remind myself that I shouldn't hit down-the-line winners on my backhand or go for an ace on add points.

I went up 5-3, and my legs began cramping. When I served, I had to straighten my right leg immediately or it would cramp as I kicked back. I was worried that my legs would give out and that I wouldn't be able to finish the match, but I managed to hold out and won the set 6-4.

"That wasn't too bad," Lukas said, then he added, "but it took you three and a half hours."

After my match, Lukas helped me stretch, and then we went to the tournament desk to examine the draw. I would play the winner of a match between a player from Germany and one from Belgium—their match had started two hours behind mine so there was a good chance the two boys would still be playing. Lukas wanted to check on one of the other players from the academy, and then he would join me. I found the court where the German and Belgian were playing and climbed the stands to watch.

The German boy was winning 6-2, 5-1 and was serving for the match. I had hoped that it would be close so that I would have a good opportunity to assess their strengths and weaknesses—how they dealt with a change in momentum, how they fought when they were ahead and when they were behind, and what patterns of play they followed. The German won his serve game easily to finish the match. I called Lukas to let him know, and he said he would pick me up in ten minutes. I noticed an argument taking place on the next court.

Two USTA referees in their khaki pants and blue-and-red official shirts stood among several coaches and the two players in the center of the court. I couldn't imagine what would cause such a commotion. It was much more than the not-uncommon dispute about lines. A player walking off the court to get a referee who then stood at the net post and monitored the line calls was about as dramatic as it could get. If a player argued with the referee, the player risked being disqualified by the referee right then and there. Once a referee ruled against you, you had no recourse to overturn his decision.

A few more players and coaches had gathered to watch the dispute. I walked down a row of bleachers to get a closer look. I nearly fell off the stands when I saw that one of the boys on the court was Bowen.

I asked a coach who had been watching, "Is this a sixteen-and-under match?"

"No, it's the fourteens."

Bowen was at least seventeen now. But sure enough, there he was. He had grown another inch or two, but he was still thin and willowy. His hair had grown long again, and he still wore his trademark bandanna, but instead of a piece of yellow cloth, it was a bright red Nike bandanna. I saw that all of his clothing was from the brand-new Nike winter collection. He played with the same racket he had used in Beijing, but now it had a large red "W" stenciled on the strings—the mark of a player sponsored by Wilson. I almost yelled out to him, but I stopped myself. His opponent was much smaller; in fact, he was almost half his height and based on the scorecard on the court, it looked as if Bowen was about to win the second set easily. Two coaches with the British flag on the shoulder of their jackets were gesturing at Bowen and disputing something with the referee. The referee was trying to tell the coaches that they could lodge a formal protest, but there was nothing he could do. The match should go on. The two coaches were almost screaming—they had traveled from the UK at huge expense—only to have one of their players lose a match to a player who was clearly ineligible. They did not believe for a second that Bowen was fourteen.

Bowen stood without showing any emotion. How had he gotten to the States? I remember his telling me that his father would have to work one or two years to earn enough money for a one-way plane ticket. A man who I assumed was his coach sat in the stands carefully watching what was going on, but he didn't walk down to the court. He was wearing all Nike gear.

Several times I saw him slowly shake his head when Bowen looked up at him. The referees were telling the British coaches yet again that they could lodge a formal protest, but they could not disrupt the match. After realizing the coaches weren't going to budge, one of the referees went to get the tournament director. I walked down to the court. Bowen lifted his chin in recognition. He didn't seem surprised to see me. He must have seen my name in the draw. He must have known that I was there.

The tournament director returned, and the two British coaches were giving him an earful. The tournament director turned to Bowen and grilled him with questions. The English was coming too fast now for Bowen, and he pointed to me. I saw the same panicked look I had seen for that brief second in the Forbidden City. Only this time it didn't disappear.

"*Yu!* Tell them you know me! Tell them I am fourteen!"

But I had already disappeared.

In the moment that I caught his eye the consequences of his situation materialized like dark clouds sprinting across the sky, a moving storm that was headed straight for me. I wanted to help him, I really did. But at the same time I was overwhelmed with fear of what might happen if I allowed Bowen to pull me down with him, what might occur if I lied for him again. My mind conjured up images of college coaches crossing me off their recruit-ing lists. But worst of all, I imagined trying to explain it all to my father. Trying to explain to him why I had allowed Bowen to derail my future for a second time. How I had allowed him to lay waste to all of the hard work that I had put in and all of the effort my father had made to ensure that I would go to a good school and have a bright future. And the danger of jeopardizing my re-lationship with my father, maybe even more than my future, ter-rified me. I panicked and fled. I left Bowen to fend for himself.

That night as I lay in bed, I went over and over what I had and had not done. Lines of thought converged and crossed and dou-bled back. I tried to convince myself that I had acted correctly. I tried to tell myself that I had done the sensible thing this time, that it was unfair for Bowen to lie about his age, that enabling his lies would only serve to hurt both of us in the long term, that it was unfair to pull me into this. I came up with every possible argument to convince myself that what I had done was right, but no matter what I told myself, there was one thought I could not avoid—my friend had needed help and I had turned away. I understood what the consequences of my decision were. I knew that if Bowen were caught lying about his age he would lose his scholarship and any chance he had of making it as a professional. Bowen had never had anyone to help him the way I had. He was trying to survive in a way I had never had to. And yet, even know-ing all that, I turned away.

I knew my father would have agreed with my choice. I thought back to how indifferent he had always been about the futures of Bowen and the rest of my teammates. He had seen more of the hardship in China than I ever had, and if I brought up the unfairness of their situation I knew he would remind me of the people who had starved during the Great Leap Forward, or of the hundreds of millions of Chinese who still lived below the poverty line. He would tell me that for every Bowen I came across, he could point to ten million young men just like Bowen, in fact, not as fortunate as Bowen. Maybe my father had seen so much that he had become numbed by it—the way a journalist in a war zone can leave a child stranded by the side of the road and not see it as his duty to do something. Or maybe in the singular pursuit of goals he had learned to keep emotions quarantined from reason. Or maybe he just understood the unfair algebra of life's opportunities.

But I wasn't like him. I couldn't ignore the pain of others. And that night as I tried to sleep I felt the return of the horrible guilt that I had last felt in the weeks after my brother died.

When I showed up for my match the next day, Bowen's name had been crossed off the tennis draw.

三十九

I have thought about that day for a long time. What I did, and what I didn't do. I've had to live with those decisions since that day, and the guilt often returns when I'm least expecting it. I could be walking to class or sitting in an airport or bending down to tie my shoe. The punch in the gut never offered a warning.

Four years passed. I graduated from Dover and was accepted at Yale where I earned a place on the tennis team. It was the first time since Beijing that I had practiced with a team, but the boys on the team were so different that it was hard to equate the two. The boys in Beijing looked in one direction. The boys on my college team looked everywhere. Tennis had helped them get into college, but now they were thinking about other things—going out drinking, applying to law school, finding a girlfriend. One kid quit on the first day of practice.

I had not returned to China. My school holidays and summer vacations were filled with and exhausted by tennis tournaments. And I suppose, too, I wanted more distance before returning to Beijing. It had been a lonely, hard time and I knew if I went back I would want to find my old teammates, but I was afraid to discover what had become of them. Most of them probably would have moved on. My guess is that of all the boys remaining on the team when I left—Random, Sun Li, Little Mao, and Dali—none of them would be there anymore. Random didn't have his heart in it. For different reasons, Little Mao and Dali would have been moved to some provincial area to help coach—Little Mao, because he didn't have the talent, and Dali, because he was lazy. I knew I couldn't see the boys and not tell them about Bowen. Still I continued to work on my Chinese.

In the year following my months in Beijing, my father had mended his relationship with Mr. Zhang and had been able to resuscitate the big real estate deal they had been working on. The deal paid huge dividends after one of the large lots of land they had bought had been selected as an ideal site for the Olympic village and a second lot was conveniently located right next to the Olympic basketball arena. My father confided in me that he was fairly confident that the land they had bought in Shanghai would be purchased by the government at twice what they had paid as a location to host the Shanghai World Expo that had been planned for 2010.

In the summer of 2008, the summer after my second year at Yale, Mr. Zhang invited my father, his new fiancée, and me to Beijing for the Olympic Games. It was a historic event and incredibly important to the Chinese. The opening ceremony was planned, just as Victoria had said, for August 8, 2008, at 8:08 in the evening. I hadn't heard from Victoria in over a year, so I e-mailed her that I would be coming. A few weeks later she e-mailed back. Victoria and her husband had moved back to Guizhou where she was teaching at Guizhou's first international school. She told me that they had decided to have a child in the end and that her baby daughter had just been born. I asked her what the girl's English name was, and Victoria said that her husband had given her the name Chaos—for all the trouble she was sure to cause. I remembered the old page of writing we found that day at the old writing school and it made me happy that Victoria had a daughter to pass it on to. Victoria said that she would try to come to Beijing to see me while I was there, but she was not sure she would be able to because their daughter was too young to travel.

Two days before the opening ceremony we flew into the new airport that had been built for the Olympics. It had been designed by the famous British architect Lord Norman Foster. It was the largest airport in the world. Lord Foster had said that the design of the new Beijing had been inspired by the form of a dragon. Our flight landed in the afternoon, but it was cloudy, and I did not get a view of the airport from the sky. I remembered Mr. Zhang's describing his designs for his building as a dragon, too.

The new airport was elegant and ultramodern. It had been designed to be vast and airy and built of light material. The ceilings were high and swept upward in gentle curves, dotted with triangular skylights. Most of the walls were glass and huge yellow columns rose from the floors, supports for the giant structure. As we passed by, the columns changed from yellow to orange to red. Everywhere you looked there was color and light. My father said the airport had been designed to deal with the fifty million passengers a day expected by 2020. That number was just shy of the population of the United Kingdom.

Over the past few years there had been an incredible amount of construction in Beijing. I remembered my father saying that the Chinese had plans to put up skyscrapers covering ground three times the size of Manhattan in three years. I had questioned him: "A new New York City every year for three years?" My father was confident it would happen.

Though the airport had opened, it wasn't quite finished. There were no signs telling arriving passengers which way to go. Young men and women, dressed in matching navy blue uniforms, had been positioned every ten yards to direct travelers and answer questions in crude English. I had read somewhere that fewer than three thousand high school students in the States take the Chinese AP exam. That one day, I guessed there were more English-speaking young Chinese in the airport than there were Chinese-speaking young Americans spread out across all fifty states.

We went through passport control with passengers from other arriving flights. There were separate lines for all of the Olympic athletes. We saw members of the Israeli swim team and the Brazilian men's volleyball team. One of the Brazilian players was over seven feet tall. Even though many of these athletes were well traveled, the Olympics was, for many of them, their first time in China. This time when I handed the immigration officer my passport, there was no trouble with my visa. The woman spoke good English and briskly stamped my passport and smiled and waved me on.

Our luggage came swiftly. My father's office had arranged for a driver to meet us at baggage claim, and once our bags had arrived, the driver led us to a private elevator that took us down to a VIP exit where his car was waiting. As the black Audi pulled out of the airport and onto the highway that led to the city center, I gazed out of the window at a landscape that was familiar but different.

The sides of the highway had been planted with grass and

flowers and shrubbery. The landscaping reminded me of the entrance to exclusive gated communities in Florida. The landscaping wasn't just at the entrance of the airport. It continued on both sides of the road all the way to the city. I could only imagine the number of people required to plant these miles and miles of flowers and shrubs. I also noticed newly planted bands of trees. I asked our driver if the trees were for the Olympics. He shook his head and said, "To stop the sand from coming." I had remembered Victoria pointing to a large swath of land that had been cleared near the airport. She had explained that the government was planting a ring of trees around the city to trap the sand and prevent it from entering the city.

The traffic wasn't nearly as bad as I had remembered. There were two highway lanes dedicated solely to Olympics-related travel, and we flew toward the city center without the usual stop-start rhythm of Beijing traffic. My father explained that the government had put into effect an alternating system of odd and even license plate numbers, so, in theory, the amount of traffic should have been cut in half. It was still heavy but not as bad as when I had lived there. The pollution had improved as well. My father said that the government had shut down a number of factories six months earlier to improve the quality of the air. Some of the Olympic competitors in track and field had dropped out because of the pollution in Beijing. One marathoner was interviewed and said he was fearful that he could suffer permanent lung damage. He was not willing to take the risk. It had taken me over a year to get over the cough I had developed in Beijing. My father looked up at the gray sky and said that they were seeding clouds in an attempt to create more rainfall that would also help purify the air.

In the five years that I had been away, the city had changed dramatically. An entire district had been redeveloped to serve as an area expressly for Western tourists. It was filled with familiar restaurants and shops and new nightclubs and bars. I asked our driver if he could take us to the old tennis center where I had practiced every day. He was confused by my question. He assured me that the Beijing tennis center was on the outskirts of the city. I realized they must have built a new center and asked him if he could take us to where the old one had been. I was amazed to see that the old tennis center had been totally transformed into the site of several new clubs and bars. I got out of the car and walked toward the old stadium. The main gate was gone, and with it, any sign of the machine-gun-toting guards that I had passed by every day. A huge neon club sign sat atop the building that had housed the gym and thin women in glinting cocktail dresses tiptoed past in their stiletto heels. I heard laughter and voices speaking in English behind me, and I turned to see a group of American teenagers stumbling in my direction. The tall five-sided statue was still there, but it looked wildly out of place now—a relic from the past that someone had forgotten to remove, or maybe it was too heavy. The indoor tennis stadium, where we had run and sweated and bled until we were on the verge of unconsciousness, was now a nightclub called Club Latte. I went back to the car and motioned to the driver that we could leave.

When we arrived at the hotel there was a message from Victoria. She would not be able to come to Beijing. Her baby was sick, and it was difficult to get train tickets. She sent me an e-mail with a picture that she had found and had been saving for me. It was an image of an airplane that had been mislabeled BUS. Underneath was the nonsensical slogan "Wherever we go the passages are always our God." Victoria said in her e-mail that she had never stopped looking for the absurd signs to enter into our *Translation Olympics*. I replied that I could hear her laughing.

My father and I unpacked our suitcases and decided to walk down to the Forbidden City and Tiananmen Square. Both were packed with people. At the entrance of the Forbidden City, gone were all the beggars. I suggested to my father that we go to Starbucks. He told me that the Starbucks had closed. About a year ago, an anchor at CCTV had started a blog against Starbucks being in the Forbidden City. His blog had received over half a million hits. Many Chinese felt, as he did, that there was something disrespectful about having a Starbucks inside the Forbidden City.

On the eve of the opening ceremony, Mr. Zhang invited us to a party at a penthouse apartment in one of the buildings he had built on the land next to the Olympics. I don't know if I was more amazed by the Olympic buildings or Pangu Plaza. There, on what four years ago had been a vast field of rubble, was a five-building complex that was in the shape of a dragon. Of the five buildings, the middle three were thirty-nine stories tall and identically shaped. They formed the body of the dragon. On top of each were penthouses that were modern interpretations of courtyard houses. The three buildings were flanked by an office tower, twice as tall as the other buildings with a top in the shape of a dragon's head, and a fifth building the same height as the three identical buildings but which looked half the width of the apartment complexes and represented the tail of the dragon. Unlike Lord Norman Foster, Mr. Zhang's interpretation of a dragon was as literal as possible. Pangu Plaza had been named after Pangu, the mythic Chinese god who is said to have created the world by separating heaven and earth.

We arrived at Pangu Plaza behind a gold Rolls Royce from which two Chinese men emerged. My father recognized both men, K. L. Tang, a wealthy Hong Kong businessman who had made a fortune in real estate, and Timothy Chan, also from Hong Kong, who owned a private bank. My father greeted both of them as we waited for the elevator. K. L. Tang was finishing off what looked like a hamburger wrapped in McDonald's paper, and he was looking for a place to throw away his wrapper. "I had to stop by McDonald's for my Big Mac," he said, laughing. "I can't survive these parties without my Big Mac, but I can't arrive with this." He laughed, waving the crumpled wrapper. His British–Hong Kong accent produced sharp, exact words. He stuffed the wrapper in the pocket of his bespoke suit as he entered the elevator. Just as the elevator door pinged open, he invited my father to a private dinner he was hosting several days later in the Forbidden City at a royal garden he had restored.

Mr. Zhang was waiting for us. It wasn't the first time I had seen him since leaving Beijing. After my father had salvaged the deal they had been working on, they had gone on to partner on several other projects and he had come to stay with us once or twice. He greeted us warmly and insisted on giving us a tour. He ushered us into the center of his apartment. It had indeed been designed around a central courtyard. A large flat piece of glass covered the ceiling. People were scattered throughout the apartment. In addition to the Chinese, judging by the accents I heard, the other guests were a collection of Americans, Russians, and Brits. Mr. Zhang took us over to a dining table where some guests were finishing dinner. He introduced my father and me to

Lord Foster, who had been describing to everyone how the Chinese had built an entire airport in three years while the English, after a decade, were still working to finish Heathrow's Terminal Five. Mr. Zhang patted him on the shoulder and said that they both had been inspired by dragons.

Mr. Zhang escorted us to the balcony, which overlooked the swimming complex referred to as the Water Cube and the Bird's Nest Stadium that would host the opening ceremony the following evening. Mr. Zhang remembered the tour he had given me and Victoria four years earlier. "You remember," he said, enthusiastically waving his hand out in front of him, "none of this existed."

"Watch," he said as he pointed to the Water Cube. First it turned blue, then silver, then white. Lights forming the five differently colored Olympic rings traveled swiftly around the middle. Mr. Zhang clapped his hands like a delighted child. We turned to reenter the penthouse apartment. I looked down again across the city. From such a height, cars looked like squares of a broken mosaic that disappeared behind bands of buildings.

四十

There was a lot of talk that evening about the opening ceremony, especially about the security. Everyone said the security was going to be so tight that there was no chance anything would go wrong. The government had designed a special computer system that used cameras at the immigration desks in the airport to scan the face and measure the pupils of every person who entered the country. Placed around Beijing were tens of thousands of cameras that scanned every face in a crowd and matched it up to a face in the computer database. Apparently these high-tech computers could even see through sunglasses. With this system, any threat to security, any dissident or terrorist, could be identified and located within a matter of minutes. However, even with this intense security system in place, everyone had to come to the stadium via official buses. A few people said they suspected that the bus drivers were military officers.

The following day we moved from the Grand Hyatt to the Diaoyutai State Guesthouse. There were nineteen state guesthouses laid out on a one-hundred-acre plot of land with lakes on what was once the site of an imperial mansion dating back to the 1200s. During the Cultural Revolution, Mao's wife, Jiang Qing,

had made it her permanent residence. Now, visiting foreign dig-
nitaries and provincial government officials were housed there.
My father had been invited to stay in one of the guesthouses by
a prominent Chinese businessman. The entrance to Diaoyutai
looked like a park enclosed with a high stuccoed wall. At the entrance four armed guards checked our passports. We were ordered to get out of the car and walk through a metal detector
while the car was checked carefully for bombs. We drove down
a winding lane that crossed two small lakes. Villa Seven was a
plain two-storied rectangular building with a Chinese-style portico. We walked inside. The entire staff of twelve was lined up to
greet us. We were given a choice of several rooms, all of which
were decorated like high-end hotel rooms. We even had a television with CNN.

Later that afternoon, we were driven to a hotel in the north
of Beijing and joined other guests of Mr. Zhang's on a luxury
coach bus. The bus left at 4 p.m. and we reached the Olympics
site forty-five minutes later. The bus passed through an opening
in the high chain-link fence that surrounded the entire site and
deposited us at the entrance to a football field–sized hospitality
tent where we were offered dinner. At 6 p.m. the gates to the
Bird's Nest were opened and we, along with thousands of others,
walked toward the stadium. I felt as if I were taking part in one
of those movies I had seen of massive ancient armies marching
to seize a city. To the left of us was a less imposing chain-link
fence that separated the spectator area from where all the per-
formers were preparing. I noticed hundreds of young Chinese
men dressed in long, flowing, light gray robes that reminded me
of the garments that choir boys wear.

As we were walking along, I thought I heard someone call

my name. I turned around and looked but didn't see anyone. Again I heard my name, "Chase! Chase! Hey, Chase!" My father was ahead of me talking to another banker. I looked around but couldn't figure out who was calling my name. Someone grabbed my arm from behind. I turned. It was Random. He looked the same as he had four years before.

"I can't believe I saw you," he said.

"Are you still playing tennis?"

"No, I'm in business selling shirts with my father. We are making fashion shirts now." He tugged at the white shirt he was wearing. "I am in charge of this line."

"Nice," I said. "Only white?"

"For now, but very good quality."

"How about the other boys?"

"No, none of them," and then he mentioned the names of two Chinese men players whom I had never heard of.

"Bowen isn't playing?" I hadn't heard anything about Bowen, nor seen him at any tournaments since the incident at the Orange Bowl. I assumed that he must have gone back to China.

Random shook his head. "He's in Tianjin."

"On the men's team?"

Random lifted his shoulders and frowned. "I don't think so."

The crowds were condensing, and I feared I would lose sight of my father as the undercurrents of the converging people were getting stronger and stronger. "Hey," I said, "I've got to go this way. Where are you sitting?"

"We are in lower section K4."

"I think we are in the top," I said, "with Bank of China."

The opening ceremony began, as most of the world saw, with 2,008 *fou* drummers running single file into the stadium. They were dressed in gray robes, and they pushed their large square drums mounted on wheels. Row by row they filled the entire stadium. In formation they lit their drums to form giant digits for the countdown to the Games. These young men arched their backs and flung themselves over their drums with a dancer's grace and flexibility. They performed the same movement in exactly the same way. Our host at the Bank of China told us that the boys were soldiers and that they had practiced for over two years. I had never seen such synchronization. And they made me think about Bowen. Bowen could never have been one of those 2,008 drummers.

The ceremony lasted four hours, one set more fantastic than the last, but the only thing I could think about was what had happened to Bowen.

By the time we got back to our hotel it was 3 a.m. I had been given tickets for a fencing match the next day, but I had other plans. I decided instead to take a morning train to Tianjin. I wanted to find Bowen.

I arrived at the train station at about 11 a.m. It was packed. The old train station had been razed. In its place a much larger and modern station had been built and had opened a few days before the Olympics. I had never been in such a clean public space. There was not one piece of discarded litter to be found anywhere. Upon entering the train station, I passed through a metal detector, and my backpack was searched. I asked, *"Zai nar mai houche piao* (Where do you buy tickets)?" The security official seemed surprised I spoke Chinese, but after a brief pause, he pointed to the left. I headed off in that direction and after about twenty meters saw the line to buy tickets. There must have been several hundred people queuing in eight lines. I stood at the back of the first line and waited. As I advanced closer to the ticket booth, I heard the same series of disappointing announcements I had heard four years before. The first said that all the trains before 11:45 a.m. were sold out. I must have bought the last ticket for just as the woman behind the ticket counter pushed my printed ticket toward me, I heard an announcement that the 11:45 a.m. train was also sold out. I purchased a return ticket on the high-speed train leaving to Tianjin at 6:15 p.m.

We lined up to board. The train station was new, but the behavior of the passengers had not changed. Boarding was a free-for-all. The doors of the arriving train had barely opened when people began pushing and shoving to get on the train, showing absolutely no regard for the passengers on the arriving train who wished to get off. I eventually made it onto the train and found my seat occupied by an overweight man. I showed him my ticket, and he shook his head. It wasn't worth a fight so I stood in the space between cars and had my ticket ready to show the ticket taker. This train had a top speed of 330 km/h, and the journey was just over forty minutes. Compared to the two-hour trip I had made four years ago, standing for only one-third of the time would be easy. I found it surprising that even in the middle of the day so many people were traveling between the two cities—but then again the train ran between two cities, both of which had populations of over ten million people. Tickets were extremely cheap. A ticket on the high-speed train was only 50 RMB (a little over six U.S. dollars), less than one-twentieth the cost of a ticket on the high-speed train between New York City and Washington, D.C.

We arrived in Tianjin at precisely 12:25 p.m. As in Beijing, the old train station had been demolished and a much larger one built. I walked out into the sunlight to a vast concrete plaza the size of four football fields. In the middle stood a tall clock tower with all of the mechanics exposed. Around its base, travelers wearing backpacks sat with a sense of permanence, as if they had no plans to move. The sun shone brighter than in Beijing. I hadn't seen any other Westerners on the train, nor did I see any around the plaza. I bought a map at a kiosk and opened it up to get my bearings. The tennis complex was not far from the train station so I decided to walk.

I reached the tennis complex after about half an hour. It was just as I had remembered it. A group of young boys and girls were practicing. I waited for the coach to notice me. He walked over and asked me what I wanted. I told him I had played in Beijing with the boys' team four years before. I was trying to find one of the players who was from Tianjin. "Do you know Bowen?" He shook his head and pointed to the office. "You can ask in there," he said.

I found a woman at a desk in a small office. I explained why I had come.

She shook her head. I asked again. She said, "Wait a minute," and brought in one of the other coaches. He nodded his head. "Bowen. No play," he said. "Working."

"*Ta zai nar* (Where is he)?" I asked.

"*Bu zhidao* (I don't know)." He looked away when he answered and I could tell that he was lying. I switched to English.

"I'm an old friend of Bowen's. I came all the way from Beijing to see him."

"Bowen no here. I don't know," the coach repeated.

"Is he with his family? His father?"

Maybe because he wanted to get rid of me, or maybe because

I had proved by my knowledge that I was a friend of Bowen's, he decided to help me. He nodded and pointed north. "He works over there, I think. New buildings. Very big."

"How far?"

"*Hen jin* (Very close), ten minutes?"

I left and headed in the direction that he had pointed. I couldn't imagine Bowen being so close to the tennis courts and not playing.

After a few blocks I saw the tall high-rises. I counted twenty-eight buildings. About half were finished, the others were under construction. The buildings were grouped in clusters of four with shared courtyards. I saw a group of men building a wall at the far side. I walked slowly and then stopped and watched.

There was Bowen, sitting down on a half-built wall with the other workers smoking a cigarette. I watched him throw his cigarette butt down and stand up to return to work. His hair was shaved close. He wore dusty cargo pants and a once-white tank top. His skin was tanned and his thin shoulders and arms were sinewy with muscle. He worked while the other men rested.

The sun was high, and the August air was hot and thick. I looked around for a spot in the shade, but there was none. The building next to where Bowen was working had a fenced-off playground that was part of a primary school housed on the ground floor. I found a bench on the other side of the playground and sat down. The tangle of so many children on swing sets and jungle gyms screened me. I listened for a moment. A high-pitched laugh or shout would peak above the gentle static of the children's voices as they tried their skill at the monkey bars, or pushed each other on swings, or played king of the mountain on the sliding board.

I don't know what I had hoped to find, but I didn't expect to find Bowen like this. I leaned over and held my head between my knees to find a way to breathe. I closed my eyes and heard the joy in Bowen's voice when he gave me my Chinese name—Yu—and when he first told me the Chinese name for America—Mei Guo—the beautiful country—Mei Guo—he had repeated it several times. I sat back up and watched Bowen as he bent down and picked up one heavy concrete block and laid it across a joint. He adjusted it slightly and then began to smooth a thin layer of cement across the top and side. He turned to pick up another concrete block. He kept his back flat as he bent down. He straightened his body and set the concrete block in its place on the wall. He gently pushed and pulled each side until it was lined up just right. He took a step back to examine it. Unsatisfied, he made one more tiny adjustment and then smoothed a thin layer of cement across the top of the next block. He turned to retrieve another concrete block.

He didn't work with gloves. His fingers and palms would now be so callused that he would not be able to hold a racket the way he used to, when the racket was an extension of his arm. He would no longer be able to feel the speed and weight of a tennis ball. He would no longer be able to play the game the way that he had, the way that so many people dreamed of playing, but so few ever could.

For three hours I watched Bowen single-handedly complete one side of the wall, concrete block after concrete block. Bowen worked with the steadiness and precision of a machine. When he had completed his side of the wall, he turned to help another worker, an elderly man who was thin and stooped.

A teacher emerged from the primary school, leading a troupe of children single file. She clapped her hands and shouted to the children and they broke ranks and scattered, running and laughing, across the playground. The playground was now almost completely darkened by the shadow of an adjacent building. The children ran in circles around her until she called out again. They dropped into a loose arc around her. She led them in songs and clapping games. Some of the children stood up and jumped around and waved their arms as they sang. With each successive song the teacher slowed the tempo, and the children were calmed as if a light had been dimmed.

Why had I come?

I checked my watch, it was almost five. I looked back at the construction site and saw that the other workers—all, that is, except Bowen—had begun to pack up their belongings. The sun was making its slow descent, but Bowen remained. He worked alone now, building the wall, brick by brick. There was no joy in the way he worked as there had been in the way he had played tennis. But he worked in a way that was different from the other men who had slapped cement on the bricks without care and never checked to see if they placed them on the wall crooked or straight. I remember the pride he had shown when he had spoken about his father as a master craftsman. I remembered the story he told me about his beginnings in tennis—about how he practiced every day by himself, hitting a ball against a wall, here in Tianjin. I wondered if the wall he was building would ever serve the same purpose for another young player.

Even though he was alone, I could not find it within myself to go over and speak to him. Three times I almost got myself to go over and talk to him, but each time I found some reason to turn back. I told myself that Bowen would not want me to see him laying bricks, that it would hurt his fierce pride. I told myself that even if I went over and spoke to him, that I could make no difference in his life—Bowen who had so desperately wanted to be a world-class tennis player. He and I both knew he could have been one of the best of our generation. I gave myself a thousand reasons not to go over and speak to him, but in the end it didn't matter. They were probably all wrong.

I knew that in many ways I was responsible for Bowen's fate. I was scared, I supposed. Scared of what he might say to me. Scared that he might not say anything at all. I thought about the letter my father had given me before I left for Beijing almost five years ago. "Courage is about always doing the right thing." The definition was simple and clear—four words—*do the right thing*—but the difficulty was in the identification of what was right and what was wrong. By the simple definition I had done the right thing. I tried to help a friend who had lied to me, and I had refused a friend when he asked me to lie for him. I couldn't be faulted, but deep in my heart I knew what Tom would have done, and I knew in the same way that I had failed to *venture forth*—I had failed to find the courage to take a risk, to act when only one part of me was certain what was right and what was wrong. I've come to understand that each person has to work out their own personal algorithm of courage. No two are the same, and it's no use trying to borrow or copy anyone else's. Guided by his own algorithms of courage and determination, Bowen had made it as far as he was capable of on his own—and then he had turned to me for help, and I had failed him.

The children were now singing a slow, gentle song that had the rhythmic simplicity of a lullaby. After each verse, they repeated the refrain "*yue er ming, feng er jing* (the moon is bright, the wind is calm)." When they were finished, the teacher asked them to stand up and form a line. She led them—quiet and subdued—inside.

I took the 6:15 back to Beijing. I watched the countryside shudder past—flat, dry fields and small blockhouses scattered here and there, orange under the final light of the dying sun. Next to me a small child slept in her mother's lap while her mother sang to her. I recognized her song as one of those the children at the school had sung in the playground that afternoon.

As we pulled into the Beijing station I noticed that someone had scrawled graffiti across a door in the station wall. I looked at it more closely and recognized one of the quotations that Victoria's husband Z had on the ceiling of his restaurant.

我们将治愈我们的创伤，我们将继续战斗直到结束。

We will heal our wounds, and we will fight until we come to the end.

Acknowledgments

I owe a debt of gratitude to all the people who helped me along the way.

To the boys in Beijing who welcomed me as their teammate and whose work ethic and discipline have always inspired me to work harder.

To the family I lived with in Beijing, who gave me a home on the other side of the world.

To Karel Fromel, who taught me the meaning of hard work.

To Fritz Mark, Jean Yu, Manjula, and Stuart Solomon for the advice and support they gave from the very beginning.

To Ron Carlson, who read the earliest draft of this novel and told me to stick with it.

To my wonderful teachers Bret Anthony Johnston, Amy Hempel, and Mark Poirier, from whom I learned so much.

To the Office for the Arts at Harvard for supporting me.

To Andrew Wylie for believing in me.

To Jeff Alexander and Ann Patty for all their help and advice, without which I would not have made it to this point.

To my editor Maya Ziv for all her hard work and for taking a chance on me.

And to my mother and father for instilling in me a love of literature and for always encouraging me to pursue this path.

About the Author

J. R. THORNTON studied history, English, and Chinese at Harvard College, graduating in 2014. He lived in Beijing as a teenager and returned to undertake a fellowship as a writer-in-residence at the International Writer's Center at Beijing Normal University. He was an internationally ranked junior tennis player and a member of the 2012 Ivy League–winning Harvard men's tennis team. He has been the recipient of the LeBaron Russell Briggs Fiction Prize and Harvard's Artist Development Fellowship. He will return to China in the fall of 2016 as a member of the inaugural class of Schwarzman Scholars. *Beautiful Country* is his debut novel.